Nicole Watson is a member of the Birri-Gubba People and the Yugambeh language group. She has a Master of Laws and has worked for Legal Aid Queensland and the National Native Title Tribunal. She is currently a researcher at the Jumbunna Indigenous House of Learning, University of Technology, Sydney. *The Boundary* is her first novel.

NICOLE
WATSON

THE
BOUNDARY

UQP

For the real-life Charlie Everselys.
Renaissance men and women.

First published 2011 by University of Queensland Press
PO Box 6042, St Lucia, Queensland 4067 Australia

www.uqp.com.au

National Library of Australia Cataloguing-in-Publication Data
The boundary / by Nicole Watson
ISBN: 9780702238499 (pbk)
       9780702246593 (epub)
       9780702246609 (kindle)
       9780702246586 (pdf)

This project has been assisted by the Commonwealth
Government through the Australian Council,
its arts funding and advisory body.

Cover design by Blue Cork
Cover photographs © Photolibrary and iStock
Typeset in 11/14 pt Bembo by Post Pre-press Group, Brisbane
Printed in Australia by McPherson's Printing Group

University of Queensland Press uses papers that are natural, renewable
and recyclable products made from wood grown in sustainable
forests. The logging and manufacturing processes conform to
the environmental regulations of the country of origin.

PART ONE

ONE

Face buried in the marble. Crown is bare and pale, skirted by tufts of black hair locked in a macabre dance with bloody tissue. Feathers circle like reefs surrounding an island. Chards of green glass whisper dry white wine. Jason breathes in the floral perfume. Subtle and classic, but young.

Nothing else in the kitchen is disturbed. The double fridge sits in the polished wood like a cave in a cliff face. Elements on the stove so clean they'd scream in horror at the sight of burning fat. Empty glass sits on the bench. Blood at its base.

Bright lights unveil dust on the boundaries of the floorboards. As he walks through the corridor, Jason is surprised by the bareness of the walls. He'd expected to see portraits of weddings and childhood milestones.

The living room is dressed in elegant understatement. The black leather couch betrays no signs of wear, crystal vase on the coffee table looks new. Orange and pink brushstrokes demand to be worshipped.

Detective Senior Sergeant Andrew Higgins is staring at the canvas with the bloodshot eyes of a dachshund. He turns to Jason.

'Matthews, do you know who painted that?'

Jason is surprised. 'No. Do you?'

'Emily Kngwarreye – one of the most successful Aboriginal artists ever.'

'How do you know that?'

Higgins smiles. 'I'm a man of many talents.'

3

'DSS Higgins, DS Matthews, we have to stop meeting like this.' Doctor Robert Thomas, the forensic pathologist, is tall and gaunt. His hair is a nest of grey. Eyes hold a youthful spark. 'Judicial killings – that's a rarity in Australia. Haven't seen one of these in thirty years.'

Thirteen hours earlier

The air conditioning is soothing on Miranda's skin. In a city where the summer temperature hovers in the mid thirties, the Federal Court is one of the few places she feels comfortable in a suit. The dense fabric irritates her skin in the middle of the day. It's worse when she's hung-over.

Sudden laughter pierces the back row. She doesn't have to turn around to know it's the cry of journalists with rhinoceros skins. Some have been following the case since it started. Their reports are predictable – black people want to take control of the city, stop the development, the ever-constant drilling, and banish the cranes that seem to live on every corner. Even if native title could achieve that outcome, Miranda thinks, it wouldn't be such a bad thing. *Brisbane is eating itself.*

The new office blocks and apartments are like hives, colonising the body of what was. Traffic is relentless, driving the city into sleep-deprived psychosis. Caffeine pulses through the veins of its inhabitants, who live to work, so that they can buy bigger houses, to be filled with everything from state-of-the-art kitchen appliances to imposing televisions that are never quite big enough.

Anxiety wrapped in murmur floats from the back of the courtroom. The Corrowa are prisoners without a dock. The outcome remains a mystery, but intuitively, they know they have been fighting a losing battle. So they bristle on the periphery of the law. Even the elderly with their arthritic joints insist on standing next to the huge wooden doors.

In the front row of the public gallery is the battalion that apparently guards the public interest – bureaucrats from the Department of the Premier and Cabinet, Crown Law, the Department of Natural Resources, the Brisbane City Council. Whatever the public is, Miranda thinks, it doesn't include the Corrowa, whose native title claim has been resisted by every level of government.

Those at the bar table have the look of steel. That look is to the lawyer what steady hands are to the surgeon. It disguises the jackhammer, keeps the client wrapped in the cotton wool of self-righteousness, pays the bills. When she was young, Miranda had felt sexy as she pranced into the courtroom like a Siamese cat declaring its territory on the couch. In those days, she had relished the enquiring looks of older men.

The four Senior Counsel for the respondents puff their chests like an army of peacocks. The most pompous of the flock is Harrison McPherson: the 'Golden Tongue'. McPherson's grey hair has the sheen of wealth. His skin is soft, caressed by elegant cologne. The Golden Tongue has shredded every single piece of the Corrowa's evidence. Spent hundreds of hours debating legal points that all share the aim of denying the Corrowa their identity.

At least she can understand McPherson. He is, after all, a gun for hire. Believes in nothing. His instructing solicitor, Dick Payne, is another matter. One of their own, he bludgeons native title claims, seemingly with ease.

This morning Payne has sent an underling in his place. One of the luxuries of professional success is having someone else to count time for you. If Payne is the most successful Aboriginal lawyer in the country, then Miranda is the poorest. She spends half of her life waiting: for the Council bus to deliver her to Court, for clients so high they may as well fly to their appointments and even then they would be late, for the petulant photocopier to work.

Today is the culmination of six years of her life. Of her family's life. Of Jonathon's. And she knows that today's result will send ripples throughout the country, will affect the future claims of strangers, will be probed and dissected by academics. But all that Miranda can think of are the psyches of those at this bar table.

What do we ever really achieve?

What is this doing to me?

And what of the Golden Tongue? What kind of a person spends his days wresting the faith of old men and women?

Do lawyers ever suffer from the bullets we fire at others?

She looks across at Jonathon. His black curls have been slicked straight; luminous blue eyes dance behind silver frames.

'Are you okay?' he says.

She smiles sadly at her friend. 'I'm fine. We're survivors, remember.'

'All rise.'

The judge's associate is a young woman of twenty-four. Her blond hair is worn in its usual bun and her thin frame swims in the long black robes. She smiles at the court reporter, whose high hair and shoulder pads seem out of place.

Justice Bruce Brosnan's face is bloated. His eyebrows are dyed charcoal, which only makes his scowl more dramatic. He takes his seat at the altar of the common law and looks into the solemn faces below. He seems to pause at the journalists in the back row and expels a brief sigh, deftly suggesting contempt, but not quite. He clears his throat and reads from his notebook.

'The matter of Corrowa People versus State of Queensland has raised a number of issues common to native title claims brought by Indigenous people in metropolitan areas. Given the complexity of the judgment that is some three hundred pages in length, I will not provide a comprehensive summary this morning. However, I will make some brief comments. At the outset, I emphasise that the role of this Court is to apply the principles of the Native Title Act objectively. It is not the business of this Court to attempt to correct history by appealing to contemporary notions of social justice. That is a political matter best left to the Parliament.

'The applicants seek recognition of their native title over an area of land now known as Meston Park that provides a boundary between West End and South Brisbane. Over the years, Meston Park has played an important role in the affairs of the West End community. It is the home of numerous events held by various ethnic groups and it is a popular meeting place for the local Aboriginal community.

'In late 2002 the first respondent and second respondent, the State Government and Brisbane City Council respectively, entered into negotiations with the third respondent, Coconut Holdings, with a view to constructing a shopping complex and luxury apartments on the land. The complex will provide accommodation for five hundred specialty stores, substantial office space and will be adjoined by a highrise apartment building.

'In 2003 the applicants successfully obtained an injunction to stop the sale of Meston Park from proceeding. Attempts by the National Native Title Tribunal to achieve resolution by mediation have been unsuccessful. It is common ground that if the Court finds that the Corrowa People's native title over Meston Park has been extinguished, the development will proceed.

'I find that a society called the Corrowa inhabited land that included the claim area at the time of European settlement. I find that all of the applicants, with the exception of Ethel Cobb, are biological descendants of the Corrowa. The earliest records that we have of Miss Cobb concern her placement into the girls' dormitory at the Manoah Mission at the age of three years. The identities of her parents and the circumstances that necessitated her placement into state care are unknown.

'In my judgment I have referred extensively to the evidence of Lesley Tagem, herself a Corrowa elder. Miss Tagem resided in the dormitory at the same time as Miss Cobb. Miss Tagem gave evidence, which I accept, that Miss Cobb was not recognised by other Corrowa at Manoah. Indeed, Miss Cobb only began to identify as a Corrowa person when she relocated to Brisbane, at the age of twenty, in 1962. I believe that Miss Cobb was a sincere witness, but in the absence of corroborative evidence, I cannot make a finding that she is a biological descendant of the Corrowa People. Consequently, I have rejected the totality of her evidence. This is particularly damaging for the applicants' case, given the reliance they placed upon Miss Cobb as an expert on Corrowa laws and traditions.'

Miranda feels a stab in her chest, but cannot look behind. The old woman is proud. And Miranda knows she expects her niece to be just as stoic.

'In order for their native title claim to succeed, the applicants must prove that they have maintained their connection to the claim area through the continuous practice of their traditional laws and customs since the change in sovereignty. The applicants gave evidence that they currently use the claim area as a meeting place. In recent years, they have begun to teach their children traditional dances and some Corrowa vernacular. The Court must determine whether or not those activities represent a continuation of traditional law and custom, or whether they are merely evidence of a cultural revival.

'I find the unpublished memoirs of the former native mounted policeman, Horace Downer, written in 1920, to be the most reliable evidence of the content of the traditional laws and customs of the Corrowa. Downer was posted to the area in 1890 and his memoirs begin in that year. He observed the Corrowa who lived on the fringes of South Brisbane. Some were employed to work as domestic servants in homes in West End, including the Downer home, which stands adjacent to Meston Park.

'By the time that Downer arrived in West End, an evening curfew for Aboriginal people had been in place for some decades. The curfew began at four o'clock each afternoon and operated for the entire day every Sunday. As a member of the Native Mounted Police, Downer was responsible for enforcing the curfew. In his memoirs, he refers to riding through Boundary Street, West End, cracking his stock whip, at four o'clock each afternoon.

'The lives of the Corrowa were changed irreparably in 1897, when the Aboriginals Protection and Restriction of the Sale of Opium Act was passed by the Queensland Parliament. As a result of this legislation, some of the Corrowa were removed to reserves throughout the State. Many of the Corrowa women, however, were forced to stay in an Aboriginal Girls' Home in Hill End, where they were prepared for life as domestic servants.

'Relations between the remaining Corrowa and the townsfolk of West End deteriorated significantly in the following years. Downer referred to starving Corrowa breaking into homes and stealing food. He also described an incident where a farmer shot dead a man who attempted to lure his wife into leaving domestic service.

'On 16 May 1906, Downer and his battalion gathered the surviving Corrowa and removed them to the Manoah Mission, two hundred kilometres north. We now reach the most critical question in this case – did the Corrowa cease to practise their traditional laws and customs after they were removed to Manoah? If the answer is in the affirmative, the Court must find that their native title was extinguished. Once native title has been extinguished, it cannot be revived.

'In light of what we now know about Queensland's former Aboriginal reserves, it is highly unlikely that the Corrowa would have been able to continue to practise their traditional laws and customs. The State's historian, Dr Ritchie, gave evidence, which I accept, that the inmates of Manoah were forbidden from speaking their traditional languages and, in time, most converted to Christianity.

'Ultimately, I find that the Corrowa ceased to practise their traditional laws and customs soon after they were removed to the Manoah Mission. Therefore, the claim must fail.'

The room is eerily silent. The Corrowa's anger is palpable, so heavy that it overwhelms voices, the sounds of chairs moving, files being picked up from the floor.

'Miranda.'

She looks up. Jonathon's face speaks of obligation. 'Yes, I know,' she says. But she's not ready. *Just a few more seconds.*

She finally turns to face the back of the courtroom. Her father, Charlie, is holding Auntie Ethel. He's wearing one of his old suits from his days at the Aboriginal Legal Service. The dark blue is faded, revived a little by the drycleaner. Auntie Ethel's black cotton dress sits just below her knees. Her glossy black hair was cut into a bob shape only yesterday. A group of uncles have gathered around them, eyes pleading for hope. Journalists begin to approach them. They hesitate.

'Judge, here are the files for next week's sittings.'

'Thank you, Anne.'

She's not quite beautiful. Acne scars live beneath translucent powder and her nose is shaped like a fish hook. But the young men in the registry behave ridiculously around her, volunteering to carry her files, engaging in small talk.

'How are your mum and dad?' Bruce says.

'Dad's still working very long hours at the firm. He slaved to become a partner and now he's working like a slave to remain a partner.' She deposits the files on the coffee table near the door. 'Mum's been busy with her volunteer work.'

'Please give them my regards.'

Anne smiles and closes the door behind her.

Justice Bruce Brosnan's room has all the trappings of judicial office. Walls are lined with bookshelves that house law reports. In the few vacant spaces are dot paintings that he and Emily purchased at an auction in Melbourne, many years ago.

He looks to the window and drinks in the exquisite shades of light pink and orange dangling above the Kurilpa Bridge.

Blue and white ferries part the khaki waters of the river. Above, the green glass of the art gallery seems to beckon.

When he was young, Brisbane was a backwater, a place where few ventured out after eight o'clock at night. Those who did were often questioned by the police. How things have changed since Expo '88, he thinks. Outdoor dining, live music and contemporary art are now standard fare. Walking bridges sprung up overnight, and at any time of the day you can see joggers running along the river's paved banks.

He understands why the Corrowa hold such deep feelings for the river. He can even concede that the law is unfair: in order for their native title claims to succeed, black families must somehow prove that each generation was unscathed by the carnage of the Europeans, an insuperable obstacle for those in the cities. But people who choose to roll the dice with the law have to live with the consequences. Besides, he can always do some social justice work when he retires. Become the President of the Human Rights Commission, perhaps. He hears a gentle knock at the door.

'Judge, I'm just about to leave. Is there anything else that you would like me to do?'

'No, that's all. Thank you, Anne.'

'You look like you were deep in thought.'

'I guess I was. Either that or dementia.' She gives the forced laugh he knows well from all his associates. 'Are you excited about next year?' he says.

'Yes and no. The hours are going to be long, but I'll be working with great people. Of course, my work won't have the same meaning as yours did.'

Like laughing at his jokes, her reference to his days at the Aboriginal Legal Service is expected. He has shared his stories from the trenches with each of his associates.

'You can always go on to pursue social justice work after a few years in commercial firms – if that's what you want to do.'

Anne smiles coyly.

'The most important thing is that you're happy, whatever it is that you end up doing.' He grimaces at the clock on the wall. 'I'm such an ogre of a boss. Please, go home.'

Her blue eyes seem to burst with excitement.

'You're not going home, are you?'

'I'm off to drinks with some of the other associates,' she says, and offers a bashful grin that would make the young men in the registry quiver.

'Have a good night then. I'll see you tomorrow.'

Silence replaces her. He pictures Anne with a champagne glass in her hand, the associates sitting around a table, exchanging war stories that are really anything but. He opens the cabinet behind him, revealing a bottle of his favourite Scotch. As he pours the amber into crystal, Bruce catches sight of his reflection in the small mirror that sits on the corner of his desk. His jowl is a puffer fish adding weight to his depression.

He savours the first gulp of Scotch. He has to admit the bastard looks good. Charlie has the hard body of an old boxer that not even death could kill. It's been a good thirty years since they last spoke. A few times during the trial, their eyes met. But there was never anything beyond faint recognition. The past only ever leaves you with fragments, Bruce thinks, withered bones of truth. His mobile phone drags him back to present.

'Emily, how are you?'

They're both surprised by the spring in his voice.

'I'm fine, thank you. I just called because I'm on my way to get Isabella.'

'Oh.' He pauses, navigating the trapeze cable that is his marriage. 'How is she?'

'What do you think?'

Her crisp answer betrays the hurt of too many late nights in the office, and later, affairs that usually left him cold.

'Where is she?' he says.

'I can't talk about it now. I've spoken with the director.

They'll take her back.' She laughs wryly. 'Provided I can get her into the car.'

'Do you need my help?'

There's no need for an answer; both know it's a hollow gesture.

'When can I see her?' he says. 'It's been weeks.'

'Look, I'll ask. But I can't make any promises,' she says, and ends the call without saying goodbye.

Another gulp of Scotch. He savours the burn, welcomes the lightness of spirit. Bruce opens the drawer and takes out a photograph of Sherene. Amber eyes sparkle against luminous skin, surrounded by thick brown hair. Ten years ago, Sherene walked into this office, brilliance overflowing. He couldn't wait to see her fulfil her potential. She would go on to politics, the Bar, scale the heights of academia. But when he ran into her six months ago, she was a shell. Her confidence had all but disappeared.

Now she's beginning to bloom again. He dials her mobile number, the one she keeps just for his calls.

'Bruce.' The anxiety in her voice cuts like a knife.

'Darling.'

'Something terrible has happened.'

'What's wrong?'

'I told Dick. Bruce, he's furious. I'm scared that he'll do something.'

'Darling, I doubt that he'd be that stupid.' Bruce knows he shouldn't press her. 'Sherene, I need to see you.'

She pauses, mind ticking over. 'When?'

TWO

The machine thunders, it tears Miranda's brain like ripping concrete. In spite of itself, the jackhammer has elegant precision. It pierces directly above her left eye, a space the size of a scalpel's head. Miranda grimaces as she lifts her cheek from the White Pages on her desk, and the familiar taste floods her mouth. Sugar and vomit in equal measure, it compares only to the cheapest plonk, napalm that slowly cooks your insides.

Most who purchase the vile brew do so sheepishly. But not the old drinkers, with grasshopper bodies cloaked in emaciated skin. A few have interesting stories, like Auntie May. Twenty years ago she was a dancer and enjoyed affairs with corrupt government ministers. But her lovers have long since departed, to the grave or to jail in the aftermath of Fitzgerald. Now she spends her nights with other shells in Meston Park, anaesthetising themselves to life. Miranda wonders if she too is destined for the wooden bench that had been stripped of paint and tattooed with meaningless rebellion. Once you reach the bench, death is imminent. You choke on vomit, get killed by predators or, more likely, you just collapse.

Stale cigarette smoke makes her queasy. The boss is going to be furious. She's smelt the distinct fumes of marijuana linger from behind his office door, but she knows he loathes cigarettes. O'Neill isn't like her. He rarely drinks to the point of intoxication, and after obligatory Friday afternoon drinks he disappears.

Her mind wanders to Dan. It's been three weeks since he

stopped returning her calls. There was no warning of their break-up. No bitter argument. Only cowardly silence.

Screams ricochet in the dungeon on her neck, her eyes are on fire and the pain in her wrists stabs. She looks around slowly. Binders crashed on the floor, hundreds of pieces of paper scattered like tiny stars. Photographs of Meston Park sit on top of the explosion like seagulls perched on barnacled wood. For all of its cruelty, the aftermath of a night on the turps offers stunning clarity. The shambles of her office is now in stark relief. Empty coffee cups are partly disguised by photocopies of judgments and articles from legal journals. She curses herself when she sees that clients' personal statements have been left exposed. The only object unscathed is the shoebox of feathers that Ethel gave her. It sits next to the filing cabinet, neglected. For reasons that she wouldn't disclose, Ethel insisted that the feathers were important evidence. Jonathon counselled them against using the feathers at the trial. In the absence of a story, they prove nothing, he said.

Guilt jabs like a needle, releasing a vaccine that should protect her from the disease of self-destruction. But never will. O'Neill is so proud of this practice, the tug that never loses its nerve in an ocean of big business and governments addicted to the market. She's let him down. Failed all of them.

The three empty wine bottles chastise her, like members of a Star Chamber. All the same brand: a sauvignon blanc from New Zealand's Marlborough region, the brand name embossed in black with golden peaks in the background. Burnt matches are clumsily piled around a torn packet of Benson & Hedges. Cigarette butts swim in wine dregs like pond scum.

She can go for a few days without having a cigarette. But once she begins to pour into the glass, the familiar urge flows, like blood pumping through her veins. Gulp the wine, suck the fumes. And tally all of life's injustices, the disappointments, the pain, because when she's drunk, she's resilient. And the wine bottles and cigarettes are a captive audience, simultaneously inspired by her intellect and overwhelmed by her humility. But in the brutal aftermath she's just a fucking loser.

Why did I go back after the first bottle? She was already tipsy. But she has the performance so well honed, it's instinctive. Brush the teeth, spray the perfume. Wear the confident façade like skin. The young man behind the counter offered his usual smile, full of teeth and empty of sincerity. She made a seemingly off-the-cuff remark about buying more wine for a dinner party. Both knew it was a lie, but what would he care?

Miranda wants to cry, begs to, but the tears won't come. She's a broken-down boxer, lying on the ring, face a war zone. The faithful are calling. But she's comatose. She tries to retrace the events of last night, but ends up with a half-finished jigsaw. Angela emerged briefly while she was still working on the second bottle and almost caught her red-handed. Then Miranda opened the packet of fags. Promised to drink only one glass of the third bottle.

A gentle light flickers through the blinds and throws a grenade into the chaos. Miranda looks at her watch – seven-fifteen. Angela usually gets in by seven-thirty. She climbs into her skirt, which stinks of demons and yesterday's sweat. Picks up her blouse. It takes a few seconds to register. She's shaking violently, but Miranda doesn't know if it's because of the toxins inside her, or the blood that's caked the white linen. Tears that seemed impossible a moment ago begin to slide down her cheeks.

Dick's face is a bomb of a car whose rattling panels threaten to fling into the air once the speedometer reaches one hundred. Baby cries, Dick's brain explodes.

'Sherene!'

Harsh light bounces off his eyelids; heat rises from his face with no place to go.

'For fuck's sake! Sherene!'

Sounds of kisses being planted on soft skin. Baby's smell

lingering from behind the ensuite door: formula, vitamin E cream, talcum powder.

Most mornings she calls out to him, 'Dick, it's your turn to change the baby.' Or her old favourite – 'Dick, you spend far too much time in your office. You'll regret it, you know.' But there will be no chastising this morning.

He opens his eyes to see his wife standing at the foot of their king-sized bed, a pathetic mixture of fear and defeat. Lines on her forehead plead for escape. Grey roams the ends of brown hair messily held together in a butterfly clip.

Sherene's matronly figure is hidden in the black dressing gown that covers even her toes. Years ago, she would have stood naked in the doorway, teasing him. Sherene had been so proud of that lean body, those silky thighs. She probably won't lose the baby weight now. He knows better than to raise it. That would only spark an endless rant about how she can't attend Weight Watchers' meetings, because he's at work. Work that paid for this house. Their cars.

The baby wriggles in her arms. She has his eyes, brown and enquiring. Sherene's milky skin. The curls aren't from either of them. Probably an inheritance from his father-in-law, at least that's what Wayne says, often. Now he doesn't know what to think. Dick silently curses himself. The child is his, of course she is.

'She's teething.' Sherene's voice is meek, but there's nothing innocent about her now. 'Dick, what happened to your eye?'

She disappears into the bathroom and rifles through the cabinet, returning with a tube of antiseptic cream. 'Put this on.'

He thunders, 'Just leave me alone', and rolls onto his stomach. He buries his head in the pillow. 'Close the blinds.'

She says nothing, offering only the familiar sounds that shroud the room in darkness.

'Dick,' she says finally. 'I've been thinking –'

'Not now, Sherene.'

'When?'

'When I'm fucking ready, alright!'

'You don't have to swear.'

He pretends to sleep, but it's pointless. She won't leave.

'I tried to call you last night.'

Sherene speaks in the little girl's voice that he had once cherished.

'Leave it alone.'

'Where were you?'

'Sherene, so help me! You got no right, woman!'

He opens his eyes to study her generous hips, and laughs. 'That old man's the only one who'd want your fat arse. Brosnan — fuck me! It's a wonder he can still get it up.'

She instantly shrinks. Her self-esteem is a piece of paper, bowled over by a gust of wind.

The jets of water sting, but Dick needs the cold shower. It makes him feel alive. He grimaces into the mirror. Swollen skin in a purple sea. Dick stopped looking at his body long ago. But he still cherishes his handsome face. He savours the smell of his freshly ironed shirt. When Sherene first hired the housekeeper, he dismissed it as a ridiculous extravagance. After all, Sherene was only working part-time. But the housekeeper excels in washing and ironing. Now he'd let go of Sherene before the housekeeper.

He makes sure his leather shoes sound heavy as he treads along the polished floorboards. Ignores the portraits on the walls, all of her family. A lone mug of coffee sits on the huge teak table. Sherene stands at the kitchen sink, with her back to him.

'I've spoken to Mum. She's going to take the baby for a few days.'

'Why?'

'I'm going to Sydney this afternoon. I'll stay with Romaine. I just need some time to think.'

He swallows a gulp of coffee, smirks. 'I hope it doesn't hurt.'

She turns the radio on as he walks out the door. He hears the clanging of cutlery falling to the floor and smiles.

The black Ferrari convertible purrs. He adores this car, especially since Sherene told him it wasn't an appropriate vehicle for a family man. She was right. The looks that he gets from women make him the envy of the other men in the office, whom matrimony emasculated. He picks up in this car. He almost got caught once by a senior partner in the car park.

He drums the wheel at the traffic lights. Gigantic walls of green and copper cellophane peer into the river. Beauty queens foolish enough to believe that their stars will always burn. Mocking laughter oozes from the cranes and cement mixers. The machines know that the skyscrapers are destined to be dethroned by ever more grandiose buildings, an inevitability in a city whose soul cannot sleep. A cathedral stands among shrines to the State's mineral wealth. Occasionally, Dick wanders inside. Even though he is not a Catholic, he enjoys watching the men and women in suits, grasping their rosary beads.

His office is only a hundred metres away, but he knows it'll take at least another five minutes to get there. He shakes his head; the traffic in Brisbane is ridiculous. In spite of the huge amounts that people like him pay in taxes, it's impossible to get to work in a decent time. What the hell are the Council and the State government doing? This city has so much potential and yet they treat it like a precocious teenager. No mature debates about its future, only patronising clichés.

A group of workmen sit outside the Riverside Centre, finishing sandwiches Dick figures were wrapped while most people were still asleep. If you work hard, you prosper. Never mind that sit-down money. Dick saw what sit-down money had done to his family, how it corroded the moral compass of each one of them. He has more in common with these guys than his family back in Mount Isa. *Parasites.*

The house he was born in was gutted by white ants. Filled with people gutted by life. Mostly there were only ten, but during the bad times it felt like thirty were crammed in like battery hens. By the time that he turned twelve, Dad had already been gone for five years and Mum had begun her descent into madness. The misery was punctured by spurts of happiness, uncles who taught him how to hunt, schoolteachers who gave him respite.

At thirteen years of age, the boy excelled in the humanities and was a member of the debating team. His teachers were concerned that Dick would fall into the same bleak lifestyle that engulfed his family. So they rallied together for a scholarship to Elliot College, an elite school in Brisbane. Young Dick couldn't believe his eyes. He had never seen ovals so elaborately maintained and the gymnasium was a kingdom of the finest sporting equipment that money could buy.

His phone rings and he snaps it onto speaker.

'Dick, how you goin', bub?'

Lesley Tagem. The old barracouta.

'I'm good thanks, mate. How are you?'

'Good, darlin'. I'm just making sure you'll be at the meeting this morning.'

'Wouldn't miss it.'

'Alright, bub. The boss is looking forward to it. See you shortly.'

He hides fear well, a skill perfected by hundreds of press conferences and dinners with clients whose fickle temperaments determine whether or not he'll have a job to go to in the morning. But Dick smells the bubbling fear within. What will the Premier think of his black eye?

Lesley has chuckled over this plaque hundreds, perhaps thousands, of times. The faded brass looks like a neglected garden, overgrown by weeds, forgotten by the hands that had once lovingly tended it. It tells the world that the Executive Building was opened by Premier Johannes Bjelke-Petersen on 23 July 1971. But Lesley is probably the only person in the world who still gives a shit.

I remember when you used to ride your horse into Manoah. You wanted to control us blackfellas. Well, now a black woman is working in your fuckin' building mate. What do you think of that?

Child inside her giggles. That's when the dizzying feeling hits:

Like her favourite scones (not pumpkin, mind you), the euphoria consists of a small number of ingredients. All high quality, of course. A morning win on the pokies, sifted with the thrill of sticking it to that old dictator. Add a cup of the atmosphere of George Street. She enjoys watching the men in elegant suits and polished shoes, others huddle in coffee shops, speaking animatedly and in no rush to leave. It's not like Sydney, she thinks. She went there once and vowed never to return to the madness. Lesley had to endure the indignity of three taxis passing her by with their vacancy lights on. A huge lump of sugar, that place: humanity artificially soldered together. Manners evaporate in an instant.

Lesley smiles at the two security guards as she approaches. Mike is in his fifties, pot belly nurtured by his hobby of cultivating home brew. Derek, on the other hand, is in his late twenties and lean. Thick brown hair dangles over olive skin. Mike and Derek often work the same shift and they strike her as quite the odd couple.

'Morning Derek, how you goin'?'

'I'm good thanks, luvie. How are you?'

'Oh, I'm coping. How you goin', Mike?'

'Good thanks, darling.'

Lesley swipes her card and makes for the lift.

Mike and Derek are the only sign of the importance of this place. The dark brown building is inconspicuous. Few ever stop to gaze at the place from which the Queensland Government wields its power. The ancient beings trapped underneath the bitumen mourn for recognition, but their grief is in vain. Power demands fidelity to the status quo. For black people, that means remaining the poorest and most despised.

Every now and then, Labor's spin-doctors muddy the waters with publicity shots of the Premier and photogenic Aborigines. And when the dysfunction in the dirt-poor communities attracts too much heat, the Premier calls another enquiry. A group of white bureaucrats is herded into a room to solve the 'black problem'. Black public servants are cosmetic spokes in the wheels, except for the Premier's Senior Indigenous Adviser, Lesley Tagem. At least, that's what Lesley likes to think.

Lesley's grey curls resemble a tea-cosy and her body a tea-pot. During meetings she perches her tiny arms on her belly and delights her colleagues with slang and gibberish. Sometimes, she'll turn her head to the right and pout her lips, for dramatic effect. She also has the rare quality of being completely without scruples.

The former checkout operator had been a member of the Caboolture branch of the ALP for twenty years, which was no easy feat in the former National Party stronghold. Lesley attended every single branch meeting and threw herself into election campaigns with gusto. When the Labor Party swept into power after decades in the political wilderness, Lesley was not about to let the Premier forget that she was among the party faithful, whose blood and sweat had secured his victory. So she rang him and demanded her purple heart.

At first, the Premier was furious that she had inveigled his personal telephone number from his staff. In fact, he thought that she was one of those crazy fogies who wrote him letters warning of an impending UFO attack. But one of the strengths of his political life had been the ability to divine skills hidden behind the veneer of first impressions. While hearing her tirade about life in the trenches, the Premier realised that he was speaking to a woman whose ethical flexibility matched his own. How he loathed briefing notes that spoke of Australia's international human rights obligations and rah, rah, rah. Once the dust settled on electoral victory, the Premier's only priority was to secure the next. Lesley understood that.

So he offered her a job with the fancy title of 'Senior Indigenous Adviser', and a pokey desk with a view of the tea room. Lesley's expertise was within the realm of 'community consultation'. Aboriginal people were usually defined by what they lacked – houses, infrastructure, services, long life-spans. But they had an abundance of meetings; community cabinets to plan youth centres that would exist only on paper, round tables to talk about partnerships that would be anything but, and, after the advent of native title, an endless series of meetings whose purpose no one knew. This was Lesley's world. Her rule of thumb was that if you wanted to have a yarn with blackfellas, you had to fill them up with good tucker first.

'Lesley, how are you?'

Ralph Parkes, the Premier's Chief of Staff, is sitting at her desk. She's angry that he's invaded her territory, but remains cool.

'Good thanks, bub.'

As she sizes him up, Lesley figures that the lad doesn't have much going for him. He's too tall, gangly, and she's heard on good authority that he has the morals of a bandicoot.

'The Premier can't come to the meeting.'

Lesley hides her disappointment behind her matronly smile.

'Why's that?'

'He's got a press conference with the Police Commissioner. Haven't you heard?'

'Heard what?'

'Justice Brosnan was murdered last night.'

'Oh, that's terrible.'

'I thought you would have heard it on the radio this morning.'

She figures it's best not to tell him that they don't play the morning news in the casino. She pats him on the back and heads for the conference room.

'Lesley, how are you, darlin'?'

'Dick, bub. What happened to you?' she says, peering into his swollen face.

Dick offers Lesley a charming smile. 'I had a gym accident. I was working out with the personal trainer last night and I dropped one of the weights.'

Parkes stands at the doorway. 'What gym do you belong to?' he says. 'I'll make a mental note never to train there.'

'Actually, my trainer comes to my house. I have some weights in the garage.'

Dick's lie isn't melding with reality, but Parkes doesn't care. 'The Premier has passed on his apologies,' he says.

Dick's instantly relieved. He's embarrassed by his face; it makes him look like just another violent blackfella. But Dick Payne is an important man whose time is precious. 'What did you say?'

Parkes ignores him and spreads out some papers on the table. 'The Premier has asked me to make sure that everything is ready to go for the launch of the Aboriginal Employment Initiative.'

'Look,' Dick interrupts, 'I gave up my valuable time to be here. I'd like to know why the Premier saw fit to cancel.'

'As I just explained to Lesley, the Premier is giving a press conference with the Police Commissioner.'

'What the fuck for?'

Ralph looks like he's just been winded. 'Bruce Brosnan was murdered last night. Haven't you heard? The press is going crazy.'

Dick is surprised, if not elated. Fuck with Dick Payne and you fuck with the gods. He grins at Parkes. 'Let's start then.'

Parkes is confused but presses on. 'The launch will be held next Friday at ten o'clock. You'll need to be here by nine-thirty. The Premier will make a brief speech, followed by you.'

He looks squarely at Dick. 'Nothing fancy. Only three minutes.'

'Okay, Ralph. I'll give a short speech, just for you.'

THREE

The orange and blue letters of the Brisbane Transit Centre are depressed. Even the scraggly palm fronds are ready to quit. Up the escalator, the food court reeks of stale air and cheap fat. Roma Street is a wasteland, abandoned to backpackers. Signs promising budget tours throughout north Queensland and cheap gift shops have replaced the grand old department stores. But the lawyers and police remain, like cockroaches that could survive nuclear fallout.

Jason is intrigued by the young man at the traffic lights. Earphones on his head, hands in his pockets. Every so often his head sways to the private rhythms. In the sea of impassive faces, his is the only smile. Don't these people realise it's Friday? The contraptions of flesh and bone cry out for the city's second most precious lubricant – caffeine. The first is alcohol. Bottle shops exist on every corner and barflies drink beer with breakfast.

The Giant stands on the footpath outside Police Headquarters, savouring what is perhaps his tenth cigarette of the day. Higgins is a far cry from the pup Jason befriended at the Academy, who regularly trained in the gym twice a day. Back then he was so lean that the hollows in his face looked like they had been chiselled by a sculptor.

He was also the brightest in their class, often helping Jason on their more challenging assignments. At first, Jason was perplexed as to why Higgins chose the police force. Jason had limited options, but Higgins could have pursued any number of careers. But with a father who was a legend in the force, Andrew Higgins' future seemed pre-ordained.

By the time they became friends, Higgins Senior was a shell. A drunk who had lost his way, his career a distant memory. For those at Headquarters now, his name is a litmus test of regret. Silence follows any mention; faces say, *there but for the grace of God go I.*

Jason looks at his friend. He still has the dachshund eyes, balls of off-white that hover above an ocean of red.

Higgins extinguishes the cigarette with his shoe, offers a rascally grin.

'What time did you get up?' Jason says.

'Six. The baby started crying a lot earlier, but it was Lisa's turn this morning. Why do you ask?'

'You look like shit.'

'You obviously woke up on the wrong side of the bed – and I couldn't give a fuck what time that was.'

As they cross Adelaide Street, they notice Steve Jones, a barrister who frequently goes to bat for members of the Police Union. Jones is tall and thin. He rarely speaks outside of Court, smiles even less. Jones enters the Criterion, a favoured watering hole of the legal profession. Higgins inspects his watch, shakes his head.

'Jesus Christ, how do those blokes manage to perform when they start this early in the day?'

'Years of practice,' Jason says, wryly.

Bar Merlo screams in neon pink. Coffee clouds float above animated conversation. Loners type furiously on their laptops. Army green hangs against the back panel of the lift, another testament to endless construction in the city.

The firm's name, Richardson and Wright, is embossed in sky blue on the glass wall next to the doorway. A young woman sits behind the desk, thin blond hair ironed straight.

'Greg, I've got the Registrar on line two.

'Michelle, Larissa Chalmers is on line three.

'Transferring you now.'

By the time there is a lull in the traffic she appears rattled, but then quickly regains her composure. Higgins offers the smile that many women have found attractive over the years. The receptionist greets it with indifference.

'I'm Detective Senior Sergeant Andrew Higgins and this is Detective Sergeant Jason Matthews. We're here to see Chris Jennings.'

Twenty minutes later, Chris Jennings emerges. He's in his mid thirties, but his gaunt body and pale skin remind Jason of an old undertaker from a cult horror movie. His handshake is brief and superficial. He offers no apology for the delay.

'Emily is ready to see you now.'

Jennings' office is small, but these days, any office is a trophy, awarded after pounding a computer like marathon runners pound bitumen. Most professionals are housed in workstations that resemble makeshift settlements. The dividing walls are like pieces of tin, with only the bare necessities of computer and desk inside. Through the window of Jennings' office they see the massive silver tentacles of the Council Library, above its base of pea green.

Emily Brosnan is tiny and her hair is cut above her ears, making her look like an elf. She seems nervous and takes a seat close to Jennings.

'Mrs Brosnan, why don't we just start from the beginning again?' Higgins smiles and it seems to calm her. 'When was the last time you spoke to your husband?'

'It would have been about six-thirty,' she says. 'I rang him at his chambers.'

'What did you talk about?'

'I told you last night. I said that I was going out and I'd see him at home.'

'How did he sound?'

'Fine. Normal.'

'What time did you get home last night?'

She sighs deeply, as though expelling air will expel her fear. 'It would have been ten o'clock. Yes, that's right. I left Greenslopes at about nine forty-five and it usually takes me fifteen minutes to get home.'

'What were you doing in Greenslopes?'

'Visiting a relative . . .' She shifts in her seat and looks at Jennings. 'She's not well.'

'I'm sorry to hear that. We'll need to get the name and contact details for this relative.'

'Why?' she says.

Jennings gently touches her shoulder, suggesting a familiarity beyond a professional relationship. He looks across at Higgins. 'We'll get that for you.'

'Mrs Brosnan, can you describe for us what happened when you arrived home?'

'It's a blur now. I walked inside and, obviously, I went to the kitchen. I don't remember finding Bruce. I can only remember being at the neighbour's house.'

Higgins checks his notebook. 'Right, that's Rebecca Collis at fififty-nine Wadley Street, MacGregor?'

'Yes.'

'Mrs Brosnan, we talked about this last night, but I want to raise it again – the blood on your blouse and skirt. Can you tell us how it got there?'

'I don't know.'

Higgins waits for her to continue, but she remains silent. 'Do you know of anyone who would want to hurt your husband?' he says.

'No, no, of course not.'

'Mrs Brosnan, I think it'd be useful if we did a walk-through of the house. It might help you to remember.'

Jason sees the shock in her eyes, or the indecision. He's seen it before. She doesn't know whether to believe this is all happening.

'When would that be?' she says, finally.

'They'll be preoccupied with the crime scene for a few days. Let's aim for Tuesday morning.

'There's a question that I have to ask you. It's standard in these situations. Did Bruce leave a will?'

'He did. I drafted it myself.' Jennings' voice is confident, authoritative.

'Beneficiaries?'

'Only Emily and Isabella.'

Higgins turns to Emily. 'Isabella's your daughter?'

'Yes, that's correct, Detective Higgins.'

'Does she live at home?'

'Why do you ask?'

Jason recognises them – the eyes of a lioness, defending her cub. 'Well, your husband drove a late-model Mercedes Benz and I understand that you have a BMW. Who owns the old Pajero in the garage?'

'She's gone away for a few weeks . . . left the car with us.'

'Have you been in touch with your daughter recently, Mrs Brosnan?'

'I plan to visit her this morning.'

Voice smells of defensiveness. 'Why not last night?'

'I wanted to break the news to her in person.'

'Where is she, Mrs Brosnan?'

'Detectives, this is very stressful for my client,' Jennings says, standing up. 'I suggest that we continue this discussion on Tuesday morning.'

The morning sun has ripened into unforgiving heat. As they cross the street, Jason watches barristers stride into the Supreme Court, followed by their instructing solicitors and clerks.

'Let's find out more about this Isabella Brosnan,' Higgins says.

Jason nods in agreement. 'Why isn't she here, supporting her mother?'

'I was asking myself the same question. I'll start making enquiries.'

'Alright. I'm going to Brosnan's office,' Jason says.

'You'd better. If I hear that you're at the pub with Jonesy . . .'

Jason offers a cynical smile, but he's too late. Higgins already has his back to him.

The brass and green panels of Santos are a disaster from one of the old Copperart stores. As he saunters past the herd of motor-bikes on the corner of Turbot Street, Jason ponders what became of the man in the Copperart advertisement, whose seemingly permanent smile could very well have been made from tin. On the other side of the street, two barristers alternately laugh and inhale. Jason is certain he's been cross-examined by both of them, but can't remember when.

The Harry Gibbs Building is a colourless box. The huge blocks at the entrance remind Jason of a castle, overtaken by the kingdoms of Santos, Telstra and Hitachi.

Inside is bathed in neutral colours – black couches, grey car-pet, polished timber. The national emblems are hung throughout, along with Aboriginal artifacts. In the corner, a black woman rocks a toddler in a pram. Hard living is stamped on her face. She sits beside a cabinet that showcases vases from Hermannsburg, but apparently hasn't noticed them. Jason reasons that those who spend hours in a place like this are either poor or lawyers. The rich pay their lawyers to do their waiting for them.

The Registrar looks like a surfer who doesn't quite belong in a suit. Rebellious ginger hair is combed back, above skin that's been baked.

'Hi, I'm Detective Sergeant Matthews.'

'Steve Burns.'

Handshake is firm.

'We've been expecting you. Would you like to go straight up?'

'Yes. Thank you.'

The Registrar says little as he leads Jason through the offices that house the judges and their staff.

'Did you see Brosnan yesterday?'

'Yes. In the morning, I sat in on the Corrowa judgment. But I left soon after it was delivered.'

'You didn't see him later in the day?'

'No.'

They pass a group of women huddled in the corridor. Mascara that had been so carefully applied earlier sits beneath their eyes. The Registrar pauses outside a light blue door.

'His office has stayed locked, just as you asked.'

He watches Jason put on his gloves, intrigued.

'I'll be downstairs if you need me.'

Justice Bruce Brosnan's office is several times the size of Jason's cubicle at Police Headquarters. Hundreds of law reports, canvases similar to those in the Brosnan home. A small lounge suite and coffee table are at the entrance and a bar fridge is nestled into the corner. At the back of the room is a large black desk. A photograph is turned on its face in the centre.

Jason walks over and picks it up. The woman in the picture has long dark hair, an attractive smile. She's at a restaurant or café. Other faces at her table blur into the background.

'Please put that down . . . It was his favourite.'

Jason turns to see a young woman dressed in a pink suit. Her trembling hands clasp soggy tissues.

'I'm Anne Grey, Justice Brosnan's Associate.'

'You shouldn't be here,' he says.

Even though he's spoken with the bereaved so many times, Jason is still awkward. He takes her arm and leads her to the adjoining office. She offers no resistance. This room is much smaller than Brosnan's, but like the rest of the building it too feels sterile.

'Sorry, I'm Detective Sergeant Jason Matthews.'

'Hi.'

Her voice is soft. Shyness, he figures.

'Were you at work yesterday, Anne?'

'Yes. In the morning he delivered the judgment in the Corrowa case. The trial was pretty draining for everyone involved, especially the elders. I felt sorry for them, but the law has to be applied equally, without fear or favour.'

She pauses, suddenly conscious of her sermon.

'When was the last time you saw him?'

'I left the office at about six o'clock. He was sitting at his desk.'

'Did anyone come to see him yesterday?'

Her eyes turn sheepish for only a second, but it's not lost on him.

'I don't know. At least, I'm not aware of –'

'Good morning, Detective Matthews. I'm David Westin, Chief Justice of the Federal Court.'

David Westin is tall and wiry. Face sombre. He's not accustomed to waiting for others. Anne takes her cue.

'I'll be down the hall if you need anything, detective.'

'Shall we talk in my office?' Before Jason can answer, Westin is heading for the door.

His suite is similar to Brosnan's, but slightly larger. Jason wonders if the rooms are measured to reflect one's place in the judicial hierarchy. Westin gestures they take a seat on the more generous sofa.

'This is such a tragedy. I haven't been able to speak to Emily yet. Do you know how she is?'

'We interviewed Mrs Brosnan earlier this morning. She's understandably distraught.'

'Such terrible news. Please ask if there is anything I can do.'

'How well did you know Bruce Brosnan?'

'We shared chambers when we first went to the bar. We had a long professional association.'

'How would you describe his relationship with Emily Brosnan?'

'I really wouldn't know. As I said, my relationship with Bruce was of a professional nature.'

'Are you aware of anyone who might have had a grudge against him?'

'No. But, once again, I didn't really know anything about Bruce's personal life.'

Jason doubts the conversation will be anything but a waste of his time, but then he remembers. 'Did you ever meet Brosnan's daughter, Isabella?'

'Detective Matthews,' Westin says, frowning, 'I do understand the importance of frankness, but . . .'

'I assure you that discretion is a crucial part of my job.'

Westin sighs. 'About ten years ago Isabella was in a very bad way. She had a drug addiction. I understand that she was even homeless for a brief period. But the extent of Isabella's problems didn't come out into the open, until the criminal charges.'

'Working on a Friday afternoon – Homicide's the gift that just keeps giving.'

Jason knows Higgins is only half serious. Between them, Higgins was the first to decide on Homicide, inspired by a father who had spent two decades seeking answers for and from the dead.

'You can really make a difference in Homicide. Do things no one else can,' Higgins insisted, as other young men indulged in drinking games. Jason was intrigued by the passion in his friend's voice. He was just as touched by Higgins' unswerving belief in his father. Whereas Jason had always struggled to reach an understanding with his own father, Andrew seemed to worship the ground that Higgins Senior walked on. It led Jason to believe that, of the two of them, Higgins was the better man. He was the one who had charisma, compassion for those he worked with, and married at a time when the idea of a life-long commitment still scared the hell out of Jason.

Higgins takes a left and pulls up at a red light. 'Have any luck reaching Sherene Payne?'

'No, her phone keeps going to message bank.'

'And it was definitely the last call to Brosnan's mobile?'

'Yeah, seven twenty-nine.'

Higgins frowns. 'Who is she?'

'A lawyer. Married to that big shot Dick Payne,' Jason says, glancing out the window.

The yards in the established suburb of MacGregor are generous, accessorised with pools, landscaped gardens and pergolas. They pass a Scout hall in a park and Jason thinks he could probably have a good life here, albeit a quiet one. Will he ever settle down?

Jason looks at his partner's groggy eyes, and thinks perhaps not. 'How are things at home?'

'Shit.'

'What happened?'

Higgins pauses. 'Lisa and I had another argument.'

His words hang in the air with no place to go. Both have seen too many men give everything to the job, only to retire to the loneliness and dust of boardinghouse rooms.

The light-coloured bricks of the two-storey house were popular in the 1980s. The balcony on the top floor is bare apart from a poodle, yapping wildly. Seven garden gnomes stand at the foot of the front door.

'Fan of Snow White?' Higgins says, knocking on the door.

'Maybe. I'm surprised no one's flogged them.' Jason glances over the fence at the Brosnans' house, next door. 'Have you heard those stories of people being sent postcards from their kidnapped garden gnomes? There was this one from –'

'Good. You're on time.'

Rebecca Collis is tiny in the door jamb, the sash of her blue dress wrapped tightly, light powder pressed into a face that speaks of clean living.

She slides bony hands from yellow gardening gloves. 'You must be Higgins.'

Higgins smiles and extends his hand. 'Mrs Collis, thanks for agreeing to see us.'

'It's Miss.' She turns to Jason. 'And you're Matthews. An Aboriginal detective, hey?' She sizes him up like a bidder inspecting art at an auction. 'I think Aborigines can achieve whatever they put their minds to.'

Voice whistles as she speaks.

'Thank you, Miss Collis.'

'I went to school with an Aboriginal boy. What was his name ...'

Higgins smiles impatiently.

'Come in, then.'

The dining room could have come straight from the window of a furniture store. The white vinyl chairs and glass table are flawless. Tall black vases stand in the corners of the room and portraits of children adorn the walls.

'Grandchildren?' Higgins asks.

'God no! I wasn't that stupid.'

Bashful grin dances on creases.

'Nephews and nieces.'

Jason and Higgins sit at opposite ends of the table. Rebecca takes her place in the middle.

'Miss Collis, perhaps we can start by talking about last night.'

'I did what I do every night. I had my dinner in front of the news and then I watched the *7:30 Report*.' Rebecca draws close to Jason. 'That Kerry O'Brien is a dish. If I was twenty years younger, I'd let him put his shoes under my bed.'

Higgins laughs heartily while Jason tries his hardest to remain serious.

'I heard a car pull into the driveway next door. I think that was during the last story on the *7:30 Report*. Yes, that's right. I just assumed it was Emily or Bruce.'

She looks wistful; it's all too recent.

'Did you hear or see anything unusual last night?'

'After I got my nightly dose of Kerry, I started doing the washing up. That was when I heard the argument.'

'Where?'

'Bruce and Emily's house.'

'Did you recognise the voices?'

'Hmm, it was a man and a woman. I couldn't really understand them. To be honest, I felt uncomfortable hearing it. None of my business. So I rang my sister in Sydney.'

'How long did you speak?'

'It would have been half an hour. By the time I hung up the phone, the arguing had stopped. I sat in bed reading a book for an hour. It's Peter Corris' latest. I really love that Cliff Hardy . . . none of that new age *CSI* rubbish.'

Higgins starts coughing as though he's about to choke. Rebecca disappears into the hallway, returning with a tray of glasses and a jug of water.

'I would have been asleep for half an hour before I heard Annabelle.'

'Annabelle?'

'The dog.' Rebecca speaks with the certainty that all dogs should be called Annabelle. 'She's a good pooch – never barks unless there's a stranger outside.'

From behind his mask, Jason finds that very difficult to believe.

'Then I heard the thumping. It sounded like someone was going to knock the door down. I was so surprised when I saw Emily. At first I thought she'd been attacked. She was a frightful mess. She didn't make any sense until I forced her to sit down. She wanted me to go to see Bruce, but I wouldn't. I didn't think it was safe. We rang the police together.'

A flash of pain appears on her face.

'I hope I did the right thing.'

'How long have you lived next to the Brosnans?'

'Oh, I moved here when I retired. It's fifteen years in April.'

'Were Emily and Bruce already here?'

'Oh yes. People around here tend to stay.'

'Did you know them well?'

'Not really. We'd chat over the fence occasionally.'

'Did you ever hear them arguing?'

'No. To be honest, I rarely saw them together.'

'Did you ever see their daughter?'

Rebecca smiles. 'Isabella is a lovely girl. She always brings a present for Annabelle, mostly bones. But every Christmas, she'll buy her a new outfit. You know it's amazing . . .'

'When was the last time that you saw Isabella?'

'Hmm, actually, it was yesterday. I was sitting in the garden, having my lunch. Isabella was standing near the fish pond in the front of Emily and Bruce's house.'

'Did you speak to her?'

'That's the interesting thing. I called out to her a few times, but she just ignored me and went inside.'

FOUR

No sound bites of screaming children, no mass casualties. No eyes of the world staring in indignation. Native title is the most sophisticated weapon they have fired at us yet. Break our minds with invisible bullets, until we can no longer believe that we are who we say we are. This judgment will poison our insides like Agent Orange. Deform our children before they are born, so that they will never see their own reflection, only the distorted image the law sees fit to provide them.

If we no longer have our traditional connection, then who are we?

Refugees who have never left our own land?

Six years of my life for nothing.

'Where's your Auntie?' Charlie's sneer is coated with blame.

'I don't know, Dad.'

'I thought she was coming with you.'

'No, Dad – she didn't say anything.'

Charlie mutters under his breath. It's inaudible, but there's no mistaking. He knows that alcohol is putrefying her soul. And flesh. Miranda feels like a character in a post-apocalypse film. A drone cloaked in grey skin.

She stares at her father's back as he walks away. Charlie is short, his body hard from the boxing of his youth. Soul is hard too. The faithful gather around Charlie. A young woman looks hungrily into his eyes. Her jeans are faded and tight. Other men have been staring, albeit surreptitiously, but Charlie appears oblivious. When the woman speaks, Miranda recognises the Manoah accent, its exaggerated vowels bounce off the walls.

Everyone from Manoah has the accent, a virus that lives in

a huge cloud over the mission, resistant to vaccine. Fifty years of living in Brisbane seems to have had no impact on Auntie Ethel's, Miranda thinks.

The soothing aroma of milky tea wafts. The elders have been sitting down for the past half-hour, sipping from chipped porcelain. Every so often, Miranda hears a gasp, followed by silence then a stampede of voices. Standing at the very back of the hall near the kitchen is the younger generation, too young to remember the euphoria on 3 June 1992.

But Ethel's not here.

'Missed you in the office today, mate.'

O'Neill is fifteen years older than Miranda, but he looks so much younger than she feels. The playfulness in his hazel eyes is gone, replaced by apprehension.

'I called Angela,' she says. How she hates her gravelly voice. 'I felt so exhausted.'

She knows her words smack of desperation. Christ, she *had* been desperate this morning. Throwing her bloodied blouse into the wheelie bin. Lying to Angela about flu-like symptoms. Spending what felt like hours staring into the toilet bowl, nursing a body filled with pain and regret.

O'Neill just nods slowly. 'Did you hear the news?'

'What news?'

'Bruce Brosnan was killed last night.'

He pauses and she knows he's letting her digest it.

'The Premier and the Police Commissioner held a press conference this morning. Word on the street is a home invasion.'

'Are you serious?'

In the corner of her eye, she sees Jonathon. It's his height that she notices first and the smell – he always wears Lynx deodorant.

Jonathon throws her a quizzical look.

'You look surprised to see me,' he says. '*Hellooo*. We discussed this last night. Don't you remember? My meeting got cancelled, so now I'm giving the talk about the appeal.'

She feels deflated when O'Neill walks away. She wants to

follow him, wants to redeem herself, but has no idea where to begin.

'Jonathon, how you going?' Charlie offers a handshake, happy to see him, as always.

When has Charlie ever looked at her that way?

'Good thanks, Uncle Charlie.'

'Which one of you is speaking?'

'I am,' says Jonathan.

Charlie grins in approval. 'Do you know what you're going to say?'

'I thought I'd just give a quick spiel about the principles of the Yorta Yorta decision and how they'll affect any appeal.'

Jonathon's face is so earnest. Miranda has often wondered if he has ever nursed a grudge. Would he even know how?

'It's pretty grim, Uncle Charlie.'

Charlie shrugs his shoulders. 'I've never believed in this native title bullshit anyway. It's just crumbs. All the while, our attention's being diverted from the real things – sovereignty, land rights . . .'

Jonathon looks wounded, and asks, 'Where's Auntie Ethel? I haven't seen her.'

Charlie sighs in exasperation. 'She was supposed to come with this one –' he says, nodding towards Miranda – 'but she hasn't turned up.'

'That's strange. Auntie Ethel never misses a community meeting.'

Jonathon speaks as though he's a member of the black community, and in a way that's true. In the past few minutes, aunties have kissed him, uncles have shaken his hand. Even some of the young girls have gushed in his direction.

'We have to start,' Charlie says. 'Can't wait for Ethel any longer. She'll probably turn up later.'

As she watches Charlie and Jonathon take their seats at the front of the hall, Miranda feels the chill of shame. She tries to convince herself that last night was an aberration, a traumatic response to a traumatic event. After all, she spent six years fighting in a trench with only Jonathon sharing the burden. But right now, the jackhammer inside her brain is merciless. Recklessness defines her. Always has. Over the years, she's taken drinks from strangers, jumped into cars with inebriated men at the wheel, woken in her bed with no recollection of how she made it home the night before. Mum was the lucky one.

Miranda can't remember what her mother looked like. She can only recall the security of being on top of Carys' shoulders, and the glare of the sand that day at the beach. Was she four or five? Miranda will never know. She's not even sure if it's real or imagined. It pains her that she can remember the green lights of the machines that kept her mother alive those last few months, but not her smile. Or her voice. It was soft and melodic, Miranda thinks, or was that her imagination too? She knows why her mother is on her mind. Chemicals fucking with her brain, melancholy shredding what's left.

Charlie opens the meeting with his usual acknowledgment of the traditional owners. Each one of them feels its poignancy. The law had determined that the 'traditional' Corrowa society no longer existed. Who are they now? And what of the man who determined that their traditional connection had been lost?

Cameramen point their equipment into reluctant faces. The media are here to see if they can catch a delicious sound-bite, wild and vengeful natives who take joy from Bruce Brosnan's death. But the Corrowa are far too dignified. Brosnan's death is felt, but not acknowledged. Miranda had no great affection for the judge, but she has sympathy for his family. She had spent enough time listening to courtroom gossip to know that Brosnan had a daughter. No doubt she will be suffering terribly right now. After ten minutes of their probing, Charlie asks the press to leave.

Jonathon speaks with his usual aplomb: native title is a bundle of rights kept alive by the continuation of traditional law and custom. Empowering words, Miranda thinks, if you forget that it's the judges who decide what traditional law and custom actually is. The Corrowa are just as powerless as their countrymen's artifacts kept in sterile glass cabinets, scattered throughout the Federal Court.

Native title is shrouded in complexity. Ask five native title lawyers for an opinion and you'll receive seven in return. Can they win an appeal? Miranda looks around the room. Intuitively, each knows that it's a pipedream. It's the feeling in the gut, fed by bitter experience. Watching black kids grow up in jails, black mothers fighting bureaucrats for their kids, elders being told that their hard-earned money will languish in government coffers. All law courts are cut from the same cloth.

As Jonathon closes, the crowd claps. They may not believe in his medicine, but they have great affection for the practitioner. Charlie hugs Jonathon, whose eyes are misty. Charlie seizes the podium.

'If you want to pursue an appeal, then I'll support it with everything I have. But I have to level with you mob. Native title is crumbs. They throw the crumbs from their table of caviar and champagne and then they sit back and watch, while we tear each other apart. Brothers and sisters, we have to see through the smoke and mirrors.'

The crowd is deathly silent. Miranda is taken back to her father's speeches during the Commonwealth Games protests, when he kept hundreds spellbound. Charlie never wrote any of it down; he didn't even know what he was going to say until the microphone was in his hand.

'In the last few years, I've watched our mob being made to feel less welcome in West End. Most of the hostels have closed and so few of our families can afford to live here anymore. Brothers and sisters, Coconut Holdings just cares about profits. They talk about giving jobs to our people with this Aboriginal Employment Initiative rubbish. But they'll be paying our people with the very money that the government stole from our grandparents. Coconut Holdings has no honour and neither does the Premier.'

'That's right, brother!'

'Too deadly, my brother!'

'On this very piece of land, our ancestors fought a brave battle against the native mounted police. They may have been overwhelmed and removed to Manoah, but their dignity and courage live on in us. I say that we stay true to the values of our fallen warriors – our judges.'

Whistles come from all corners.

'We need to get back to the ideas of the 1970s. When we were calling out, "What do we want?" I don't remember anyone answering "native title". This place is the last piece of land we can call our own. We're not going *anywhere*.'

Ethel is pleased that she can still fit into the child's swing. Those brisk walks through Orleigh Park must be paying off. Each morning, the zestful smell of grass shakes off the embers of sleep. Its huge tree trunks stand like withered sages and from the banks of Meanjin, West End peers into the old money and private river docks of St Lucia. It's in the early hours that Ethel hears the screams of the water spirits.

Your time will come.

Our time will come.

He promised.

But there are no water spirits in this place. Meston Park. Blackfellas' Park.

Even though the signage arrived only this morning, the blue and white of the Coconut Holdings logo is coated with dust. The earthmover stands inside the fenced area, reminding her of the mission superintendent's old house. Like Mr McGraorty's family, the machine lives in a compound surrounded by barbed wire.

Unlike the other parks in West End, there is no community garden in Meston Park. No bike-riding track. Or welcome sign. Families rarely bring picnic hampers to bide time on the lush green. Years ago, timber had been soldered to the ground to make seats in the hill. But there are never any spectator sports played here.

Three sides of Meston Park are surrounded by industrial estates and the northern boundary faces a block of mansions built in the nineteenth century. In other parts of Brisbane, the grand old homesteads would have been converted into apartment buildings. But here they remain inconspicuous, like guards at the watchtower.

Light from cigarettes unveils the drinkers. Huddled beneath the trees, they fill the night with bickering and laughter. She knows the drinking would have begun this morning. They will continue until their exhausted bodies collapse. This place is dense with misery and yet there are no bodies in the earth, Ethel thinks. But you don't need decayed bones to feel the pain of this place. It pelts down like torrential rain. Only during the huge festivals is the pain drowned out by thousands of feet and music that thunders from portable stages.

She turns and sees the shabby white timber of the hall in the western corner. Soon it will disappear completely under night's blanket. Miranda and Charlie will be wondering where she is. All of the mob will be looking for her. For them, this place is the last bastion. They fear that once they lose it, they too will be erased from West End.

But this is also the safe side of the boundary.

Hear the stock whip. Curfew. Get to Meston Park before nightfall.

He had come to her.

Fifty years ago.

Red Feathers.

Childbirth had torn Ethel apart, but she felt nothing, only disbelief that those tiny lips would never draw breath. Eyes closed as though he was in a deep sleep. She begged and begged.

Please wake up.

Matron smiled as she said that it was God's will.

Ethel found a leather strap from the stables, the remnants of an old bridle. She concealed it in her apron and kept it tucked between her old mattress and its creaky frame. The next day, Ethel sat on the steps of the mission church, staring at the mango tree. When she was small, the older girls in the dormitory would lift her into its bough.

Lesley snored softly that night. The light in the hallway reflected on her cherub face. Even when she was heavy with child, Ethel had allowed Lesley to remain in her bed. *This is what a mother does*, she thought. *If I can be a mother to Lesley, then I can look after my own baby.* But that night Ethel made Lesley sleep in her own bed. Her heart filled with sorrow as she chastised the sobbing child.

When she knew Lesley was soundly asleep, Ethel slipped outside and silently made her way to the hole in the fence. It was concealed by the boulder, but all of the dormitory girls knew about it. Matron probably did too. But you had to be brave or stupid to crawl through. After Gina was caught with her lover, Matron shaved her head and made her dress in a sugar bag for two months.

Like Ethel, Gina had been sent to work for a white family, only to come back with a swollen womb. She didn't know what happened to Gina's baby. No one ever talked about the babies of the dormitory girls. For Ethel, that was the cruellest punishment of all. She craved some acknowledgment of the little one she had loved and tried her hardest to keep alive.

Ethel climbed the mango tree that night and sat on top of the bough, making a noose from the strap. She knew her body would probably be found by one of the men, up at dawn to begin work. So long as it wasn't Lesley who found her, Ethel didn't care. No one else there had ever accepted her. Twelve years ago, a protector had pulled into the mission and deposited Ethel. She had no country, no name.

She wondered whether she should say a prayer. Anger welled. If God really did exist, then why had he taken her baby away? She tried to lift the noose over her head, but couldn't. Her hands were weak, as though an unknown force was trying to keep her alive. Then she heard the sweet melody of the Paradise Parrot. Emerald green and red belly, tail almost as long as its body. It was sitting on the bough. Next to *him*.

He had a regal face full of pain. His long legs almost touched the ground. Ethel was afraid at first, but Red Feathers smiled timidly as he took the noose from her hands. Drew her to him and blew air into her face. And for the first time, she was at peace.

Fifty years ago.

Now, Ethel sits on the grass in Meston Park, remembering. Her heart sang when she saw him again, at the Court yesterday, flying above the judge's head. She waited in her room last night, biding her time, until she heard the soft chirping of the Paradise Parrot. She had so much to tell him. Yes, she had been waiting for him. Had never lost faith. Some stories she'd shared with the mob, the lawyers, but other secrets, like his name, the purpose of the feathers, she'd kept. And she'd keep those secrets locked within, until he told her otherwise. Oh yes, Ethel could be trusted with secrets. *Been keeping them for fifty years.* But he wanted only to fly. It was exhilarating, but she had forgotten how cold it could be at that height.

He told her that his journey back through time had begun with an immense blow to his chest, as though reliving the moment when the bullet had entered him. With his chest aflame, a multitude of hands appeared, dragging his body. When they left him, Red Feathers could feel the cold earth against his face. He was terrified when he opened his eyes. The metropolis of concrete and filth was overwhelming. The lights, the traffic, the noise. Thankfully, one of the water spirits had seen him. It was the water spirit who told him that he had returned to the bosom of Meanjin. He had made it home.

Now, Ethel watches Red Feathers sitting on top of the slippery dip, his huge legs just touching the gravel. The glare of the streetlight reveals a long face. It's a ridiculous sight – the giant in the child's playground. But Ethel knows better than to laugh. She feels his pain, breathes in his torment.

Red Feathers looks at the hill where seats now wallow in loneliness, the place where he and the other men had charged against the police, the curfew, the boundary, over a century ago. He had stood in front of his wife that day, so his body could shield her. But the horrific pain in his chest drained his mind of thought. As he lay on the ground, his life force ebbing, Horace Downer stood over him. The man's eyes were crazed, as though all logic had been sucked out.

Few of the living ever hear the screams of the dead. Red Feathers, on the other hand, is followed by voices constantly. And he sees everything. The living and the dead. Whenever his feet touch the bitumen, the cries of the spirits vibrate beneath him. The most chilling are the parents who wander the streets, calling out the names of lost children.

Last night, Ethel and Red Feathers saw Downer's spirit loitering at the top of the hill. At first, Red Feathers thought that Downer had chosen to spend his death protecting the boundary. He wanted to confront him, but Red Feathers soon realised that Downer was on the hill by way of punishment. His body had shrivelled, so that he was the size of a boy. Downer drank laudanum from a dirty flask, with an unquenchable thirst.

Ethel and Red Feathers flew to Downer's home above the hill. The two-storey mansion was long and narrow, like the man who had built it. The iron lace on the rooftop balcony had remained virtually unchanged. Countless nights, Downer had sat, clutching his gun. Enforcing the boundary. In spite of the obvious danger, the black men and women took their chances after curfew. They were domestic servants who could no longer bear the separation from their families on the other side of town, lovers who took the ultimate risk, and then there was Red Feathers, who just despised the boundary for all that it represented.

As they watched from high above, the cries of a spirit woman sent a chill down Ethel's spine. They could see the image of Downer's bullet plunging into the back of the hapless domestic. She had just seen her baby girl walk for the first time, and her heart was singing. Red Feathers knows their secrets. In the space of a second, all of that joy, all of that potential, snuffed. Ethel begged him to leave, to take her home.

Night has finally fallen. Ethel walks over and buries her face into one of his gigantic arms. Red Feathers tells her that the business has begun. She has no doubt that he is strong enough, but Red Feathers is nothing if not compassionate. Compassion for warriors who had turned into drunken beggars was what had ultimately led to the failed rebellion. Watching people who believe they have no power to change their circumstances is more painful than any injury that could be inflicted by bullets. She knows that Red Feathers believes that change is always possible, so long as one draws breath.

He waited, he tells her now, for the dead man's people to come for him. He expected the old, pompous white men and their fragile looking women, but was stunned to see the black woman standing behind them. She was young, perhaps fifteen, and her eyes were stained by tears. When Justice Brosnan rose from his body there was an exchange of awkward nods but he was aghast when he saw her. So his Aboriginal ancestry had been kept hidden, and he was not welcoming the revelation.

Red Feathers wanted to touch her, to assure her that in spite of everything, she still had her humanity. But that kind of contact was not appropriate. As Red Feathers took the pouch from his back, the relatives formed a circle and spoke in hushed tones. By the time his work was done, all of them had disappeared.

They hear screams from the drinkers' tree and look across the park. A streak of grey darts, followed by the sounds of a radio. Bodies fall to the ground surrounded by anxious yelling.

Red Feathers seizes Ethel's hand and they soar above Downer's hill again. As they watch the young black man being pushed into the police van, she knows that Red Feathers has finally realised.

The boundary remains.

FIVE

John Tipat's mother taught him to use the toilet by burning his hands on the stove. At age six, he drowned the neighbour's cat. Twenty years later, Tipat drowned a little girl. Detective Senior Sergeant Andrew Higgins beat him through a telephone book in the watch house for over three hours. Tipat's confession would have been thrown out of Court, had Detective Sergeant Jason Matthews not been prepared to lie in the witness box. Now, Jason looks back on that sorry chapter as just another casualty of war, a war that began in the womb. Insanity was the constant precursor to murder. The notion that one had to plead it has never made sense to him. Sane people don't kill the innocent at random.

He and Higgins spend their working lives protecting society from the dangerously insane. But when he is in this room, Jason feels like the prisoner. He knows that after the first forty-eight hours, the chances of finding the killer are slim. It has been five days. And the clouds of futility are gathering momentum.

Coffee and cigarette smoke waft. Black sandbags live underneath bloodshot eyes. You can't spend years in the underbelly without being shaped by it, he thinks. Study enough monsters and surely you become one. Is he a monster? He doesn't intentionally hurt those around him. But his soul is impervious. Over the years, he's enjoyed many short-term relationships, some spanning weeks, a couple for three months. But she always leaves, bundling unfulfilled expectations together with her clothes and CDs.

Jason craves the solitude of Homicide. But the others have partners, children even. Yet here they are, stress flowing from every gesture. Bodies are beacons of the violence that human beings are capable of. Pencils tap on desks, smokers cough and loners sigh. The whiteboard at the front is blank, the only comfort this room has to offer. Higgins scrawls onto it, conscripting it back into the war.

'Morning people.'

Higgins removes his black suitcoat and rests it on a chair. Even though it's eight o'clock in the morning, wet patches have already gathered underneath his armpits. The white business shirt that his wife pressed last night is untidily tucked into his black pants.

'Boss, have you seen this yet?'

Henly offers a copy of the *Queensland Daily* to Higgins. The headline on the front page reads, 'Black leaders placed a curse on murdered judge.'

'Didn't take them long,' Higgins says, dismissively. He pauses to boot up the laptop on the desk. In seconds, photographs of the crime scene bounce off the whiteboard. 'The deceased, Justice Bruce Brosnan, was found lying face down on the kitchen floor. You can see the broken wine bottle and its contents next to the victim. A wine glass was on the bench above the body. Unfortunately, no print was recovered from the glass.'

Higgins cocks his right eyebrow as he focuses on the base of the glass. 'At first glance, we thought it was blood. Turns out it's a rock that's been ground to a paste.'

'Like ochre?' Henly says.

'Perhaps. They found the paste on some of the feathers as well. Hopefully, the Forensic Services Branch will be able to provide us with some more information soon. Alright, we need more information on the feathers. I've never seen this before. We need an expert who can place them.' He turns to a female officer, Lacey, sitting in the middle row. Her brown hair is spiked with hair gel. Toned arms speak of many hours in a gym.

'Lacey, can you look into this? Your first port of call will be Dr Bernes at the Environmental Protection Agency.'

Lacey looks deflated at the task, but nods immediately.

'Nothing else in the kitchen appears to have been disturbed. Perhaps Brosnan was about to enjoy a glass of wine, and the killer came from behind, by surprise.'

Higgins has aged rapidly since arriving at Homicide, Jason thinks. But that's normal here, perhaps expected. On rare moments, he catches a glimpse of his partner's former self. The flamboyance that dances in his eyes like a solar eclipse is infectious. But too many stories have gained him notoriety, the kind that live through harried whispers in corridors.

All originate in the war, but alcohol gives them fists.

'We've received the autopsy report from Doc Thomas. As you already know, this was a particularly vicious attack. The victim's neck and lips were slashed repeatedly. Two of his front teeth were completely knocked out.'

Higgins pauses to read from his notes. 'Brosnan's associate said goodbye to him just after six. The neighbour, Rebecca Collis, reported hearing a car pull into Brosnan's home at some time between half past seven and eight o'clock. She also heard an argument between a man and a woman coming from Brosnan's home, sometime after eight o'clock. Then Emily Brosnan runs to Collis' house just after ten o'clock. Emily's alibi is dodgy – she claims to have been visiting a relative up until nine forty-five, but is yet to provide us with the details of this mysterious person.'

Higgins pauses to clear his throat. 'Collis also reported seeing Brosnan's daughter, Isabella, enter Brosnan's home at midday. Now, Isabella has an interesting past. Ten years ago, she was charged with the attempted murder of her former dealer.'

Higgins sweeps the room for recognition, but only dredges shock. 'Yeah, I have to confess it was news to me too. Apparently there was an argument over drugs and the dealer ended up with a knife in his chest. The Brosnans got the best lawyers money could buy.

'They argued self defence and Isabella walked. Fast forward

ten years and Isabella appears to have cleaned up her act. Until two months ago, she was employed as a counsellor in a homeless people's shelter. But the million-dollar question is – where is she now? Her car was left in the Brosnans' garage. Emily Brosnan was only prepared to say that her daughter had "gone away".

'Another thing, Brosnan took a call on his mobile at seven twenty-nine from one Sherene Payne.' He turns to Jason. 'Matthews, still chasing the elusive Mrs Payne?'

Jason nods and Higgins quickly moves on. 'There were no signs of forced entry so Brosnan probably knew his killer. This could point to Emily? It might also point to Isabella. Given that her car's still in their garage, she presumably has a key to her parents' home, or at least she might know where the spare's kept. We need to check. Henly, you've been to Isabella's last address?'

'Boss, the place was deserted. I've spoken with the landlord. Isabella cleared out four weeks ago. She left the place in a shambles. The only forwarding address is her parents'. I knocked on the neighbours' doors, but came up with nothing.'

'Matthews, any luck getting a copy of the will?'

'Jennings finally sent it through this morning. He was right – the only beneficiaries are Emily and Isabella.'

'Alright, now, another controversial aspect is that Brosnan dismissed a native title claim on the morning of his death.'

Higgins looks down at his notes. 'Here we go . . . ah yes, the Corrowa People.' He grasps the *Queensland Daily*, waves it around in a circle. 'Which means we'll get shit like this. So we're going to keep the feathers out of the public domain. Let's just concentrate on the facts, rather than this voodoo bullshit.'

Higgins turns to Henly. 'I want you to go back to Isabella's old employer. See if anyone's heard from her.' He pauses to check his watch. 'Matthews, we gotta go.'

Higgins is behind the wheel as per usual. Jason doesn't mind. It's an opportunity for him to reflect.

'I wonder how they managed to keep Isabella's trial out of the headlines,' Jason says.

'It never made it to the jury. The Crown entered a nolle prosequi on the first day.'

'But I still would have expected some publicity from the committal.'

Higgins screws his face like a pin cushion. 'It pays to have friends in high places.'

'Hmm.'

'What was that?'

'Loses her job and her home. No doubt the inheritance will arrive at a fortuitous time.'

Emily will always cling to the memory, even though it's jaded. Court One had a musty smell and the listlessness of artificial light. The place was a rambling tow-truck, clearing the city's streets of the downtrodden, whose engines had died long ago. The old black woman sat in the dock, face filled with indignation. Her body was stiff, folded arms shielding wounded pride. Bruce stood at the bar table; his body tall and strong. Emily had only heard of him, was yet to feel the touch of his eyes, or the rush of excitement when he spoke to her. He turned to the dock, murmured gently to the old woman and placed a reassuring arm on her shoulder. The woman smiled. Perhaps it was the first time that anyone in that desolate place had treated her as a human being. In those few seconds, Emily fell in love.

'Is the air conditioning too heavy?'

She smiles into Chris' warm eyes.

'I'm fine, thanks.'

Chris has always been grounded, so unlike her Isabella, whose life constantly teeters on the brink of disaster. She's always thought that about him, even when he was Bruce's associate. Had naïvely hoped that he and Isabella would form a relationship. They were roughly the same age, shared the same family background.

'There's no need for us to get out of the car until the police get here,' he says.

It's been less than a week, but the house is like an abandoned mansion, something that she would expect to see in an American Civil War epic. The grass is overgrown, hedges require trimming and the pond is choking on leaves. But it's the silence that causes a tremor within. It's the silence of a ghost who swallows its pain, who revels in the familiarity of haunted dreams.

When she had first seen it, Emily imagined standing perched against one of the four white columns, greeting him when he came home. But it struck her as odd that the three of them could possibly need so much space. Bruce nudged her lips and whispered, 'We'll need a big house for the other babies.' Her heart sang.

Early in the marriage, they had made love daily. The look he gave her was a combination of affection and hunger. But the look had disappeared long ago. She'd given up on having more children. Bruce was already gone when Issie woke in the mornings and she was asleep by the time he walked through the front door, wearily carrying tomorrow's brief.

'For how long were you here?' Chris says.

'Twenty-five years in June,' she replies.

Emily threw herself into their baby home. She painted the interior, spent hours selecting the right shade for the curtains. Within a year, Emily had breathed order into the garden that had been rack and ruin. But the babies never came. When she had the last miscarriage, Bruce was in Court, defending a rock star who'd assaulted a flight attendant. So Emily invested all of her love in Issie. And the house.

Bruce may have slaved to become the star of the Bar, but Emily and Issie had paid the real price for his success. Emily was determined that the debt be discharged. The luxury pool became a necessity, as was the new kitchen. Then there was the matter of the sauna. Emily had almost managed to convince herself that she was happy, until Issie began her downward spiral.

'They're here.'

She smiles nervously at Chris.

'I'll be with you the whole time. It'll be okay,' he says.

Higgins opens her door.

'Mrs Brosnan, thank you for meeting us here.'

Emily enters the garage at the western wing of the house, just as she did five nights ago. She pauses when she sees his fishing rod standing next to the bikes. Bruce took up fishing on his fiftieth birthday, his first and only hobby, she tells them.

Higgins moves forward. 'Are you alright?'

'Mrs Brosnan, take your time.' The stench of disinfectant irritates her nose. Emily expected to see bloodstains, but the marble is clean.

'Mrs Brosnan, do you remember anything?' Jason says.

Emily scans the room, begs for hidden memories to enter her mind.

'Take your time, Mrs Brosnan.'

But the fishing rod is where he left it. We're going to Stradbroke next weekend. Bruce will tell you. He'll want me to protect Issie.

Feebly, she shakes her head. 'I'm sorry, detectives.'

Higgins asks her to check whether any valuables are missing. Emily is adamant that nothing has been removed. 'Did Bruce store any money in the house?' he says.

'He always kept some cash in the top drawer of his desk in the study.'

They walk up the stairs and into Bruce's study. Photographs of the young barrister adorn the wall. He's standing between an older man and woman, their cheeks rosy against the yellowed paper.

'Bruce's admission ceremony.' She keeps her head bowed. Emily is certain that his smell is still here. A combination of aftershave and Scotch.

'Mrs Brosnan, the drawer isn't locked.'

'It never is. This is a safe neighbourhood. At least, it used to be.'

Jason rifles through the drawer. A pile of old receipts, but no cash. 'How much money did Bruce keep in the drawer?'

'Oh, a few hundred I suppose. Why, how much is there?'

'Nothing.'

'Did anyone else know about the money?' Higgins says.

'No, no, of course not.'

'What about staff?'

'The cleaner comes twice a week and the gardener drops by to mow the lawn every Tuesday. But they've worked for us for over ten years.'

She leans on Chris as they walk into the sunlight. Emily doesn't look back at the house. It's no longer her home.

Higgins stops them in the driveway. 'Mrs Brosnan, you still need to provide us with the details of the relative you visited before you came home on Thursday night.'

She stares at him blankly.

'We need that information.'

'I told you, she's sick.'

'Who are you protecting, Emily?' Higgins says. There's a new hardness in his voice.

'No one.'

'Where is Isabella?'

She steps away from Chris. Folds her arms across her chest, as though she could lock out all of them.

'Do you have any idea how difficult it is for a person to change her life, detective? I'm proud of my daughter. She's a good person.'

Higgins shakes his head, he's incredulous. 'Emily, your husband was murdered.'

'Of course I know . . .'

'It's my job to find out who did that and that requires me to ask you questions. Emily, my questions are reasonable. Where is Isabella?'

SIX

'Bub, the Premier was very apologetic for missing our meeting. He said to let you know.'

Dick draws his chin into his right hand, offers her the look he's perfected in front of the mirror.

'The Premier is very excited about the AEI,' she says.

Acronym rolls off her tongue, smooth as velvet. Everyone in Indigenous affairs craves acronyms, everyone, that is, except those on the ground, he thinks. Acronyms won't deliver jobs, won't wean them off the sit-down money.

'I don't want that happening too often.'

'Dick, the Premier's a busy man.'

He can always tell when Lesley is nervous, anxiety yapping at the bottom of her voice like a chihuahua biting its heels.

'If it happens again, I'm pulling the pin.'

'Bub, bub – I promise, it won't.'

He knows Coconut Holdings has no intention of withdrawing from his Aboriginal Employment Initiative. It wants free black labour that can be disposed of on a whim. Dick's wants coalesce with those of his client. *He* needs his mob to taste his hardness.

Lesley is biting her top lip. Doughy eyes. She's gone from a chihuahua to a labrador who can't understand why its master won't take it for a walk. Dick enjoys the charade. It's one they've played a hundred times. Will perform a hundred more.

'So what are you offering?'

'Bub, that's why I'm here. The boss has suggested you and I do the community consultations.'

They've worked the community meeting circuit so many times. She has such an angelic face, one the debt collectors always believe when she says, ever so softly, 'I'll send you a cheque next week.' But as soon as Lesley stands to speak at a community meeting, the metamorphosis begins. With arms waving like balloons tied to a speeding car, her tongue deftly sows seeds of conflict.

Handiwork that will hit the audience like a fallen wasp nest.

'It'll be fun. Just you and me.'

Dick leans back in his chair. 'Tell me more.'

He has no doubt Lesley will be useful, at the very least a great photo opportunity. Dick imagines the chief executive of Coconut Holdings posing with his arm around the quintessential black matriarch.

'We'll be flexible, work around your commitments. Everyone knows how busy you are.'

Her voice is desperate, like the mother coaxing the screaming brat on the supermarket floor.

'What about my fees?'

'Bub, the Premier's Department will handle that.'

He rises from his chair, walks to the window. Hands in his pockets, he speaks with his back to her. 'When do we start?'

'As soon as possible after the launch.'

'We'll have to discuss this with the Feds at some point. Those young fellas aren't going to work if they can get sit-down money. If it was up to me, no one under the age of thirty would be eligible for welfare. Survival of the fittest, Lesley, that's what it's all about. Black people have to learn to be individuals. Individuals don't get held back by bludgers and drunks. I mean, look at me. I made it to this place from nothing. Never spent a day of my life on fuckin' sit-down money.'

Behind him Lesley is cringing. The reality that Dick will be paid a fortune to give five-minute spiels irritates her. After all, she'll be doing all the legwork. On her meagre salary. Lesley smiles when it dawns on her that Dick's fees are probably 'sit-down money' too. It's not as though he'll be breaking into a sweat for it.

As if reading her humour, Dick turns around. 'What's wrong?' he says.

She nods enthusiastically. 'Oh, nothing, nothing at all, bub.'

He smells her fear. Grins. 'I'll have to discuss this with the senior partners.'

'How about you get back to me tomorrow?' she says.

'It may not be sorted by then. But don't worry. The partners understand the importance of my work. They'll give the go-ahead.' Dick studies his expensive watch, the usual cue for her to leave.

'Bub, I've already taken too much of your time. I'll see you at the launch on Friday.'

'If I don't run into you at the casino sooner.'

Her face burns with embarrassment.

'Oh Auntie, I'm only having a joke with you.'

She turns to leave, head hung a little lower. 'Give my love to Sherene and the baby.'

It's the same parting words each time. Lesley barely knows Sherene, is too low in the food chain to be a real part of his world. But she clings to whatever familiarity she can and uses it to bolster her own sense of importance. Dick watches the door close. Slams his hand on the desk. The woman is trouble. His wife.

When they met she had been so excited by life. Sherene spoke of studying art in Paris and trekking across the Sahara. Of course, a great deal of it was puffery, like so much of what lovers share in those early days. But her passion was intoxicating. Now she's lost her exuberance, has no dignity. If she had remained the woman he married, he'd have no need for his playthings. The fact that he went home to her, night after night, was proof of his goodness. Dick was faithful to the institutions of marriage, family, if not to Sherene.

But since last Wednesday, she's gained a new dimension. Until then, he had never thought of her as dishonest. He didn't think she was capable of darkness. At least Dick had always harnessed his darkness, used it to power his crusade. He had walked through the door just after midnight, smelling of perfume and wine. She sat staring at the kitchen table.

No book in front of her, no magazine.

'I know what you've been doing.'

He chose to ignore her and opened the fridge door, looking for a glass of wine. Just one more before some shut-eye.

'I've been doing it too.' Tears were streaming down her cheeks. Voice quivering. 'I'm having an affair,' she said.

'Dick, Sherene is on the phone.'

'Thanks, Holly. I'll take it.'

How did Sherene know he was thinking of her? Perhaps he really is gifted.

'Dick, how are you?'

He hears the timidity in her voice, but has no desire to put her at ease. 'Where are you?' he says.

'Still in Sydney.'

'What about the baby?'

'I've rung Mum twice a day.'

He has no comeback. Dick hasn't contacted his mother-in-law once since Sherene left.

'When are you coming back?'

'Tonight. On the eight o'clock flight.' She pauses. 'I'll miss Bruce's memorial service this afternoon, but I don't think it's appropriate for me to go.'

'No, his widow hardly wants to come face to face with his whore.'

She breathes deeply, and he knows she's expecting him to salvage their conversation. But Dick wants nothing to do with a salvage operation.

'How are you getting home from the airport?'

'I'll get a taxi to Mum and Dad's apartment.'

Her voice seems a little brighter. Perhaps she's heartened that he cares about her transport arrangements.

'Have you been talking to them about us?'

'Dick, you know that I don't discuss our marriage with my parents.'

Damn right. The last time, three years ago, he belted the living daylights out of Sherene. The following morning, Dick addressed a fundraiser for International Women's Day. The irony still brings a smile to his face.

'I'll see you at home then,' he says, and hangs up the receiver. No clichés like 'have a good flight' or 'love you'. The whore deserves silence.

The top button on his pants is the crust of a volcano about to erupt. He eases himself out of the chair, walks to the window. His clothes are tighter than usual. He's been enjoying his nights with Harrison, perhaps too much. Eating at restaurants with river views, drinking fine wine.

The Gateway Bridge is a mere speck on the magnificent glass canvas that consumes an entire wall of his office. The Storey Bridge is a fossil whose flesh was eaten while the city was still young. Cars and trucks pass in and out, rattling the ancient bones. Dark clouds suggest an afternoon storm.

Dick has looked at the apartment buildings on his left every day for the past five years, but, for the first time, they remind him of the ant mounds back home. Like the ant mounds, the luxury apartments are rifled with holes for the living. Underground parking spaces are the ants' hidden catacombs. One has to see the red earth to believe it, an artist's impression of Mars come to life.

Home never really leaves you.

The ocean floor of his mind is being dredged, sediments of the clever men rising to the surface. He laughs as he reminisces about cousin Rod, who'd looked so guarded when he spoke of their ability to bring the rains. Others even claimed that the clever men could fly. Of course, like all other myths, no one had ever seen the deadly assassins. Dick had taken in such myths so easily when he was a child. As an adult, he realised that he had needed them to anaesthetise him to the pain. Pain that drenched you like a thunderstorm – the deformed for whom medical treatment was a luxury, mothers who grieved for young boys whose brains had been fried by anything they could stick into their mouths, noses, veins, people who carried so much pain that you could almost see the millstones tied around their necks.

The light reflecting on the khaki has transformed the river into a diamond mine. Thirty floors above, Dick is mining. He enjoys taking raw thoughts and processing them into wisdom; wisdom that will wean the black man off sit-down money, booze and smoke. Christ had turned water into wine, fed the masses with fishes and loaves. Dick Payne will perform miracles too. Fuck, he could do with some coke. Where's the number for that dealer? He's working his BlackBerry when the landline hollers.

'Dick, there's a Detective Sergeant Jason Matthews on the phone for you.'

'Holly, I don't know him. What does he want?'

'He said it was a personal matter.' She sighs. 'Actually, Dick, he's left a few messages for you to call him.'

'Put him through.' Dick taps his hand on the desk while he waits.

'Mr Payne, good morning.'

'I'm in a hurry, make it quick.'

'I'm trying to contact your wife.'

'Why?'

'I've left messages on her phone, but she hasn't returned my calls.'

'Why do you think Sherene could help you?'

'I'd prefer to discuss that with your wife.'

'My wife is in Sydney until later tonight.'

He slams down the receiver, his mind a beehive.

He wants to slap her, make her terrified. Punish her for everything she is and all she can no longer be. Perhaps she was never that person to begin with. She was just fucking with him, to trap him.

He feels his pulse racing, the heat skipping off his jowl.

The file on his desk keeps beckoning; Coconut Holdings' next development in Western Australia. He needs this; it will propel his name into brighter lights. Lights that will save his people, inject pride into their veins. Help them to become like him.

He paces the carpet, drinks in his domain. First black man to breathe the hallowed air up here. Did it all on his own.

His shelves are filled with glossy native title texts, most of which quote him. The personal bathroom always brings a smile to his face. It is, after all, a symbol of his success. But it also reminds him of the women. The whores he's fucked, every which way, in that tiny shower cubicle. Thoughts of them make him feel emptiness, but not guilt. He's not like Sherene, whose lover had been a mentor. A friend. Dick's women are playthings. Walking codeine to dull the pressure.

And he's so skilful, he's got the routine down pat.

Like a farmer in a coop of battery hens, Dick mechanically plucks them of their naïvety. He begins by offering his prey a glass of wine. Over three bottles of semillon they plot her ascent in the glamorous world of native title litigation; she will travel to the furthest parts of the country and pursue test cases in the High Court. Most importantly, however, she will provide him with personal support. Blushing cheeks on the fawn's drunken face are his green light. After lifting her onto the desk, he'll drape the inevitably long legs over his shoulders and swiftly relieve his swollen sex. She will go half an hour later, clutching a twenty-dollar note for the taxi ride home. Dick seldom remembers their names. What's the point? One, however, left an indelible impression. Whiny voice.

She was nervous and giggly, more a child than a woman. As the weeks progressed, whiny voice became manic. When were they going away for that romantic weekend he had promised? After three weeks, she stopped calling. Life was proceeding normally, until the afternoon that whiny voice appeared in the flesh.

He was seething. Then whiny voice opened her overcoat and allowed it to fall. She did it so elegantly that, later, he wondered if she had rehearsed untying the strap and shaking the dense fabric from her shoulders. He drank in the sight of her pubic hair, before throwing her around. She leaned into the desk and giggled as he undid his fly.

'Dick, baby, when are you leaving your wife?'

Excitement instantly boiled over into rage. He screamed at her to leave. She cried that she loved him. He responded by calling her the pathetic slut that she was. She grabbed the overcoat and ran, a spluttering mess. White women are supposed to have fewer complications. Dick Payne can't afford complications. There is only one complication that he'd embrace. Perhaps it's because he knows that this complication has become an illusion. Like Sherene, Miranda is no longer the woman he once wanted so desperately. He reflects on her disgusting office that night. Air heavy with cigarette smoke and dust. She looked like a bag lady, breathing decay.

He touches the swollen skin around his right eye and grimaces. Had he known what would happen, he'd have stayed the hell away.

Ten years ago.

They came from all walks of life: pensioners who spent their retirement writing leaflets in the hope of change, schoolteachers and the occasional suit. He was reaching for his glass of water when he noticed her in the front row. She wore a black jersey and tight denim jeans with boots. The toned contours of her body pleased him but it wasn't just her looks that he found intoxicating. It was the feistiness that she exuded. She spoke animatedly to those around her, who hung on her every word. He imagined her arguing with him and then descending into fits of laughter, making love like there was no tomorrow.

When he finished his dry analysis of the Native Title Amendment Act, the audience clapped enthusiastically. They always did. He was so desperate to make contact with her that he answered questions from the floor with only monosyllabic replies. As he shuffled his notes, Dick pondered what he would say to her. Suddenly there she was, standing above him. He smiled as he breathed in the scent of her perfume. It was subtle and reminded him of the jasmine beneath the window of his boarding school room.

'Mr Payne, I understand you're speaking at the Wexley Institute tomorrow night.'

He smiled into blue eyes that were even more alluring up close. 'Sorry, I don't believe that we've been introduced.'

'Miranda. Miranda Eversely.'

He pictured her gyrating above him, pert breasts. As if reading his thoughts, she scowled.

'Can I just say how very disappointed I am that you are working with that disgusting right-wing think-tank. Mr Payne, are you familiar with the saying about absolute power?'

'Let me think. Is it along the lines of absolute power corrupting absolutely?' he said, wryly.

'Yes.'

'Is that an indirect way of insulting me?'

'If you want blunt, I'll give you blunt – you're a sell-out.'

'What . . .'

'You heard me. I hope the fifteen seconds are worth it.'

He can't remember what happened after she dropped the sledgehammer on top of his heart. Obviously, she walked away.

Was she gloating? Some nights he drives past her office, watches her through the window. Often she holds a wine glass.

At the last minute he decided not to go to Court for the judgment. He understood why she had fought, but he found her self-indulgent. Why fight a battle that's impossible to win? Walking the negotiator's tight-rope was so much more difficult than the carefree life of a revolutionary. Radicals danced on the floor of principle, but that was all they ever did. He, on the other hand, lived and breathed change.

That night, after the Corrowa had lost, he sat in his car

watching her. She looked so frail. Even from the street, he could see she was crying, face buried in her hands. As he scurried up the steps, he imagined their future together. He would rescue her from self-destruction. She would finally learn to appreciate him.

But he walked into the carcass of an old dream. Mascara had run down both of her cheeks and her eyes were bright red. Skin grey and haggard. Miranda lunged at him like a wounded animal and he had to do all he could to restrain her. Once he'd thrown her into a chair, she just sat there, staring blankly as though she didn't even know him. He didn't realise what she'd done to his eye until the following morning, when Sherene noticed.

Miranda could have lived the life most women only dreamt of. He would have seen to it that she wanted for nothing. Miranda was a fool. A fool undeserving of him. Undeserving of his love. He should have called the cops that night. Made a complaint to the Law Society.

Perhaps he still will.

SEVEN

Human traffic filters in and out of the Greek delicatessen below. Miranda envies the ease with which they engage in conversation. She receives few invitations to go out for coffee. Or anywhere else. She has no real friends apart from Jonathon. And he has his own life. On the rare occasion that she socialises, Miranda is usually gripped by fear. Scared that people will think she looks dowdy. Fearful they will find her intellect lacking.

The judgment is divided into two piles on the corner of her desk. She can remember very little of what she's read already. That night is a blur. If she's brutally honest, Miranda would concede that much of the last six years has been a dust storm.

There had been talk of a land claim in the southeast, but no real impetus until the Corrowa caught wind of the proposed sale of Meston Park. Once the injunction temporarily put the sale to bed, the Native Title Tribunal attempted to mediate. Inside the plush reception room, Miranda was surprised to see Lesley seated at the front with Dick Payne. Lesley may have been a bureaucrat but she was Corrowa too. Only much later would they realise the extent of her betrayal.

Payne looked uncomfortable in the white shirt that accentuated the bloated mess his body had become. Miranda likened him to Darth Vader, one who had been seduced by the dark side of the force and was now beholden to an evil emperor. That morning, however, she felt sympathy for a man who was drowning in his own success. And now he's soon to drown in their old people's money, under the guise of the Aboriginal Employment Initiative.

Auntie Ethel had worked as a domestic throughout her teens, before she could escape from Manoah. But she never saw a cent. The protector even followed her to Brisbane, but she was safe. The mob kept her within their sight at all times. They were the Murri version of Harriet Tubman's Underground Railroad, but history would never celebrate their heroics.

They had been fighting to recoup their stolen wages for decades, only to be told by smug officials that all of the records had been destroyed during the flood of 1974. Only remnants remained, held in the dubiously named Aboriginal Welfare Account. Now, those crumbs would fund Dick Payne's brainchild.

'Withdraw the claim and we can talk about jobs for the young people,' Dick said at the tribunal. 'Coconut Holdings really wants to help.'

'If your client wants to be so bloody helpful, then why doesn't it recognise our native title?' Charlie said.

Dick eyed him with contempt. 'You'll have no chance in Court, old man. This is your one opportunity to do something positive for your children.'

The mercenaries wanted them to sign so badly, dollar signs dangling in their eyes like jackpots in pokie machines. The very machines that Lesley had spent thousands on.

'Look around you,' Dick said. 'Look at the Asians who clean toilets so their kids can go to private schools. Look at the Greeks who work seven days a week so their families never go without.' Dick had the eyes of a snake, spat words like venom. 'You mob disgust me.'

Containing her anger at the memory, Miranda wonders what has become of fair play. Meston Park was the last piece of land left to the Corrowa. How many more shops did the newcomers need? How many more things could they possibly fit into their homes? How much more construction could the city eat, before it succumbed to heart disease? The Corrowa said no. Their dignity carried no price tag.

The trial that followed was like a swimming carnival – but in order to win, they couldn't get wet. And cross-examination was like opening your skull and inviting a stranger to dissect everything within it. The Golden Tongue painted the Corrowa as extinct, belonging in sterile museum boxes rather than a bustling city. A demolition job dressed in eloquent legalese.

Miranda lifts the judgment from her desk and looks for some space on top of the filing cabinet. The place is such a shambles; she'll have to bring order to it, one day. She places the judgment on the telephone book. It's still open at the page she slept on. An address has been circled – *Brosnan B and Brosnan E, 58 Wadley Street, MacGregor.*

'Sorry to disturb you, mate.' She turns to see O'Neill at the door. 'Have you got a moment?'

She sees the concern in his eyes, the anxiety that's slowing his body like lead.

'Sure,' she says. 'Come in.'

He takes the chair usually reserved for clients.

'How are you?'

'Fine, thanks.'

'There's no easy way to say this.' O'Neill pauses, swallows. 'On Friday morning I had to come in here, to get the Levy file . . . I was pretty bloody shocked.'

Miranda slumps into her seat. 'I'm so sorry.'

'The smell! Jesus, you must have been on the turps for hours.' The disgust in his voice cuts like a knife.

'You've been so good to me and I've let you down.'

O'Neill has indeed been very good to Miranda. Hired her as an articled clerk and then kept her employed as a solicitor. She's never had to look for work in the past ten years.

'Mate, I've seen this a hundred times. Alcoholism is a disease.'

Is she really an alcoholic? She's never used that word in relation to herself. Miranda can't think of any lawyers who do. She's met drunks worse than herself. And they're at the Bar.

'You need to get help.'

'Did you have something in mind?' Her voice is shaky, barely audible.

'I was hoping you'd come up with something yourself.'

'I'll make some enquiries.'

He's struggling with eye contact. This is excruciating for him too.

'Mate,' he says. 'I think we should have a few conversations about this.'

Miranda's mobile phone rings and she picks it up.

'It's Auntie Ethel.'

'Ah, well don't let me keep you from the Queen.'

She can see the relief wash over him. The business is concluded. For now.

'Bub, I'm at the Native Title Tribunal,' Ethel says.

'What are you doing there?'

'Didn't you hear the news about that mongrel dog?'

Miranda is stunned. Ethel's never used such language before.

'Aunt, who are you talking about?'

'Golden Tongue. Who else?'

'Auntie Ethel, I don't understand what this is about.'

Ethel's voice becomes distant. Miranda can hear her admonishing some unfortunate soul.

'Miranda, are you there?' Ethel says.

'Yes, I'm still here.'

Where would I be going?

'That mongrel dog just got a new job. He's going to be the President of the Native Title Tribunal. How could they give that job to a paedophile?' Ethel exclaims.

Miranda doesn't have the energy for this. If it were anyone else, she'd have said goodbye and hung up.

'I hadn't heard that. Auntie Ethel, I still don't understand why you're at the Tribunal. What are you doing there?'

'Protesting, bub. I'm not leaving until that paedophile stands down.'

'Auntie, I don't think you should be calling him a paedophile unless you can . . .'

'Bub, you there?'

'Yes, Auntie. Look, I think that you should stay put. I'll come and get you.'

Miranda clenches her teeth as she opens the door. She wonders whether the others had been there on Friday morning when O'Neill went into her office. How much do they know? The articled clerk, Angela, smiles as she walks past. She will never know how much Miranda appreciates that small gesture.

The offices of the Native Title Tribunal are a stone's throw from the Supreme Court, making the surrounding cafés second homes to the law's patricians. Rosy-cheeked barristers sip lattes and bask in the curiosity of passers-by. She's been here so many times, but never to save Auntie Ethel from defaming the new president of the Tribunal. Although it's probably the Tribunal's staff, rather than Ethel, who are in need of rescuing.

Miranda recognises the young woman at the reception.

'Hi, Miranda. We've been expecting you.'

'Yes, I believe that you have.'

At the heart is an open space that houses mostly Aboriginal staff. Hallways lead to chains of smaller offices containing suits. Miranda is surprised by the apparent absence of concern over Ethel's protest. An elegant black woman laughs demurely into a telephone, while a handsome young man with sun-bleached hair trims the leaves of a pot plant.

She's led into the office of Glenda Fitzgerald, the Corrowa's former case manager. Glenda's brown hair is cut into a short bob that sits just below her ears. Thick dark glasses accentuate foundation too pale for her face. Glenda appears nonplussed, perhaps a little tired. On the other hand, Auntie Ethel seems to be enjoying herself. She's chatting animatedly with Glenda about her favourite football team, the North Queensland Cowboys.

'Bub, I'm so glad you're here. You remember Glenda?'

Miranda nods at Glenda. 'Auntie, let's go home.'

'But he's here, bub. Golden Tongue.'

Glenda releases a sigh of frustration. 'No, he's not, Auntie Ethel,' she says. 'Harrison McPherson was here this morning, to meet his staff . . .'

'Well, there you go. True God, tell me, Glenda, how do you feel about working with a paedophile?'

'Okay, that's enough. We're out of here.' Miranda seldom raises her voice at Ethel. But Ethel rarely defames rich and powerful men. To her surprise, Ethel rises from her chair.

'See you, Glenda. Next time we run into each other, we'll have a real yarn then.'

As they venture into George Street, they run into Jonathon. Even though he has just been in Court, Jonathon looks fresh, like he's woken from a deep sleep.

'Jonathon, how are you, bub?'

'Auntie Ethel, what a surprise.'

'You're lookin' well, but you're getting a bit thin, my boy. What do you think, Miranda?'

Miranda gives Jonathon a cheeky grin. She's relieved to be away from the Tribunal. There is no one here for Ethel to defame.

'I agree. Auntie, I think you should cook your deadly shepherd's pie for Jonathon.'

'But I'm a vegetarian,' he says.

'You're what?' Ethel is horrified.

'I have been for the last ten years. What are the two of you doing in the city?' Jonathon speaks as though the city is a different country from their homeland of West End.

'We've just been to the Tribunal.'

'Oh really?' Jonathon's eyes widen with curiosity.

'Actually, we're on our way home.'

Miranda's firm voice dampens his interest. 'Would you like me to hail you a cab?'

'What a gentleman. Miranda, why haven't you settled down with a nice man like Jonathon?'

Ethel's words were not calculated to hurt, but they do.

Charlie's sitting on the verandah. Three places are set on the old table of splitting timber. Miranda can smell the tea-leaves in the pot. His jaw is clenched, but that's nothing unusual. Unlimited compassion for those in the community. Only cynicism and bitterness left for her. Charlie raises his eyebrows, the way he used to when Miranda lied about brushing her teeth.

'Heard you had words with your boss.'

'What did he say to you?'

'Nothing.'

Miranda hates these cryptic discussions. 'Then how . . .'

'You have to give up the grog. You look like a fifty-year-old woman.'

His candour stings. Her self-esteem is already a pile of bones. Ethel puts her arms around Miranda.

'Charlie, leave this girl alone.'

'Ethel!'

'Charlie, I mean it. She's had a tough week.'

He sighs in frustration.

'Charlie, where's my chocolate biscuits?' Auntie Ethel says.

'You don't need them. Besides, your doctor said you have to cut back on sugar. I thought you were worried about diabetes.'

'But I've been walking, every morning at six o'clock.'

'In the fridge.' Charlie's voice hums with resignation.

Ethel disappears inside, leaving Miranda without her shield.

'I have to go. Bye, Dad.'

'Anytime you want to talk.'

'I'll keep it in mind.'

Boundary Street is the theatre of a cold war between the new rich and old poor. She walks past rundown houses that carry million-dollar price tags. Miranda had always wanted to buy her own, but that's a pipedream now. She notices the doors of Justice Products are closed, as if in mourning. But fragments of the old West End linger. Inside the windows of one of the few hostels left, Aboriginal flags sing in defiance.

She's so angry that steam could escape from her ears. A boss could never be an equal friend. In the event of a clash of wills, O'Neill would always prevail. She'll have to grin and bear it. Miranda has no doubt that O'Neill genuinely cares. Charlie too. In his own twisted way. But she's a mature woman of thirty-eight.

'Hey, stranger.'

Miranda turns to see the woman from the old converted flats next door. She has a large frame and her hair is cut in a mohawk. Lives in cargo pants and singlets. They say hi occasionally, when Miranda's sitting on her back patio, wine glass in one hand, cigarette in the other.

'Hey, Tegan. How are you?'

'Great. And I'm glad I ran into ya.'

Her neighbour often busks in Boundary Street. Has the look of a busker, unkempt hair, feet naked. Something dancing in her eyes, a silhouette that teases without spite.

'Oh really?'

'Yeah, I've got an exhibition opening next Wednesday. Was hoping you'd come.'

Tegan has the rough voice of one who's seen life's underbelly and emerged without regret. A survivor.

'Sure, I'd love to come.'

'It's at the Ochre Lounge . . . the flash place that sells bush tucker at city prices.'

'I know the place.'

Tegan continues on her way and Miranda is calm now. She even looks forward to the exhibition. Mobile phone screeches.

'Hello.'

'Miranda.'

She recognises the voice of the corrupt evangelist.

'What do you want?'

'Miranda, that's no way to speak to someone who has the ability to cause you a great deal of embarrassment.' Payne's voice is playful, but cruelty swims through it.

'What are you talking about?' she says.

'You really have no idea?'

'Just cut the bullshit.'

'Miranda, please don't tell me you've forgotten about our little tryst in your office last Thursday night. You know, I have been thinking about going to the police. After all, assault is a very serious matter. How would the Law Society view a solicitor who was not only charged with assault, but is also a pathetic alcoholic?'

She knows he's relishing the fear in her silence. Payne is like a vulture feasting on road kill.

'My fucking eye, Miranda!'

The heightened pitch in his voice is suddenly terrifying. She's always thought that Payne is unbalanced. As though he really does believe the ridiculous platitudes that politicians and journalists throw at him.

'What do you want?'

'Geez Miranda, your clients must cringe when they smell the grog on your breath. I'm surprised you haven't been struck off.'

'You have five seconds to tell me what you want.'

'Now that's no way to speak to your new lover.'

'I'm hanging up.'

'A private meeting. That's what I want. You and I have some issues to resolve.'

'Where?'

'My office. Tonight.'

'I'll consider it.'

'I look forward to it. By the way . . .'

'What now?'

'Wear something sexy.'

She imagines him in his office, with his feet on the desk.

'Come at nine. Call me when you're downstairs.'

'What if I don't turn up?'

'Then you'd better get a new job. Or maybe you won't. Perhaps you'll become another black whore. Turning tricks for grog.'

She hears Payne's confident laughter before the phone goes dead.

The woman pushing a pram walks past her, ventures to the very edge of the footpath. She can sense Miranda's anger, her fear. The afternoon breeze has only just arrived; it's too early to drink. But her mouth pines for the taste.

The public bar of the Boundary Hotel reeks of spilt beer and spilt lives. Gravelly voices should be omens. But all that Miranda can think of is the three bottles of wine in the plastic bag.

Her apartment, Miranda realises, is more a tomb of broken dreams than a home. Old furniture that should have been replaced years ago lives alongside photographs from a time when smiles were genuine. Empty bottles are kept hidden underneath the kitchen sink, only disposed of late at night when the neighbours are asleep. Every corner holds memories of drunken tears.

It's not as though she hasn't attempted to address her loneliness. She's tried to meet men at nightclubs, but that only ever ends in cheap and nasty flings. So she joined a dating agency for the princely sum of two thousand dollars. Once a month, she'd climb into a ridiculously expensive dress and shoes that made her feel a metre taller. She did her best to appear casual and asked her dates thoughtful questions about themselves. Even though each man had said that he enjoyed dinner, not one called. So she gave up.

She doesn't believe in God. Has she ever? And Karma's a load of rubbish too. Some of the nastiest women she's met are happily married, with healthy children. She, on the other hand, has devoted all of her adult life to a community legal practice, defending the city's discarded and forgotten. She'd never imagined she too would become expended of promise.

EIGHT

Isabella decided that if the room had a name, it would be Grim. The cheap contact on the desk is torn. The single bed groans whenever she moves. Even though the cleaner drops by once a week, the room never smells fresh.

Outside the grimy window, green fruit is stapled to the banana trees. Isabella can't remember if the trees were here the last time. She had been in a different room back then, one that had a view of the traffic. At least from here, she can stare into the garden. The alcoholics sit around a wooden table next to the fishpond. Solemn faces occasionally break into smiles.

Between them, the patients have ingested just about every kind of poison, in just about every kind of way. Ice, heroin, cocaine, the kaleidoscope of prescription drugs. But they drift towards their own. Alcoholics in the backyard, heroin addicts in the dim living room, ice addicts privately writhing.

Isabella's emotions are a carousel wheel. She's nauseous from the wooden horse that drags her from the depths of despair to euphoria. Some call the latter a miracle. Isabella had her miracle at three in the morning on the fourth day. She was going to go back to university to study dentistry. Losing her teeth had been one of the worst aspects of her old life. Without her parents' money, she'd still be in excruciating pain. Surely her clients at the shelter deserve the same care? Isabella would return a hero. She could visualise it so clearly; she was convinced it was an epiphany. But by the afternoon, depression had hit like an elevator whose cables had snapped. She was a junkie who had made it to the other side, only to become an alcoholic, a shipwreck undeserving of its sandbank.

Without the chemical crutch, Isabella has to deal with being Isabella. Shy. Painfully shy. When she was a little girl, she would scamper to her room at the sound of the doorbell. Mum and Grandma would appear minutes later, in the doorway, to see tiny feet stuck out from under the bed.

'Emily, that child is paranoid,' Grandma would say.

Some couldn't pinpoint the moment that life crashed, when chemicals became fused with feeling. Isabella can. She had just topped Year Eleven English. She so desperately wanted to share her news with Dad she didn't bother to ring him first. Isabella practically ran from the lift and stormed into his office – only to see Dad and his secretary, Lucy. Lucy was sitting on his lap, Dad's face buried in her naked breasts.

Some memories had been destroyed by chemicals, others by the sheer need to survive. Like the putrid breath of the old man who bounced on top of her. Lying in the gutter, face bloody, teeth mere stubs. The night that began with an argument over twenty dollars and ended with scores of cops and a body bag. Those memories are locked in a huge wooden chest. Occasionally they pulse, but the latch will always remain soldered.

She had fought so hard to recover from the drugs, only to end up back here.

It had begun innocently.

Each day she listened to men who had lost their families, children unable to distinguish between affection and exploitation, faces lined with adult hardness. She had chosen that world. For Isabella, it offered absolution. A solvent to wipe the slate clean, not only for that night, but for the hurt she had caused Mum. But Isabella herself was a sponge, soaking up the pain. So she bought a bottle of wine from the drive-through in her street. Sitting in front of the television, she sipped the first glass. She enjoyed that couch. Like everything else in that apartment, she had paid for it herself, without any assistance from Mum and Dad. Swept up in the idiocy of reality television, Isabella had soon finished the bottle. Within weeks, Isabella was drinking two bottles per night. She'd just rekindled her friendship with Darlene, the only childhood friend who had stuck by her, when she was homeless herself. But Darlene liked to party. Every Friday night they'd hit the clubs. At first, it was only a few harmless giggles, dancing to her favourite eighties tunes. But after a few months, Isabella was in free fall. It became normal for her to wake on a Saturday morning with an exploding head, next to a man whose name had been lost in neon lights. Now she needed a drink just to function. To feel normal. Darlene hasn't visited since she arrived here.

Life here is hard. No independence, living with others' rules, being told that she has a disease the only cure for which is lifelong abstinence. But she has made friends, like Peter, the doctor. He'd always enjoyed a Scotch after work, countless drinks at Saturday afternoon barbecues. Reality bit when he crashed his BMW into the neighbour's letterbox. Peter's face has the appearance of permanent sunburn. There have been times when she's seen him in the yard, crying to himself. His family never visits; he rarely mentions his career, or what is left of it. But when he listens to her, it's as though there are only the two of them. If it is ever possible to achieve normalcy in this place, Isabella was on her way. Now, she's not sure what normalcy is.

'Your dad had many flaws. But he really did love you, Issie. He'd want you to stay here until you're well.'

Mum's voice was restrained but not cold. Whenever there is a family crisis, Mum just deals with it, because there is no one else to carry the burden. At least, not since Grandma passed away.

Isabella hardly slept last night. It's not the creaky bed, or the hushed voices in the hallway. It's guilt. Guilt that's dragging her down like wet concrete.

'Issie.'

Mum stands in the doorway, wearing a long black dress and an elegant matching jacket. Her embrace is firm. Face full of concern.

Much later, Isabella would try to remember the drive to the church. She could only picture the sudden rain, torrential rain caressing everything in its path. It was as though Dad was making his presence known. But it was the old Dad of her childhood, the one who still loved Mum. Although he was rarely there, when he was, he could be wonderful. Sometimes, when he came home early, Dad would fall into character while reading Dr Seuss books.

There's little shelter, most stand underneath black umbrellas. Mum is summoning her strength, like a swimmer just before plunging into the pool on a winter morning. Father Michael opens Isabella's car door. She's taken aback. The ginger hair of his youth has turned completely grey.

'Emily, Isabella, I'm so sorry.'

Isabella manages to smile slightly. Everyone will be using those words today.

They're greeted with hugs and glances of acknowledgment. But she doesn't know these people. Isabella is staring into a sea, watching waves, each indistinguishable from the last. In the corner of her eye, she sees the television cameras. Cringes. The scent of incense in the church is overpowering.

'Isabella.' The man's voice is gentle. Strong hands on her waist. 'I'll help you to your seat.'

She peers wistfully at the holster beneath his suit coat, before sitting down. Jason recognises it. The look. The one that begs to cut the strings of the invisible hundred pound weight of knowing. Knowing that one phone call could have made all the difference. The witness sees the murder, but is gripped by fear. The killer might even contact her, show up outside her kids' school. So the witness carries it around for thirty years, until it rots her insides. When she's just about to croak, that's when she finally makes the call. But Isabella Brosnan won't be waiting that long. Jason knows she'll spill today.

The memorial service for Bruce Brosnan is just as he expected – all pomp and canonisation. The legal profession has turned out in force, along with the Premier and half of his cabinet. Bruce Brosnan is painted as a saviour of the downtrodden. Much is made of his contributions to the board of Legal Aid Queensland and his role as the former president of the Bar Association. But the real measure of the man, Jason thinks, is in the faces of the two women he has left behind.

Isabella Brosnan is so thin she could be blown away by the storm outside. Her short blond hair is brittle and her face carries an awkward expression. Perhaps she doesn't believe what's being said about her father. Emily's arms are tightly wrapped around Isabella's shoulders. Lioness with her cub. Emily flinches when she sees him.

Jason and Higgins walk to the street, maintaining a decent view of Emily and Isabella. The women are surrounded by well-wishers. Isabella stares at them and speaks to her mother. While Emily is distracted by the Premier, Isabella heads in their direction.

'Detectives?' Isabella has a strong face, a prominent jaw. 'I'd like to speak to you, if I may.'

She has a quiet strength that neither detective was expecting.

Higgins smiles warmly. 'Certainly. Is there somewhere we can go?'

'I'm supposed to be at the wake in half an hour. There's a coffee shop down the road.'

'Isabella, I'd prefer that you wait until Chris is free,' Emily calls, striding across the car park.

Isabella frowns. 'I don't need Chris, Mum.'

The milk bar is as lacklustre as the burnt coffee. A middle-aged man, who appears to be the owner, stares gruffly into space.

'The truth is I've been in rehab,' Isabella says, peering into her coffee, her face laden with shame. 'Alcohol. This time.'

Jason offers a warm smile. 'I'm sorry.'

'Why do people always say that? It's not as though my

addiction is your fault.' She shakes her head. 'Everyone has been saying that today. As though they carry some responsibility for what happened.'

'It's been a huge day for you,' Higgins says, trying to calm her. His sympathy is real, at least, it appears to be.

'The night that Dad died . . . Mum and I were at rehab. I escaped for a few hours.'

She laughs to herself, a mixture of pain and disbelief.

'Mum had to rescue me from one of my old haunts.' She shrugs. 'Didn't even try to hide in a new place.'

Jason flips open his notebook. 'What time was that?'

'You'd have to check with the rehab centre. They record all of that kind of thing.'

'We'll do that. Rough guess?'

She shrugs her shoulders again. 'I'd say early evening.'

Isabella looks wistfully into the street. The storm has lulled, cars crash through puddles.

'It had been building up for a while. First I lost my job. Then Mum and Dad took my car because they were worried I'd drive when I was drunk.'

Jason didn't expect to feel pity, but he does.

'I couldn't pay the rent anymore, but I didn't care. All my money was going on alcohol. Then Mum walks into the apartment. The front door is wide open and I'm lying on the couch, naked. She convinced me to go to rehab then.'

'What did your dad have to say about it?'

'He wasn't exactly a hands-on father.'

Isabella pauses as new customers walk past their table. She lowers her voice. 'Look, I need to get something off my chest. The day I escaped, I went to their house . . . I stole some money from Dad's desk.'

She wipes her eyes, her voice breaking. 'What kind of person steals from her own father?'

* * *

The car's doorhandle is like a hot pebble in the road. As Jason welcomes the air conditioning, his phone rings.

It's Higgins.

'What news do you have for me?'

'Isabella's alibi – it checks out. I'm just leaving the rehab centre. Isabella arrived here at seven thirty-two.'

'Well, I guess Isabella's off the hook. Emily's unlikely to make a statement about the stolen money. It's not in our interest to pursue it. What about Emily?'

'Emily drove her there. Emily left the centre at nine forty-one. I've just done a run from here to the Brosnans'. It took thirty-five minutes. Emily would have done it quicker at that time of night.'

Higgins pauses, then says, 'We're sure she didn't leave the centre at any point?'

'The director didn't think so, but couldn't be certain.'

'Where does that leave us?'

'Isabella's no longer a person of interest. Emily probably isn't.'

'What of the elusive Mrs Payne?'

'Arrives in Brisbane tonight.' Jason stops.

'What is it?'

'Her husband sounded defensive on the phone.'

'Yeah, well he comes across as an arrogant prick on TV.'

'Perhaps there's another reason for him to be defensive,' Jason says.

'What are you thinking?'

'Sherene Payne leaves all of a sudden the morning after Bruce Brosnan is murdered. Fails to return any of my calls. What's she hiding?'

'Hmm, I think we should discuss this over a beer.'

'No can do. After I drop this car off, I'm heading straight for the gym.'

Sweat pours down his temples. Jason groans as he pulls the chest press. The spin instructor hollers, urging the small handful of zealots to keep sprinting, up the imaginary hill. Jason feels old and slack. It's a week since he's been here.

'Long time no see.'

The trainer's yellow hair is tied up messily in a bun. Jason appreciates her muscular physique and alluring grin. But he would never pursue her, or any other woman in this place. His church.

He walks over to the leg press and loads the weights until he reaches 180 kilograms. Moves his body into the seat and lifts his legs up to a forty-five degree angle. As he pushes against the weights, Jason imagines the muscles in his legs contracting and the oxygen being pumped through his body. Thoughts hidden in the crevices of his mind often emerge during his workouts.

After finishing his third set, Jason wanders to the exercise bike. Takes the headphones from his pocket and plugs them into the audio device. Only reality TV on the monitor on the wall, so he opts for radio.

'Brian, this has been a very disturbing week for many Queenslanders,' an interviewer says. 'You're not surprised when a judge is killed in a South American dictatorship. But in Brisbane! What's going on?'

'Alexander, obviously I don't want to say anything that would pre-empt the police investigation.'

'Come on, Brian. The Labor Government is soft on crime. Am I right?'

'Look, I agree with you. That's why the Coalition is promising to get tough on crime. When violent offenders get sentenced to ten years in jail, they should serve exactly that.'

'Do you also agree that violent crime is on the rise?'

'Alexander, I think it's time to get to the roots of the problem.'

'Brian, let's not beat around the bush here. You're really talking about welfare dependency?'

'Yes, Alexander. These dysfunctional families are often welfare dependent over generations. They need to be targeted.'

'Now some do-gooders are going to accuse you of stigmatising the innocent. What do you say to them?'

'Bruce Brosnan was an innocent victim too.'

'Indeed he was. Brian, I want to focus on welfare dependency just for a moment. One of the great Australian thinkers of this century is Dick Payne, who also happens to be an expert on this issue.'

'Ah yes, I'm a great admirer of Dick.'

Jason does his stretches and then hits the shower. The jets of cold water are like pine needles on his flesh. He walks into the humid summer night.

At home, her fine cheekbones are pink, lips scarlet. She whispers French into a telephone as rain plummets behind a white curtain. The subtitles are annoying, but Jason isn't watching the flatscreen television for entertainment. When he walked into the store the sales assistant ignored him. The jerk could not have been a day older than eighteen and his face was pocked with acne scars. So Jason walked up to the TV he had spotted in the catalogue and casually produced four thousand dollars from his wallet. The sales assistant instantly transformed into a gecko, whose beady eyes blinked as he salivated over the cash.

As much as he's enjoying his new purchase, Jason knows it looks out of place in his apartment. Paint that was once white has yellowed and the arch between the kitchen and living room is more 1970s than twenty-first century, as are the dark brown kitchen cabinets. Each veneered edge stands cocked like a dog's ear, revealing the cheap chipboard beneath.

He sits back into the futon, whose sagging centre is beginning to resemble an hourglass. The deformed couch is one of his few pieces of furniture. He seems to exist rather than live, Jason thinks. Photographs, trophies and the other footprints of his life sit in scraggly cardboard boxes strewn throughout his living room. Soon he will unpack them, but he knows he's been saying that for three years.

Dinner is nothing to brag about – pizza with less flavour than the cardboard it came in. Jason reflects on the rare occasions that Mum and Dad took him to the local pizzeria when he was a boy. In those days, you had to wait for forty minutes for the pizza to cook. It was worth it – fresh ingredients and a base that lingered on the tongue, as opposed to the rubber he's just eaten.

He sprawls across the old bed and buries his head in the soft pillow.

Jason can see light underneath the door, but he's afraid. Rebecca Collis opens it and beckons. He trusts her without knowing why. Isabella is standing below the canvas, holding wads of cash. Head hung in shame. The light in the kitchen is overpowering, the radiance of the marble floor hurts his eyes. Higgins is yelling, face red with anger. But he can't hear him. The tallest man Jason has ever seen. His head touches the ceiling. Arms out of proportion with the rest of his body. Long finger points below. Jason lies on the floor, head swimming in blood. And red feathers. Mobile phone drags him from sleep.

'Mate, get up. You need to get here now.'

Higgins' voice is a sudden blast of cold air.

'It's Dick Payne. He's dead.'

PART TWO

NINE

The lights are too bright, taunting her eyes.

'Mrs Payne, can I get you a glass of water?' Higgins says, reaching for the jug in the centre of the table.

'No. Thank you.'

The smell is stale, like their first home. Windows and doors closed for three months, not even the cockroaches stayed. But Sherene loved the old streets of St Lucia, near the university.

'Dick, if you don't start studying by the time the jacaranda trees are in bloom, you'll fail. Don't laugh, darling. It's true.'

'I trust the baby can stay with your parents for now.'

She nods, remembering her mother's voice on the phone, pleading for reassurance.

'May I call you Sherene?'

Higgins reminds her of a Great Dane. Cheeks running down his sides like arms. He's spent too many nights drowning his sorrows, scoffing down grease that passes for food. But he's earnest. Humour's probably rough.

'Sherene, we'll ask you to give a sworn statement in due course.'

She looks at this one. Matthews. His brown eyes bore into her soul. Why can't she see into his?

Matthews is an ice cube. Thick hair gelled back, denim shirt neatly pressed. Body wrapped in taut brown skin. Eyes covered in smog like the windows in the police car. It felt sterile in the back. She watched them take their equipment inside the foyer. Nightclubbers stood by gawking.

Higgins removes his jacket. Her nose is hit by a concoction of rain and cigarette ash.

'You should really quit, now that we have the baby, Dick.'

Sherene wants to run outside, stand in the rain, the cleansing rain.

Rain in the ferryman's oar.

Black cape flowing into rotting timber.

Long spidery fingers gliding the oar.

Is Dick with the ferryman?

'Now you understand that anything you say to us may be used . . .'

'Detective, I know my rights.'

'Would you like us to contact your legal representative?'

'No.'

Eloquent language skims off his tongue, like rocks kissing water. The audience is clapping, the Premier marvels at his brilliance. They believe that Dick is one of history's great men. Dick believes. He can have anything. Anyone.

'Sherene, this conversation will be recorded . . .'

The first time was the half-empty box of condoms in his overnight bag. Lacy underwear in the glove box.

'Yes, yes, I'm aware of that. I'm sorry. I'm just anxious to see my daughter.'

Matthews' face is a question mark.

'It must have been difficult to be away from your daughter for a week.'

His concern is bait she won't take.

'Why did you go away, Sherene?' he says.

'Dick and I were having problems. I needed time to think.'

'We spoke with your housekeeper. You left in a hurry.'

'When Dick was angry he was difficult to be around.'

'Why was Dick angry?'

Adrenalin floods her tired bones. 'Dick was angry because I was having an affair.' Her voice becomes soft, barely a murmur. 'With Bruce Brosnan.'

'So you left for Sydney the morning after your lover was killed?'

Her clothes are drenched in perspiration. She's been wearing them since seven o'clock this morning. Lethargy seems fitting in this place.

'I know what this looks like.' She glances at Matthews. 'Dick had so many affairs over the years. Part of me had wanted to get even. But I also had feelings for Bruce. He was a good man. In the end, I couldn't live with the lie. So I told Dick.'

Wine bottle in his hand smashes to the floor. Eyes full of hate.

'You're nothing without me, you hear me!'

Oh Jesus, he's getting the glass. Not my face. Please, not that.

'Bruce begged to see me one last time. We arranged to meet at our usual place.'

'When?'

'Seven o'clock . . . the night he was killed.'

Higgins cocks an eyebrow, unspoken code.

'The Mantra in Grey Street,' she says.

'So you checked in?'

'Yes, our room was booked under "Mr and Mrs Brosnan".'

A blush blooms across her face when her eyes meet Higgins'.

'When did Bruce arrive?' he says.

'He didn't. I waited for about twenty minutes. I called his mobile, but he never returned my message. It wasn't like Bruce to do something like that.'

'Did you go anywhere after leaving the hotel?'

'Home. Straight home. The nanny stayed with me until just after nine.' Tears stream down her flushed cheeks and Higgins offers her the dilapidated Kleenex box.

'I never spoke to Bruce again.'

'When did you decide to go to Sydney?'

'Soon after I got home from the Mantra. My mind was just a mess. I rang one of my old girlfriends and made arrangements to stay with her.'

'And your husband was happy for you to go to Sydney?'

'I don't know. To be honest, I was desperate to leave. When

I saw Dick in the morning he looked like he'd been in a fight. His face was all swollen and he had a black eye. He wouldn't tell me anything about the night before. I was listening to the radio when I heard the news about Bruce. I assumed Dick had done something terrible.'

Matthews rises from his chair. He paces like he's the one who's drained the carpet of life. Mockery dances in his eyes.

'We'd been trying to contact you for days.'

'Oh, that must have been on my personal mobile. I only used that phone for Bruce's calls.'

Sherene looks at Higgins and knows he's scrutinising her. He can't see her in a courtroom? Can't believe what he's heard – she's one of the best family lawyers in town?

He thinks I look frail.

Sherene straightens herself in her chair. 'There was no point in taking the phone to Sydney.'

'What made you decide to come back last night?'

'I missed my daughter.' She pauses, then finally says, 'And I wanted to see if it was possible for Dick and I to make amends.'

'But if you were concerned that Dick had done something terrible, wouldn't you be afraid, if not for yourself, then for your daughter?'

Sherene shakes her head wearily. 'In spite of everything, he was the father of my child. At the very least I had to try to put things right.'

'Alright, but if you had concerns that Dick might have been involved in Bruce's murder, why didn't you call us?' Matthews says.

Sherene needs to escape his eyes, they're like an x-ray machine to her conscience. She turns to the clock on the wall. It's wrapped in cheap plastic, faded black hands carry no sound. Everything in this room is meant to be rough. Breathe in misery like cancerous fumes.

'Sherene, when was the last time you spoke to your husband?' Higgins says.

She turns to face him. 'This morning.'

She looks back at the hands of the clock; sitting at one, they're as tired as she is.

'I mean yesterday. Just after nine o'clock in the morning. I told him I was catching the eight o'clock flight home that night.'

'How did he sound?'

'Not happy.'

These leeches will suck her dry. Give them something. *Anything.*

'I think we both had this idealistic view of marriage. Neither one of us was really prepared for the challenges. Then there was Dick's public profile.

'It's not healthy for anyone to be told that he is a genius. But they all said it. Politicians, businessmen, journalists. Dick lost his perspective.'

'What time did you land in Brisbane?'

'It would have been nine-thirty. I caught a taxi to Mum and Dad's place to collect my daughter. They weren't very happy about me taking her while she was sleeping.'

'Grandparents can be like that.'

Higgins sounds sincere, but she has no doubt he's reading from a script.

Good cop, bad cop. Do they think she's stupid?

Dick thought I was stupid.

'Where do your parents live?'

'They have an apartment in Albert Street in the city. While I was there, I rang Dick on his mobile, but he didn't answer. I tried him at home, but no luck there either.'

It unleashes a new wave of tears and she reaches for the tissues. 'Dick often worked late. I left my daughter with my parents and drove to Dick's office.'

'What time did you arrive?'

'It would have been just after ten.'

She's drowning in dread now. It's a familiar feeling.

Ever since we got engaged, I wanted to come here, see Dick's home.

But I'm scared.

It doesn't feel right here. This place is too still, too quiet.

'Please, Dick. Let's go.'

The water must be ten feet deep, but that man is standing.

Ice in his eyes.

Like Matthews'.

She looks directly at Higgins. 'I saw the light on in Dick's office. I've never seen so much blood . . .'

Her hands mask the sobbing. She knows the interview's over, there's no way she can continue. Her mind is clouded in pain.

Dick laughs when I ask him.

'Clever men aren't real. Just another stupid blackfella myth.'

None of this is real.

The scent of freshly cut grass pleases her. Takes her back to summer afternoons spent playing on the lawn. Birds singing a lullaby – the Corrowa's lullaby. Miranda's skin used to get itchy when she was a child. Auntie Ethel was always saying that Dad would have to do something about the ants. But the ants weren't as bad as those grubs that used to make a chequerboard out of Miranda's skin. Dad would scold her over that. Always scolding.

It sounds as though the traffic has settled. Still loud but not frantic. Occasionally, she hears a truck pause for a gear change. Why hasn't she ever earned her manual licence? Hears a plastic bag that's gained legs from the wind. It lands on her ankles. Miranda offers a gentle kick and hears the frantic sniffing of a dog fast approaching.

They stare at each other – shock in equal doses. The dog has the desperate eyes of an escaped prisoner, whose body has become malnourished from life on the run. Fine black hair hangs from its bones. The pound will eventually catch up with the fugitive; even the dog seems resigned to its fate. It shakes its head timidly and goes on its way.

The morning sun stings her eyes. Bowling ball on her neck threatens to roll. Her body begs to vomit, but the final vestige of dignity says no. She feels her clothing. The same white shirt she was wearing last night. Oh yes, thank God her black shorts are still there. Feels the outlines of her bra and panties. Not definitive proof that she hasn't been sexually assaulted. But it will have to do.

Her handbag is sitting at the foot of one of the huge trees. The trees in Meston Park have often reminded Miranda of old men. Grey skin stretched over bulbous limbs, generosity accumulated over a lifetime spills out into shade. Miranda hyperventilates when she notices that the zipper of her bag is open.

She rummages through the pockets for her keys. Thankfully both home and work sets are in tact, hidden beneath her mobile phone. But her purse is empty of cash. Credit card gone. Dread hits when she realises that someone must have rifled through her purse while she was out cold.

Laughter ricochets in the wind. In the southern end of Meston Park, the drinkers are either rising or persevering. Sitting on top of old cardboard boxes, wearing beanies even though it's the middle of summer. A group of joggers pound the footpath, alternately gawking at her and speaking hush, hush. Who would believe that Miranda had once been a runner too? In the days before optimism and belief had become strangers.

Adrenalin pumps.

She's afraid to think his name, let alone speak it.

Did she see him last night?

Did she really go to his office?

She checks the received calls on her phone – several new ones from a private number. She flicks to the dialled numbers. Oh Jesus, she made three calls to a number she doesn't recognise.

The glare is unbearable. Miranda reaches into her bag for sunglasses, hoping the thief didn't steal them too. She touches something cold and sticky. Her little finger feels as though it's been stung by a bee.

She seizes the black handle of the knife, and jumps.

It's the shrill call of her mobile. She grabs it. 'Hello.'

'Who am I speaking to?'

The voice is male and vibrates authority as her own voice trembles.

'Miranda Eversely.'

'Miranda, I'm Detective Sergeant Jason Matthews.'

TEN

The Premier's watermelon seed eyes blink. Sky blue, where there should be black. The make-up girl frantically mops the Premier's brow. A tight pigtail pulls her eyes to her forehead, like television antennae. He often tells Lesley that in twenty years of public life, he has never grown used to having his skin dowsed with sludge. Lesley watches the make-up girl finish her operation. She finally walks away and he offers no thanks. Lesley reasons that he's too busy moulding today's look. Stoic in grief.

Lesley knows that the Premier is in his element with an audience of journalists. Enemies he can laugh with.

A pig in shit.

Bjelke-Petersen called them his chickens. The Labor man indulges them with the same theatrics. Same contempt.

Ordinarily, the Premier is met with menacing smiles, cynical faces that dare him to draw from outside his toolbox of double-speak and spin. But today the mood is sombre. Wendy Hames, the tough and sexy correspondent from the *Queensland Daily*, is holding a Kleenex to her eyes. The air is saturated with disbelief.

From the back of the stage, Lesley watches him greet his chickens.

Come to me, my chickens. I'll protect you. Keep you safe in a world of violence.

The Premier steps up to the microphone. 'Ladies and gentlemen of the press, it is with regret that I inform you of the loss of a truly great Queenslander, Dick Payne. Dick was a Harvard-educated lawyer and a devoted family man. He was also a relentless campaigner against welfare dependency, which has had a debilitating hold on our Aboriginal communities.

'Dick Payne was a great leader of his people. He was also a much-cherished friend. One of the most profound experiences of my political life occurred while I was touring Aboriginal communities in north Queensland, with Dick, last December. One steaming hot Friday morning, Dick took me to a public meeting in Doomadgee. Some of the locals were strongly opposed to Dick's reforms, which would have forced them to sign good behaviour covenants as a condition of access to government services.

'At first I was concerned that we would be seen to be imposing our will on the community. But Dick wouldn't have any part of that. He took on everyone who questioned his reforms and he fought like a bulldog. Now, some bleeding hearts might argue that what Dick did that day was wrong. Some good meaning city folk with rose-coloured glasses may even say that Aboriginal people have the right to choose to live in dysfunction. But Dick saw things differently. Dick knew that Aboriginal people needed a saviour, who would rescue them from themselves. Dick Payne was that man.'

The Premier pauses, counts to three. Lesley has heard that he used to do this often when he was a lawyer. He'd pause just after an important point during his summing-up to the jury. He always knew he had them when their eyes followed his intently. Musicians under the spell of a conductor.

'As all of you would be aware, Dick and I were scheduled to launch the Aboriginal Employment Initiative today. Tragically, Dick will not see his legacy unfold. However, I assure you that I am more determined than ever that this outstanding Queenslander's dream is realised.'

He offers the cameras a half-smile. Not too much glee, just a drop of hope.

'The Aboriginal Employment Initiative will be renamed the Dick Payne Memorial Program. The life tragically cut short will

Huron County Library

--- Currently checked out ---
Title: A wicked snow
Date due: 17 September
2012 23:59

Title: Fortune cookie
Date due: 21 September
2012 23:59

Library name: Seafort
Branch Library
User ID: 064920015 3156

Title: The boundary
Date due: 28 September
2012 23:59

Title: Northwest Angle [text
(large print)]
Date due: 28 September
2012 23:59

Title: Bones are forever
Date due: 28 September
2012 23:59

TD Summer Reading Club:
Imagine

live on in successful Aboriginal Queenslanders, who will find meaningful jobs, own their own homes, and live like everyone else.'

The Premier casts his eyes to Wendy Hames. The black pencil skirt has been pulled up above her knees, revealing white lace, but she doesn't appear conscious of it. Hames smiles in appreciation. He reciprocates.

'I will now step back to allow the Police Commissioner to answer your questions.'

Lesley has known the Police Commissioner for over ten years. They've seen each other at various functions held at Parliament House. She knows that he's been a cop for thirty-five years, the last five in the top job. She's seen him give a number of press conferences with the boss; usually just after a grisly murder or a major drug bust. He's never at ease in front of a camera. His face is always a nest of worry.

'This was a cowardly and brutal attack on a defenceless man.

'Mrs Payne has been assisting police with our enquiries.

'We believe that the murders of Dick Payne and Justice Bruce Brosnan could be linked.'

Journalists circle him like sharks and he can do little to pacify them.

'Look, I am not prepared to say that the murders have any connection to that native title business. It's simply too early to say.'

The Commissioner sounds exhausted, his voice a lone bead in a hollow drum.

'I urge members of the public who have information to contact Crime Stoppers.'

Lesley and the Premier exchange glances. She's crying softly, her face a picture of devastation. The Premier rubs her back gently, like a brother would soothe his little sister whose ice cream has fallen to the ground.

Ordinarily, Lesley drinks in the excitement of a press conference. But today there is no adrenalin rush. No glorious reminders of how far she has come in life.

The Premier takes her elbow. 'Lesley, can we have a word?'

Journalists are placing minuscule computers into chic bags. Camera tripods disappearing like the remnants of ancient castles. Lesley hadn't even noticed that the press conference had ended.

'Lesley, it's nothing to worry about. I have some calls to make. Come to my office in half an hour.'

But I wanted to go to the casino.

I'll have my big win today.

'Certainly, Mr Premier.'

She watches the boss walk away, his minion Ralph Parkes nattering away beside him.

That boy could talk with wet concrete in his mouth.

She stares at her cubicle. Lesley has always been so proud of the little space she has made her own. Next to the computer a glass frame holds a photograph of her and the boss. She's tacked pictures of her daughter Alisha on the cheap blue canvas that covers the dividers.

She's exhausted but gets up to make herself a cup of her favourite instant coffee infused with hazelnut essence. Sipping the piping hot liquid, Lesley stands at the window overlooking George Street. Black overwhelms the heavens. She's excited by the imminent storm. Despite the smog and dust of the city, she can still taste the fresh scent of rain.

Lesley boots up her computer. There is nothing of any moment in her inbox; an email advising of new HR procedures, another confirming a team meeting tomorrow morning. At the bottom of the pile is a message from Charlie.Eversely@gmail. com. The message is naked apart from a link to www.Corrowa. com.au.

Hot coffee bounces from her chin to the floor.

'Hey, kiddo. The boss is waiting for you.'

Parkes is hanging over the divider, which threatens to buckle under his weight.

'Oh my, what a mess you've made.'

'It's nothing. I just spilt my coffee.'

She runs into the kitchen and grabs a dishcloth, her chin throbbing in pain. She should really put some ice on the burn.

'You don't have time for this. He has to see you now.'

Standing with his arms crossed, Parkes looks like the schoolyard bully. She wants to scream at him, remind him that he is only a young twerp. But she knows better. Knows her place. He's one of the new breed of Queensland Labor, born into privilege that has corroded his mind like a computer virus. The boy dresses, talks and walks like a Young Liberal. But he's Labor aristocracy.

The Premier is a handsome man. Over six feet tall. His height camouflages the weight around his middle. Hair is salt and pepper and his face is freshly shaved.

'Lesley, thank you so much for coming to the press conference. I know that it couldn't have been easy for you.'

'It's all part of the service.'

The Premier and Parkes exchange smiles. 'Lesley, I have a proposition for you.'

She offers the matronly smile that makes so many of those inside this building gush.

'I meant what I said this morning – I really am determined that Dick's program will be successful. Without him, however, things will be difficult.'

The Premier raises his left hand to invisible stubble beneath his chin. She's seen this pose many times before. He always manages to dress simple sentences in fancy clothing. And he looks so serious.

'We'll need to involve the minister.'

The minister is beautiful, graceful, but damn stupid. This is an opportunity for Lesley to shine. She'll clench it with both hands.

'I could prepare a briefing note.'

The boss clears his throat. 'What I was thinking was that you could organise a meeting with the minister and Coconut Holdings.'

Lesley nods excitedly.

'Now, Lesley, I know you'll be busy over the next few days. No doubt, you'll have, ah . . . cultural business.'

'But I can manage it.'

'Now Lesley, you know that I take the cultural responsibilities of my staff very seriously. I want you to spend time doing . . . what do you call it? Sorry business?'

'That's right, but –'

'So Ralph will be assisting you. I want the two of you to work as a team.'

Parkes smiles at her. 'I'm having lunch with the minister's adviser. I'll get the ball moving.'

Lesley feigns a migraine and heads out of the office. Ordinarily, she's excited to be here, in the central nervous system of government. All of the important decisions are made here. But today, she feels only numbness. And fear.

The boss never trusts her to deal with movers and shakers. Only blackfellas who need to be hosed down, put in their place.

Parkes was the one to break the news about Dick. He was straightforward, which she'd appreciated. No point in pretending to be caring, even around grief. Parkes couldn't give her any real details about his death. Only that the Premier had called Dick's missus and she'd appreciated his call.

She hasn't had time to cry yet. The press conference began half an hour after she was told. Perhaps she should go home. Have a shower. Make a cup of tea.

Lesley opts against using her umbrella. The rain is soothing. Across the street a group of teenage girls are dressed in the same uniform that Alisha once wore. Whatever the Premier's daughter did, her Alisha had to follow. Sure, managing the school fees had been difficult at first, but she quickly obtained a scholarship. Lesley watches the school girls until they disappear, pained longing caught in her throat.

The shock of Charlie's email is now a dull roar. Took her back to those crazy stories Ethel used to tell her when they were kids, in the dormitory.

I'm not like you, Ethel.

I'm a doer. Got eagles in my eyes.

Lesley doesn't care for cyberspace. Has never even visited Facebook. But youngsters have their own blogs now, launch pads from which they share their stories with the world. Perhaps that's all that Charlie's doing. Besides, he's a good man. He always says hello when they see each other in West End. Not like some of the others, who yell out abuse.

Ethel's in Meston Park, she's waving her finger, the way she used to when we were girls.

'Lesley, you can't mess with blackfella business.'

'Off early today?' Parkes' face is wearing its normal half-smile that radiates contempt. His black umbrella keeps his flicked brown hair in perfect order.

'Yeah, bub. What happened to the young fella has hit me pretty hard.'

Parkes trawls his brain for comforting words, comes up with dregs. 'Well, take care.' He places his arm on her shoulder to draw her into an embrace, but stops awkwardly.

'Thanks, bub. I really appreciate your kindness.'

He smiles to himself, pleased with his efforts.

As she walks through George Street, Lesley thinks about Sherene. They met only a few times, at Dick's public lectures, where conversations were more like small talk than real. Lesley always assumed they were happily married. But as much as she loved him, Lesley knew that Dick was a flawed man. When you're a leader, you carry others' expectations on your shoulders. Every so often, leaders need an outlet.

Lesley stares at her outlet, mesmerised. She revels in the glorious pain of Just Before. It's on her mind when she wakes, is woven into her dreams. The problem is that as soon as the excitement begins to fade, she's in need of the next hit. But Lesley doesn't have a problem with gambling. She goes to work every day. Why, some mornings, she's the first to arrive in the office.

The light is dim as is everything, everyone. Faces are grey and haggard. The monster that eats their coins is a life-support machine. Breathes air into their pallor. Stars on the ceiling of the main gaming room and plastic palms are a tragic testament to savannah country. This city is surrounded by icons to past. A past that never was.

If misery is a smell, the casino is its factory. Cheap aftershave and sugary alcohol swim with regret. The smell lives in every centimetre of red carpet, every particle of recycled air. It's three o'clock and the lunch crowd has left. Just the serious gamblers, those who have nothing better to do. And Lesley.

She cringes when she sees the elderly man behind her lucky machine. It's got cowboys and Indians, flashing tomahawks when you hit jackpot. She won five hundred on that machine last week. The man's walking stick is resting beside his chair. His grasshopper body crouching into the machine. Stained coffee cups sit next to a battered ice cream container that is filled with coins. Lesley sighs in resignation and takes the machine next to him. Her bones tell her that it will be a long night, even as her mind says, 'We'll be catching that bus in half an hour.'

'So this is what it all boils down to.'

Lesley turns around. Ethel's short hair is parted in the middle, the way a mother might prepare her daughter for pre-school. Lesley imagines her in a pink pinafore dress, carrying a rag doll.

Ethel's eyes are animated, like a cat about to pounce on an unsuspecting mouse. 'After all of your posturing, you're nothing but a compulsive gambler. Public servants like you need to break your own destructive cycles. What right have you got to preach to our mob?'

'Fuck off, Ethel. I'm not in the mood.'

Ethel places her hands on her hips. Invisible smoke escapes from her ears. 'Don't you ever speak to me like that!'

Lesley's had the day from hell and is ready for a fight. 'And what are you going to do? Send one of your imaginary friends after me?' Lesley spits contempt. 'Ethel, you're crazy.'

Ethel rolls up the sleeves of her blouse, slaps her left fist with her right palm. 'Let's sort this out then.'

The old man looks up from his machine, as though he's about to speak. Ethel shoots him a stare that could turn his coffee to ice. He gives a sorrowful glance to the machine and then seizes the ice cream bucket. Ethel watches with satisfaction as he takes off as fast as his walking stick will allow.

Lesley shakes her head in disgust. 'You had no business scaring that old fella.'

Ethel laughs, sits in his seat. 'Did you like the email?'

Lesley sizes her up. 'It wasn't Charlie who sent it. It was you, wasn't it?'

'You and I have some unfinished business, Lesley.'

'What are you talking about?'

'You know damn well what I'm talking about.' Ethel points at the machine the old man has just vacated. 'Is that where you put all the money you got from Coconut Holdings?'

'How did you . . .'

'There's a word for that. Now let me think. Ah, that's it – perjury.'

Anger shoots through Lesley's veins, just as fear muzzles her tongue.

'Hmm, what I can't get over is how this little machine could eat so much money.'

'What's this about? You'd better not bullshit. You hear me, Ethel!'

Ethel is calm. She's at her most terrifying when she's calm.

'I want to know why you did it.'

'Ethel, I can't deal with this now. Did you hear about poor Dick?' Lesley sighs.

'I have sympathy for his family. I really do.' Ethel is pensive now. 'But he shouldn't have messed around with blackfella business. Neither should you.'

'You got your stories Ethel, okay, but they're different to mine.'

'You remember those stories I told you?' Her eyes plead with Lesley, but Lesley won't have a bar of it.

'I don't. I swear.'

'You're lying. Just like you lied in Court.'

Lesley sighs in frustration. Damn tired of this native title business. Six years of fighting, for what? They should have signed.

They should have listened to me.

'What good is this going to do for anyone, Ethel? It's not gonna bring the young fella back. It's certainly not doing you any good. Ethel, please listen to me. You have to let this go.'

Ethel inspects the alcove, as though she's searching for something. Someone. 'But *he* won't let it go.'

'Who are you talking about? Charlie?'

'Him.'

'Who, *a clever man*?' Lesley giggles like a child whose feet are being tickled. 'I'm sorry, but you really have to leave that stuff alone. No one believes you, Ethel. Do you know the reason why no one believes you?'

Lesley can taste it: sweet victory.

I'm the leader now. You listen to me.

'Because that mob never existed.'

Lesley laughs hysterically and one of the security guards pokes his head through the doorway.

'You need help, Ethel. Go to the medical service, the flash new one. It's just down the road from you.'

Ethel hangs her head low. Whatever she came here to achieve, it's now dissipated like the dead dreams that choke the air. Ethel heads for the doorway.

She pauses, whispers, 'He's coming for *you*.'

Coins in the slot breathe ephemeral hope. Clutter of the trolley pierces Lesley's thoughts.

'Coffee, love?'

'No, thank you.'

The waitress is in her early forties but tired eyes look older. Blond hair is greying, messily held together in a bun. Her skin is sallow, as though this place is a vacuum, sucking the life out of her.

'You alright, love?'

'I'm fine, thank you,' Lesley says curtly. But the waitress is undeterred.

'You don't look chipper today.'

The woman leans into her. 'If you want my advice, you should give these machines up.'

Lesley knows the face. Redneck trash that has never been anywhere, never done anything. But will always believe that Lesley is nothing.

'Excuse me! I work for my money, thank you.'

'I didn't mean to –'

'You don't lecture the white people who come here, do you?'

'Sorry.'

Lesley smiles in accomplishment when she hears the trolley wheels fade. She studies the empty chair next to her. Why not? The old man isn't about to return. Flutter of excitement as the friendship is rekindled. Welcomes the roar of the plastic bag of potato chips.

She used to think she owed Ethel. After all, they'd been in the dormitory together. And life in the girls' dormitory was harsh. Bordered by barbed wire and locked at night, it was more like a prison than a nursery. The children rose to the cries of the first bell to make their beds and sweep the floors. Ethel was one of the older girls, and even then she bossed everyone around. Lesley had been so terrified. But at least she could sleep next to Ethel, who never seemed to mind drying her tears.

But then Ethel turned fourteen and she was sent out to work. She came back a year later. In the eyes of five-year-old Lesley, her protruding belly looked strange on her stork-like legs. She gave birth soon after, but Lesley never saw the baby. It wasn't long after that Ethel began hearing the voices.

He's come back for me.

He loves me.

You believe me, don't you, Lesley?

Ethel had terrible headaches after that. Lesley would brush her long hair to try to ease the pain. Ethel said the headaches were because of him, but not to worry, because he'd be going soon. The other girls thought that Ethel was strange, said nasty things about her.

The old world.

Men and women like Lesley are the leaders now. She takes a gulp of her gin and tonic. Welcomes the soft burn. A rustling against her neck. Light as a feather.

A red feather.

ELEVEN

Harrison McPherson, Senior Counsel, smiles into the huge mirror above the marble basin. His silver hair is damp and the grooves in his face have only made it more handsome. Age could be unforgiving, saving its most brutal scorn for women. Over the years he has noticed his female colleagues' penchant for maintenance, lineless foreheads and cats' eyes. He buttons his crisp white shirt and tucks it into his suit pants.

The roses outside his front door have begun to wither, and the grass is slightly overgrown. Leaves coat the bottom of the pond. Two more days until the gardener's weekly visit. The *Queensland Daily* is sitting in its usual spot, just inside the gate. He's not surprised by the front page. Payne is standing next to Keating, both ecstatic after the Parliament passed the Native Title Act. Payne's eyes have a youthful glow, the contours of his face are smooth and healthy. A far cry from the bloated cheeks and bloodshot eyes Harrison came to know during the trial.

Yes, it's right that he should be on the front page. Dick, after all, was an enigma. Harrison had met a few men close to Dick's calibre in the Territory. Boys nurtured by boarding school, fed a diet of Christian discipline. By manhood they wore the crests of both worlds. Some enjoyed varying degrees of success, but Dick had been in a class of his own. Kept his city audiences spellbound, while putting the fear of God into the blackfellas. He was the only person with whom Harrison could share his rare predilection. Dick had understood that the darkness within was not to be feared, but mastered.

He chuckles to himself as he reflects on their last dinner together. Dick's wife had just taken off to Sydney and Dick was anxious to unwind.

The piano is soothing, like the Möet that caresses my tongue. The whore dangles from Dick's knee. Her red dress is faded, sequins chipped. Dick's just snorted his first line of coke for the evening. He whispers into the whore's ear. She stands and announces that she's going to the bathroom. Indignation simmers beneath heavy make-up.

'Harrison, mate, you know what I think?' Dick wears a chemical grin. 'Assimilation was a bloody good thing. I mean it. Assimilation doesn't deserve the bad rap that it gets.'

Dick shakes his head bitterly. 'Those old cunts who marched in the seventies, where are they now?' he says. 'I can guarantee that none of them are dining in five star restaurants and drinking Möet.'

Dick slaps me on the back.

'I drive a five-hundred-thousand-dollar car. Labor adores me despite the shit I throw at them. The Liberals think I'm a God.'

The whore returns, stops halfway to our table. Dick glares at her.

'Slut!'

As Harrison prepares breakfast, he wonders if he'll ever find another companion like Dick. Harrison loves his kitchen – it's the size of a living room. State-of-the-art fridge looks like something from NASA. In the middle is the stove surrounded by granite, every kind of pot and pan suspended above. Guests sit in awe, watching his culinary prowess. Harrison occasionally dabbles in French cuisine, but his favourite meal is anything that comes from the huge wok.

He douses thick white toast in butter while bacon roars from the pan. Eggs poach nearby. He garnishes the twin plates with fresh parsley and feels a rush of excitement as he imagines the opportunities he will have in his new role. It'll be just like the old days, when he was the Aboriginal land commissioner in the Northern Territory. He'd been so content, before the incident. A new car for the boy's mother saw the police statement disappear. He's reminiscing about puppy eyes when the phone rings.

'Hello,' he says.

'Harrison, I'm so sorry for calling you at this hour.'

'It's only seven o'clock, Lesley.'

'Harrison, you know I wouldn't impose, unless I really had to.' Her voice is on the fringe of a sob.

'What is it?'

'I was wondering if you'd have time to see me this morning?'

Disappear, you old whore.

'I'm so sorry to hear about Dick. It's such a tragedy. But I really don't think I can see you this morning. You see, it's my first official day as president of the Native Title Tribunal. I have meetings booked until . . .' He pauses, pretending to read his diary. 'Ah, yes, I'm busy until after five o'clock.'

She's weeping now and he just wants it to stop. 'Alright. If you're quick, I can fit you in at eight-thirty,' he says, grudgingly.

'Thank you so much, Harrison.'

Harrison places one of the plates on the breakfast tray. Grumbles as he marches up the stairs. Morning sun lingers into the bedroom window. He cringes at the half-eaten packet of soft candy on the dresser and throws it into the waste paper basket. Once he ate a piece by mistake. He woke up on the kitchen floor, with a massive bump on his head. He'd lost half a day.

The boy is still buried in drug-induced slumber. A flowering moustache and occasional pimple are the buds of puberty. Soon he'll be too old.

'Get up,' Harrison says. 'I said, get up!'

The boy mumbles before opening his eyes. Only now does Harrison notice the dark caverns that surround them.

'Are you hungry?'

The boy's eyes are melancholic.

'Hasn't anyone told you that it's rude to stare?' Harrison says.

'John's going to pick me up.'

The child's voice is soft, a gentle hum.

'Who's John?'

'Mum's boyfriend.'

'When?'

'Soon.'

Harrison proffers the breakfast tray. 'Do you have time for breakfast?'

The boy answers by hungrily seizing the food.

'I have to go to work. Let yourself out when you're finished.' Harrison dispenses a bundle of notes next to the bed. 'And use the tradesmen's gate.'

As he pulls the BMW out of the driveway, Harrison wonders if the child will steal from him. He's brought scores of boys to this house. None has stolen. Perhaps their bodies are too weak to haul the loot? Perhaps he pays them too well? The song is familiar but he cannot remember its title. The singer rants about the pain of unrequited love and Harrison wonders why women seemingly cannot sing about anything else. His mind turns to that stupid, old whore. Without Dick's imprimatur, Lesley's incompetence has been stripped bare. How long will it take for her to drown? He'll enjoy watching Lesley gasping for air.

'Good morning. It's Alexander Johns on Green and Gold FM. This morning I'm in the studio, where I'm joined by the leader of the Opposition, Brian Sparkes.'

'Good morning, Alexander. It's a pleasure to be here.'

'It's always a pleasure to have you. Brian, the past few days have been incredibly tough.'

Johns' voice is so reasonable, could sell anything.

'Just over ten days ago, we had the first judicial killing in recent memory. Then one of the greatest minds in the State was murdered in his office.'

'It's terrifying Alexander, it really is.'

'Brian, yesterday we heard from both the Premier and the Police Commissioner. The Police Commissioner said that it was too early to say whether or not the murders have any connection with the Corrowa native title litigation. Would you like to comment on that?'

'Before answering that question I just want to express my sincere condolences to the family of Dick Payne. He was the most articulate man I have ever met.'

Harrison glides into the Registry of the National Native Title Tribunal with his head high, impeccably dressed. But there is no audience waiting with bated breath. The woman at the reception counter is young and obese. Her dark hair is tied up in a pony tail and she's holding the grey phone to her left cheek. Lesley is sitting on the black couch in the foyer. He's taken aback by her haggard face. Looks like she's aged ten years.

'Harrison, how are you, bub?'

'You're early.'

'That's okay. I can wait. I've been yarning with Laura. I know her mum.'

The woman at the counter smiles, revealing braces.

He glances at his watch. 'I can give you ten minutes.'

The furniture is just as Harrison had requested – elegant and understated. His large teak desk stands in front of the generous window that stares into George Street. The walls are bare, in wait for the paintings that are still in his chambers. The shelves are full of legislation and leatherclad binders. Lesley sits on the white leather couch.

'Lesley, you look like you didn't sleep last night.'

She nods glumly.

'What's this about, Lesley?'

'I've been doing a lot of thinking about the court case.'

'What kind of thinking?' She's been here a minute. A painful nine to go.

'Well, you know, I'm a positive person. I don't like to dwell on the past. The young fella was like that too.'

He offers the stare he uses to grill witnesses in Court, the one that roars contempt for fools. But she's oblivious.

'That's why I said that Ethel's story about being a Corrowa

wasn't true. I mean, how would an orphan know where she comes from? I'd always thought that the poor thing made up her identity.' She shakes her head knowingly. 'I really did think that holding onto that rubbish has been bad for her health. She should be like me, you know, move on with life.'

Her voice projects the innocence that he cherished during the trial. He bristles at it now. 'Lesley, I have another meeting shortly.'

'Sorry, Harrison. What I'm trying to say is that, well, Ethel might have been right.'

'Lesley, you listen to me. I will not be compromised.' She should have kept the money and run, stupid whore.

'I'm sorry Harrison. I didn't mean to upset you. With the young fella gone, I've got no one to turn to.'

She's sobbing now. Pathetic. 'Lesley, you have something you want to discuss with me? Yes? I'm a busy man. I have important things to do – for your people!'

'Blackfella business.' Her whisper is encased in fear. But it's petrol to flames.

'Oh please! You're beginning to sound like Ethel Cobb. There is no such thing as a clever man and, quite frankly, I'm disappointed in you.'

Lesley is dumbfounded, her long eyelashes blinking into space. She's a child who's just discovered the truth behind Santa Claus.

Harrison is pleased with his efforts. He's shaken her out of self-pity, now he needs to ease her back into reality and get her out of his office. Promises himself that he will never answer another of her calls. The professional association is spent, the façade of friendship no longer serves any useful purpose.

'Lesley, for what it's worth, my sources tell me that Sherene Payne is a person of interest.'

'No, that can't be.'

'I suggest you take a few days off.'

There's a knock on the door. A slip of a girl, perhaps eighteen, walks in carrying a tray with two cups of coffee.

'Harrison, it's a flat white with no sugar, as per your instructions,' she says, and turns to Lesley. 'Auntie, I got the same for you.'

'Thanks, bub.'

Harrison checks his watch, bristles with impatience. 'I really have to go, Lesley. You can stay here until you finish your coffee.'

Harrison takes a sip from the Styrofoam and cringes. He pulls a tiny object from his mouth. He frowns as he peers into the wet feather. Lesley springs to her feet so quickly she drops her cup. Coffee plummets on the white leather.

'What the fuck!' He wants to wring her neck. At the very least, force her to clean up the mess.

But Lesley has already gone. Stunned faces watch her scamper to the lift, like a fox running from the hounds.

At first, Jason was stunned by the symphony of cadavers releasing gases. Many times he's imagined their final words.

'Why's he doing this to me?'

'My wife's crying, pleading with me to wake up.'

'Can't breathe.'

'Blood, I've lost too much blood.'

The chemicals are nauseating but preferable to the stench of a decomposing body. Jason once found a man three weeks after he'd gassed himself. He had no family and had just been retrenched. The neighbours called only when they noticed the hideous smell. Death's scent had stayed on Jason's clothes; he never wore them again.

'Higgins, Matthews.'

Doctor Robert Thomas is his usual chipper self.

Higgins faces him. 'Hi doc, how are you?'

'Mate, you look like hell.'

'Don't worry, doc – I don't plan on ending up here for a while,' Higgins says, wryly.

Thomas' warmth makes no dint in this place. The bed of steel belongs to no one, it's only ever a transitory home. Dick Payne's face is contorted, as though he's in the middle of a sermon. Final words he so desperately wanted to breathe life into?

'The cause of death was the same as Brosnan – drowned in his own blood.'

'And it was a knife?' Jason says.

'Yes, once again.'

Jason cringes at the body, shoulders and abdomen full of holes.

'It was a particularly savage attack. Whoever did this is incredibly dangerous,' Doctor Thomas says, sombrely.

'What else can you tell us?'

'Dick Payne was a very sick man. He had diabetes, liver was in a terrible state. There's another thing – like Brosnan, he had no defensive wounds.'

'What about the scratches on his arms?'

'Already there.'

Higgins shakes his head in disbelief. 'What kind of person does this?'

Jason knows Higgins can be incredibly harsh, has beaten suspects to a pulp without so much as a moment's reflection. But the man is still shocked by ugliness, in spite of everything they have seen. And done.

'I have something else to show you.'

Jason is relieved to leave this place for the brightness of Thomas' office. A photograph of a beautiful woman in her early fifties sits on one side of the desk. On the other are the smiling faces of four young children, with Doctor Thomas in the middle. Fertile seeds in a barren place.

A small evidence bag sits next to the computer monitor. It appears to contain a tiny piece of paper, pressed into a ball. Jason's taken back three decades, throwing spit balls to the ceiling, Miss Perry's face red with anger.

Doctor Thomas opens the seal on the evidence bag and removes the paper with tweezers. 'Found this under his tongue.'

'What is it?' Jason says.

The print is smudged, almost illegible.

'It reads, QUD61. I think there could be other numbers after 1, because it looks like it was torn at the beginning of an 8.'

The froth is like a cloud. Jason welcomes the warmth of the glass after being in the morgue. Cringes in disappointment when he swallows the bitter taste of burnt coffee. 'Last time we come here.'

'If you weren't a coffee connoisseur it wouldn't matter where we went,' Higgins says, dryly.

It's a weekly pantomime. They place their order at the counter overlooking George Street. Inside the narrow hallway, dim light bounces off polished wood. It's cosy, like an old study where a professor pulls apart exam papers and manuscripts. But the air inside is cold, the wooden chairs merciless.

They walk down the winding path. Vines climb the walls of the old factory that now sells cheap didgeridoos and other sweatshop trash. The waterfall in the corner gurgles like a coffee percolator. A concrete lizard stares out from pot plants, the real ones left long ago.

The city is dotted with oases like this, reprieves from the leviathans. But demons scream in the synthetic tranquillity. Their voices live in every corner, filling the city like an orchestra. Violinists in Eagle Street, cellists in Albert. George Street is the Maestro. Demons' laughter echoes in the lawyers' chatter of murder, rape and robbery. Smirks heavy with confidence, but how much is real?

Higgins seems to savour his cappuccino. Three heaped teaspoons of sugar crystals have disappeared into an ocean of foam like the *Mary Celeste*. Demons' laughter screeches from the phone.

'Higgins.'

'Boss, it's Lacey. Doctor Bernes got back to me about the feathers.'

'And?'

'All from the same kind of bird. The Paradise Parrot. Native to central and southern Queensland. Fed on grass seeds and nested in termite mounds.'

'Take a step back. Lacey, are the feathers that were found on Brosnan the same as those in Dick Payne's office?'

'Yes.'

'Okay, how common are these birds?'

'There's the nub. The Paradise Parrot is presumed extinct under the Nature Conservation Act. The last recorded sighting was in 1927.'

'How would someone get their hands on the feathers now? Museums? Private collections?'

'Boss, the feathers were taken from live birds.'

'What?'

'Doctor Bernes was beside himself,' she says.

'Yes, I'm sure that it's great news for the EPA. Anything else? Could he tell you whether or not the birds can live in captivity? Anything at all?'

Jason can hear desperation festering at the bottom of Higgins' voice. He knows that Higgins can feel time slipping through his fingers.

'No boss.'

'Okay, Lacey. Thanks for your efforts. I'll see you back at Headquarters.'

Higgins' suit coat has become a frypan. His sweat runs like fat escaping from snags on a barbecue. George Street is manic. A man sits in between the backpacker haunts, cap outstretched, eyes glazed. No one throws him coins. They walk past the embryo of the new courts complex and Jason ponders what was wrong with the old one.

'So what do you make of a killer who leaves behind the fresh feathers of an extinct bird?'

'Should we be talking to a profiler?' Jason says.

'Fuck that. Those wankers can stay on TV.'

Higgins is old school, like his old man. He's said it a million times: 'There's no magic in these dickheads with alphabets behind their names.' Getting the hands grubby, chasing even mundane leads, following instinct that has been cultivated over so many years on the job. That's the essence of Higgins. Jason, on the other hand, will try anything new. He'll spend hours on the internet, absorbing the latest expertise from around the globe.

Higgins takes the car keys from his pocket, swings them around his head like a lasso. 'I'm driving.'

Jason feigns a look of disappointment.

'It's one of the few benefits of seniority. Come to think of it, the only one.'

'I'm still at a loss. I just can't make sense of this tragic waste. A little earlier today, his widow, Sherene Payne, gave a press conference.'

A cluttering of microphones follows background interference. *'Many people will remember my husband by his powerful oratory . . .'*

Jason glances at Higgins and reaches for the volume on the car stereo. 'Did Sherene do a press conference?'

'Yeah, this morning.'

Jason turns up the volume. Sherene Payne's petite voice teeters on collapse.

'And yes, Dick will go down in history as a courageous and visionary leader. But to me, he will always be the father of my child. The love of my life. We planned to grow old together. We had so many plans . . .'

'Listeners –' Higgins rolls his eyes as shock jock Alexander Johns takes the air waves – *'one of my greatest concerns is that now there will be a void in black Australian politics. Who will replace Dick Payne? Are we going to see a resurgence of the old style, radical leadership?'*

Johns' voice disappears, replaced by one that's raw.

'We're the traditional owners of this entire city . . .'

Jason tries to place the speaker. Charlie Eversely?

'*We've never received one cent in compensation for what was taken from us. All we ask is that you leave Meston Park. It's the only place we have left.*'

Journalists shout questions like talons striking flesh.

'*Of course, we have the utmost respect for Dick Payne's family. But we will not be cancelling Friday's march. The march will be perfectly legal. There will be no violence. We're a peaceful —*'

Higgins shuts the motor.

A black Audi pulls up outside the Mantra hotel. Jason watches as a woman piles her bags into the back and then climbs inside, enthusiastically kissing the driver. Long ago, he would have presumed that she was greeting her husband. These days he questions everything. Everyone. She could be his wife's sister, or perhaps they met on the internet. She's the mousy housewife who craves the excitement of sex with strangers.

Trees live in their concrete cells and vines grow on trellises attached to apartment buildings. Taxis queue, waiting for their dwindling supply of passengers. Teenagers dribble a basketball on the pavement, dawdling as though they have no purpose. Inside, the hotel is bathed in grey, white and olive green. Soothing music hums from the bar that extends to the footpath. A handful of diners are perched on stools, speaking, tapping keyboards. The coffee machine splutters, lamenting that its work is never done.

The reception guy's hair is cut so short it's a series of brown dots painted on his scalp. It magnifies his face. Hazel eyes shout from their sockets, lips chiselled into a grin.

'Sherene Brosnan checked in at 7:06 pm.'

'Did you check her in?'

He pauses to study the monitor. 'Yes. Actually, come to think of it, I remember that night. Soon after, she left. She was crying. Looked pretty embarrassed.'

'How long did she stay?'

'Checked out at 7:32.'

'Thanks for your help,' Jason says.

They cross the street to one of the cafés that face South Bank, taking a table under a huge white umbrella. The crowd is yet to swell. A group of young men play football in front of them, conjuring memories of life before the job. The waitress brings them coffee. Not a day over seventeen, Jason guesses. She wears an enthusiastic smile that he knows won't last.

Higgins is just about to light a cigarette when he remembers the prohibition. The phone screeches from his pocket.

'Boss, it's Henly.'

'Tell me you've spoken to the Paynes' nanny.'

'Hmm, Maria Connett.'

'And?'

'Three little kids in a tiny one-bedroom apartment. No signs of Dad. She didn't want to talk to me at first. Got a feeling it's a cash-in-hand job.'

'Well we don't work for the ATO. What did she have to say about Mrs Payne?'

'Arrived home just before eight. She was pretty upset but said nothing. Maria left at nine.'

'And?'

'Maria struck me as being very afraid of losing her job. My guess is she'd say anything to keep a roof over those kids' heads.'

'Thanks, Henly. We'll see you back there.'

Higgins shuts his phone and looks at his partner for clarity. He relies on Jason to tie all their instincts, facts and fears into a concise package of words.

Jason's mind ticks over. 'The Brosnan women are ruled out, which leaves Sherene Payne. After she left the Mantra, she still had time to drive to MacGregor. Rebecca Collis heard a man and woman arguing. It could have been Sherene and Brosnan.'

Higgins frowns. 'Motive?'

'Lover's tiff. She says she initiated the break-up. What if she didn't?'

'What of her husband?'

'Dick scared the hell out of her. It was pretty obvious she was less than frank about that. He could have threatened either Sherene or the baby. So she struck back. There was no one else in his office and the security guard was on the ground floor.'

'You don't sound convinced.'

Jason throws his hands in the air. 'Well, it doesn't explain the feathers or the note in Payne's mouth.'

Higgins cocks an eyebrow, manages to look debonair for a second. 'Could be a file number?'

'He was a lawyer; might be a number relating to one of his cases.'

Higgins grabs his phone and dials. 'Lacey, can you get the court number for that native title claim?'

Jason stares at the football game. One of the players is limping off the field. The others pause to allow him to hobble to the bench, but they're hungry to continue.

'Corrowa, that's right. Call me back.' Higgins looks across at Jason. 'So who does that leave?'

'Miranda Eversely. Payne called her four times the night he was killed. She called him three.'

'Sounds like a booty call.'

Jason shrugs. 'Don't remember what they are.'

Higgins' face screams disbelief. Jason ignores him.

'So what did she tell you? She claiming confidentiality?'

'Apparently they were discussing the Corrowa's appeal.'

Higgins chuckles cynically. 'A boat full of lawyers sinks to the bottom of the ocean . . .'

'Mate, you've told this joke at least a hundred times.'

'You call it a bloody good start.'

Jason can't be bothered pretending to laugh. His mind is elsewhere. 'We need to find out more about the Corrowa. The feathers suggest some kind of ritual.'

'Is this Miranda related to Charlie Eversely?'

Jason would do anything to change the direction this conversation is heading.

'Hey, I asked you a question, Matthews.'

'It's been fifteen years, mate.'

Jason knows it used to happen all the time: drunks perishing in cells. Ordinarily, they didn't even bother with an inquest. But after one incident, the revelations of the Royal Commission into Aboriginal Deaths in Custody were still fresh in the public mind. The Aboriginal Legal Service demanded blood and Charlie Eversely worked the press until he got it. Higgins Senior was implicated.

Jason looks at his partner. 'Mate, I know you blame Eversely.'

Higgins ignores him, reaches for his cigarettes. 'He gave everything to the job and in the end it meant *nothing*.'

TWELVE

Boundary Street is a kaleidoscope of time. Fashion on the cusp of tomorrow is housed in faded brick and roofs almost naked of paint.

Sports cars mingle with ancient sedans. Charlie sips his four-dollar latte and the taste rolls on his tongue. He sits back against the couch of garish brown and pink flowers. The music in the café is psychedelic, taking him back to another life. Head ablaze, hysterical laughter that has no reason. Angry, young black man in a world that wants to keep him in chains.

He thinks about the visit from the real estate agent yesterday. Elegant blond hair with just enough bounce, white suit unblemished. She removes her sunglasses, squints. He knows them so well, he can spot them instantly. Pigeons desperate for bread.

'Excuse me, I've been trying to contact the owner.'

'You're looking at him.'

'Oh.' Her smile reveals expensive teeth. 'Nice place you have here.' She looks around, still in shock. 'My name's Carol Anne. I'm from West End Realty.'

'What can I do for you, Carol Anne?'

'Have you considered selling?'

Both know the answer, but they still go through the motions.

His castle. Bought for a song thirty-five years ago. The suburb had a bad name back then: strictly for Murris, migrants and those who lived on the fringes of their own. Carys had fallen in love with the huge balcony and sprawling yard. Whereas Charlie saw a dilapidated house, Carys had seen a home.

Different time.

We're all slipping away from this place.

Charlie feels the unease simmering within. He hadn't spoken to Bruce for years, no longer knew him. If he ever did. But the shock is still raw.

He thinks back to that demonstration against the Springbok tour. The speeches fired him up: he was ready for whatever they wanted to throw at him. But he was only flesh and blood: bones those coppers could very well smash.

The Springboks were inside their hotel. Charlie wondered what they thought of the protest. A young white boy stood out among them. He was tall, lanky. *The coppers are giving him the eye – he's a sitting duck.* A wall of blue came crashing down and the students spilt like dominoes into the darkness of Wickham Park.

The white boy went down. One copper launched his baton into his head. *Oh Jesus, he's busted open like a melon.* The copper was built like a bullock, but Charlie knew he could take him.

They ran for their lives. *I can outrun him, but won't.* It was an unexplained bond that had no past, lived only in the next five seconds. Inside Trades Hall, Charlie's pulse kept racing.

'What's your name?'

'Bruce. Bruce Brosnan.'

An ice pack was glued to his face. *He'll be sore and sorry tomorrow.*

'So Bruce, why are you here?'

Bruce's look suggested the question was ridiculous.

Charlie had seen it so many times. White students who risked life and limb to stop apartheid in South Africa, but closed their eyes to apartheid in Brisbane.

Charlie shakes his head, drinks in rain's smell. Cars glide in and out of the coveted spaces on Boundary Street, like ants on a picnic blanket. Chaos lives alongside perfect symmetry. The occasional council bus is the elephant of the kingdom. It moves with as much grace, releases the same thunderous roar.

Carys, baby, your garden's getting a drenching. The cherry tomatoes are coming up good. You should see the chillies.

Across the street, Andrew O'Neill and Associates is painted in white on a pink background. The sign is old and weathered. He imagines the interior is old and weathered too. Hasn't been inside for years.

He remembers the new black suit that Ethel bought Miranda for her admission ceremony. Her hair was curled beneath her shoulders. It was the first time he'd seen her wear blush and lipstick.

She was sitting behind the large blue desk in her office. Bottle of champagne almost empty. Her eyes were cloudy, voice breaking into drunken laughter.

I did this.

When they brought her home from the hospital, Charlie watched her with more fear than affection. Why was she crying? Was he holding her right? Carys never worried. Carys had always been his anchor.

I sank to the ocean floor when she died.

The girl at the counter is in her early twenties. Hair braided with tiny lavender flowers, eyelids green.

'Hi, Uncle Charlie. Did you enjoy your coffee?'

Charlie doesn't know her name, doubts they've even been introduced. But the locals know him. Ethel chuckles when she calls him the Mayor of West End.

'I did thanks, darlin'.'

'Have a good day.'

He stands outside the fruit shop, breathing in the freshly squeezed orange. It's almost ten-thirty and suits are emerging from their caves. It's an uneasy truce between old and new. They walk alongside each other, sometimes on tiptoes.

Charlie has to admit that on the surface things have changed. He is, after all, a black man who owns prime ribbon. But black people don't own any of the restaurants, jewellers, real estate agencies or bars that line Boundary Street. They don't even work in them as cleaners or sales assistants. The Corrowa are watched with fear and loathing. Pebbles on the side of the road. State economy roars down the street like a hedonistic teenager.

The newcomers have no interest in past. Not even half-breathing curiosity for the boundary. Slaves who cooked, cleaned, suckled babies. They were shot dead in darkness. Old men, dignified men, marched down the street in neck irons. Metal burning their skin, indignity melting their souls.

We know what the boundary did to us, but do you know how it has scarred you?

He allows the rain to caress him as he crosses Vulture Street. Once again, his mind turns to Carys' garden. The window of the old secondhand bookshop is lined with posters of upcoming concerts, plays and protests. It sits like an exposed vein in the flawless skin of chic boutiques.

When he retired from the Aboriginal Legal Service, Charlie thought that he'd scrounge to fill time. But he's busier than ever. Most nights he's at a board meeting for some community organisation, whether it's the Aboriginal Medical Service, Legal Service or Black Housing. Then there's his work with the West End Primary School that takes one day of every week. Charlie loves teaching the kids about Meanjin. He's talked to them about the boundary too, but the version he gives them is sanitised of violence. The kids gasp in disbelief, giving him hope. Education is his passion. That's why he's so excited about the website. Charlie had wanted to launch it in time for the march, but there's still so much work to do.

The rickety gate's about to fall from its hinges. He's been saying for months that he'll replace it. He knows Ethel's sick of reminding him. The gate always takes him back.

That bus better be on time. I just know Court One will be mayhem this morning.

'Charlie, wait.'

Auburn tresses are scattered around her shoulders like a bushfire. She can never control that hair. Her smile says she believes in me. Loves me.

'You forgot to say goodbye.'

'Darling, I'm late for work.'

'Doesn't matter.'

Miranda's in her arms, Carys has just taught her to wave.

'Say bye, Daddy.'

The parched brown is gone. The grass is lush now, but long. He'll have to get the mower out this weekend. As he walks up the stairs, Charlie hears the dulcet voice of Huey B on the radio.

'I don't think that anyone should speak ill of the dead. And no one, I repeat – no one – deserves to be murdered in cold blood. But . . .'

The pause is short, dramatic.

'Dick Payne was no saint.'

The lavender paint on the hallway still looks fresh, even though it's been ten years. Charlie feels the heat from the kitchen, recognises the smell. He hears cutlery crashing into the sink. The radio sits on the kitchen bench. Huey B has been replaced by a country and western singer who laments the mixed fortunes of a lonely truck driver. Ethel's wearing her 'Boss' apron, an old Christmas present from Miranda. White threads have frayed, but she treats it like precious metal.

'Charlie, you're just in time.'

'Scones?'

'Hmm.' She opens the oven door and the aroma fills the kitchen. 'It's all over the papers and the TV, Charlie.'

He takes the pitcher of water from the fridge. Says nothing. The community is a beehive, rumours about Payne buzzing every which way. Charlie wants nothing to do with such talk. Untimely death has circled them for too long – forty-year-old men dying from heart disease, young mothers with breast cancer who are little more than walking skeletons, children who end their lives with a noose. *Carys.* Why should the loss of one man, a flawed man, attract so much attention?

'The phone's been ringing non-stop. Mostly journalists about the march.'

'Did you take their numbers?'

'On the phone table.'

'Thanks, luvie.'

She disappears into the pantry, returning with the jar of honey Charlie brought back from the Glasshouse Mountains.

'I can't believe Payne's getting a State funeral!' she says.

'I'm not surprised.'

'You or I would never get one.'

'You or I would never expect one.'

Charlie walks into the study next to the kitchen. The guest bed sits in the corner, next to the ironing board. On the opposite side is Miranda's old high school desk. Phone numbers and equations are carved into the wooden top. Did he leave his laptop on? Can't remember turning it on.

'Ethel, have you been using my computer?'

Her face is transparent, a window on every emotion, secrets that may never surface into words.

'I was just having a look at our website. It's deadly.'

He puts his hands on his hips, a silent question mark.

'Oh, don't give me that look, Charlie Eversely.'

'Well, don't you go mucking around with my work.'

'Our work! Besides, I was just curious to see what you've been doing this week.'

'Yeah, well haven't you heard that curiosity killed the cat?'

'I made some changes.'

'You did what!'

'Oh Charlie, stop worrying.'

Honey and flour melt on his tongue. Ethel's been the boss of the kitchen for the last thirty years. Occasionally Charlie tries to steer her towards healthy options, but draws the line at her scones. He winces when Ethel brings out jam and cream from the fridge. She laughs into silent disapproval.

'The police have been giving the park mob a hard time,' she says.

'Heard that too.'

'What's the Legal Service doing about it?'

'Had a meeting with the Commissioner yesterday. Same old, same old.'

Ethel is pensive, he feels the light bulb flashing inside her.

'We should bring back the pig patrols,' she says.

His mind returns to a past he's proud of, but has no desire to glorify. Too much pain to ever go back.

Charlie remembers sipping stubbies in the old Terminus Hotel.

Juke box pumping out the Stones.

Couple on the dance floor. Sister wasn't a day over eighteen. The brother was resting his hand on those tight jeans, singing softly in her ear.

Cops stormed inside. Place was emptied of black bodies that soon filled the van. No questions asked, no time-honoured warnings.

He documented everything. Gave it to Bruce in the morning.

'They'll beat me through telephone books later, might even stick a gun up my nose.'

'It won't be this way forever, Charlie. Things have to change.'

'Charlie, you listening to me?'

'Wouldn't be game not to.'

'Spoken to Miranda lately?'

Charlie says nothing.

Ethel has no time for his awkwardness. 'Well I rang her this morning.'

'And?'

'She's sick. Come down with the flu, Charlie. You should make some chicken soup for her.'

He crosses his eyes.

'You're too harsh with that girl.'

'What else did she say?'

'She'll be at the rally on Friday.'

'Wouldn't expect her to be anywhere else.'

'Well, she might have other places to go. Like Court.'

'She was Corrowa long before she became a lawyer.'

'Charlie Eversely, you're a grumpy old man.'

'What do you mean by that?'

'You should tell that girl you're proud of her.'

'She knows I am!'

His face is suddenly alive with fifty-seven years of bittersweet existence. Ethel offers him the sisterly grin that says everything will be alright. 'Have a look at what I've done to the website. I think you'll like it.'

White sand blinds her eyes.

Sunscreen cakes her skin, cotton hat held to her chin by a band of elastic.

She hates that hat, but Mum insists.

Mum's shoulders are an oasis in this desert.

Bird perched on Mum's hand.

Long body bathed in turquoise, brown, vibrant red.

Man so tall she has to look up to his face.

He's shaking his head.

'Mum, what's happening? Where is he taking you?'

Mum's favourite Joe Cocker song.

Dad's lying face down on the living room floor.

Empty bottle.

Weeping.

Miranda has been sweating beneath the only blanket on her bed. It might be the middle of summer, but she needs a shell to hide in. Darkness chokes with old cigarette fumes and wine. Nothing dulls the misery of sleeping alone. Loneliness is the undercoat on every wall, every door.

She clicks on the light of the sports watch she bought after the last break-up. Before then she relied on her mobile phone to keep time. But in the days following Cyclone Dan, Miranda chose to leave her phone at home. She knew she'd be constantly checking it otherwise, in the hope of Dan calling. She's proud of herself. It's been five weeks and she hasn't called him once. Not even during her frequent bouts of inebriation. Sent a couple of friendly text messages. But he's declined every single olive branch.

Each day was the same routine. Wake up next to each other, sip tea, exchange light-hearted emails from work, make dinner, go to bed. It all unravelled so quickly. But reality has begun to bite. The rose has dissolved and she's beginning to see that life with Dan had been far from perfect.

His family was so damned rude. Their dinners nauseating. Dan would abandon her to make small talk with his sisters. The problem was that everyone else at the table would abandon Miranda too. In those last few weeks he'd stopped inviting her. She was relieved, but it should have been a warning that the rug was about to be pulled out from under her.

Miranda always listened intently to his woes from the corporate trenches and all the other theatres of Dan's perpetual war with the world. He never conceded that he was at least partly responsible for his problems. She even sympathised when he complained about having to pay child support. For a son he hadn't seen in *four* years. Dan never expressed remorse for being an absent parent. But that too would have required an admission of personal responsibility.

Why on earth is she grieving? Dan would have drained her until she had nothing left. The embers of her dreams may very well be dying, but he would have extinguished them completely.

Miranda has been in exile since she woke up in Meston Park. O'Neill was sympathetic; even wants her to talk to a shrink.

'Mate, I never say this to anyone, but please, take the week off. You haven't had a holiday for ages. But use this time to do some research. You need to consider your options. I know of people who've had good experiences with AA.'

'AA?'

'Don't sound so shocked. Have you considered seeing a shrink?'

Any noise outside that remotely sounds like knocking sends her into a panic. Yesterday a police car was parked in the cul de sac. Miranda sat on the back patio, cigarette in her trembling hand. Would she jump over the fence if they knocked?

What if it's that Detective Matthews?

She'd heard of his reputation for being prepared to bend the rules. Knew he'd been a witness for the Crown in John Tipat's murder trial. O'Neill had acted for Tipat. Like everyone else, he loathed the man, but felt a professional responsibility to accept the Legal Aid brief. O'Neill was convinced that the confession had been coerced. But Matthews was a talented liar and the confession was admitted into evidence. Later, O'Neill asked her why a black cop would have so little respect for the rules of fair play, as though Matthews' colour should have insulated him from impropriety.

In the years following, Miranda occasionally heard his name in the courts. But last Friday was the first time they had spoken. She immediately launched into a diatribe about the Corrowa's appeal and the apparently confidential nature of her conversations with Payne. She doubted he bought her confidentiality diatribe.

What kind of a person wakes up in Meston Park without any recollection of how she got there! And the knife! Jesus Christ, this is not her. This is not the person she wants to be.

Her head is swimming in a toxic river. But as soon as the jets of water hit she feels refreshed. Hope rears its head, like new buds on a dying stem. She slides into her favourite black jeans. Dangles gold earrings. She feels a small rush of excitement as she steps into night.

As she passes the Boundary Street Hotel, Miranda's cheeks burn. The rambling building takes her back to Friday morning. Faces are illuminated by restaurant lights. The old man is struggling with his walking frame. Head shaped like a potato. Lightness of spirit reflected in those hazel eyes. He offers a friendly smile.

Even this old man, with his metal limb, is happier than I am, she thinks.

He carries no resentment for what life has taken from him.
Why can't I be grateful for what I have?
Why can't I be happy?

The Ochre Lounge is bathed in incandescent red. She's dazzled by the ornate light fittings; each holds six bulbs. Leather couches have the hardness of new furniture. Lamps sit in the corners for no apparent purpose. The tapas menu boasts chilli crab cakes and blue cheese sourdough. She remembers when this place used to be a habitat for lonely barflies. Old filth has been covered over by the Persian carpets, but ghosts linger.

Beside the entrance is a table carrying a sign: 'Tegan Chandler Exhibition Opening'. A gold cord separates the art space from the dining area. Paintings are surreal but all have a West End theme. One stands out for Miranda. The café strip in Boundary Street, but the road is naked of bitumen. A policeman on horseback cracks a whip. A black woman holds a baby; she's cowering.

'Miranda! So glad you could make it.'

Miranda turns to find Tegan, and smiles. 'Wouldn't have missed it.' She points to the painting. 'Is that the boundary?'

'Sure is.'

'How did you . . .'

'I'm Murri too.'

'Where's your mob from?'

Miranda senses Tegan's awkwardness, decides not to press it.

'Can I get you a drink, Miranda?'

'Um, actually, I'll just have a mineral water.'

'Great minds think alike.'

Tegan guides her to a table with trays of mineral water and orange juice.

'Congratulations, darling.'

The man is wearing tight white pants and a black T-shirt. Grey sideburns sit uneasily with the silver ring in his bottom lip.

'Thanks, mate. Rodney, this is Miranda. Miranda's a lawyer.'

'Oh really, where do you work?'

'Andrew O'Neill and Associates.'

His eyes glisten with familiarity. 'Wow, you guys do great work. Andrew's helped the kid I do volunteer work with.'

'What kind of volunteer work do you do?' Miranda says.

'It's a scheme called "Uncles and Aunties". Once a month I spend a Saturday morning with Tom. He's been in and out of foster homes for most of his life. He's just moved back in with Mum, but they're struggling. So I take Tom to see a movie or we'll ride our bikes in the Botanical Gardens.'

Miranda pictures herself with a little girl, feeding pigeons. Laughing.

'Rodney, you haven't said hello to *me* yet.'

The stunning brunette offers an exaggerated frown. Tiny figure in an even tinier black dress. She raises her hand and a diamond sparkles.

'Oh my God – look at that rock!' Rodney quickly embraces her. 'So when did he pop the question?'

'Last Saturday. Both of our families were there. He'd organised the whole thing and I had no idea,' the brunette gushes.

'That's so wonderful.'

Rodney turns to Miranda, offers an awkward smile. 'Miranda, meet Louise.'

'So sorry, Miranda, I must be boring you.' Louise flashes a dazzling smile. 'So how do you know Tegan?'

'We're neighbours.'

Miranda is navigating uncharted waters. The excitement of new land pulses in her veins, but it's tempered by the fear of drowning. She silently curses herself when she interrupts, wishes that she wouldn't stutter. But Miranda is revelling in the thrill of meeting people from different walks of life. Excited by the possibility of making new friends.

By nine o'clock most of the guests have disappeared. Tegan's grin is testament to the evening's success.

'Made three grand.'

Miranda smiles at her neighbour. 'Wow, congratulations.'

'And the nice thing is that I didn't have to pay for this place.'

'Even better,' Miranda says.

Tegan shrugs. 'They like to have artists hanging around. Adds to the "authentic" West End experience. Hey, sorry I couldn't spend much time with you tonight.'

'Oh, please don't apologise. I'm just happy to be here.'

'Anytime you want to come next door for a cup of tea, just yell out.'

'I will. For sure.'

The guitar spills from the café's tiny stage to the street. Patrons are swinging to the rhythm, clutching imported beers.

Walking down Boundary Street, Miranda is in her own world. She'll become a volunteer, work with kids. This could be the start of something. She can feel it. People listened to her tonight. They really wanted to know about her. Her! And tomorrow morning, she's even going to wake up with a clear head. Might go jogging. She hasn't been jogging for years.

The aftershave hits her first. Something called Allure. Dan used to dab it on his neck after dressing for work.

Black-rimmed glasses frame his stunned eyes. His stomach has shrunk and he's wearing new jeans. They're tighter than the old blue denim. He's holding her hand.

Louise from the exhibition.

THIRTEEN

They'd come in their buggy. The man has the face of a crab, beard thick like claws; the world only notices those beady eyes when he blinks. His wife's waist is squeezed into a corset, eyes squeezed of life. The woman's cheeks are unusually hollow, and her slight mouth will never complain of his cruelty. Six sons spent the journey in silence. Silence that's flimsy protection from their father's violence.

The slaves followed on foot. Skeletal bodies fuelled by hope. Hope of casting eyes on that much-cherished child, discovering that a wife is still alive, feeling mother's embrace. Their memories are a handful of sand, and the grains are slipping into the wind. Soon the archives will be empty of precious faces.

Milky white walls whisper the secrets of this place. Her loneliness. Her body's no longer taut, ripped apart by ten births. Her mind torn apart by four baby girls lost in their first month of life. She stays in her room for days at a time, reminiscing. She misses the cold air of home, streets alive with humanity. She stares into the mirror as she brushes her long hair. Cascading water over auburn and grey stones. Her tired eyes flicker with excitement. At times like this, she can see hints of the girl from London. Tonight, they will enjoy the company of the men from the Department of Lands. Their first visitors in five months.

She's obsessed with the floorboards, commanding the black girls to sweep until she can see her reflection. They hide their bewilderment as she pretends to see her harsh face in the timber. This morning she argued with Cook. His oriental tongue throws sparks of loathing. Loathing is everywhere here, in the black girls' stares and the boys' sordid eyes.

Dinner is a success. The chicken was baked to perfection. The mulberry pie attracted so many compliments. None of which will be relayed to Cook. Generous quantities of wine lubricate conversation. She retires to allow the men to enjoy a final drink.

She quickly prepares for bed and blows out her candle. Stifles her tears with a pillow, as she hears them walking out the door.

How she despises the legacies of his indiscretions, those coffee-coloured babies. She will not have them anywhere near the house. Discipline is firm. She breaks in each girl with an iron brush. They walk with congealed blood in their hair. No one says a word.

Perhaps the brush compensates for her own subjugation? Perhaps she has pitched herself in a perverse competition with her husband? When they first arrived he kidnapped a little boy. Not a day over five. The chains were too big for his tiny neck, so the child was locked in the poisons shed. He has been with them for twelve years. The absence of his right ear and permanent limp are testament to her husband's cruelty.

The young woman's blanket is thin and smells of smoke. She tries to keep it clean, but like everything else in the blacks' camp, it is caked in dust. She feels the tightness around her neck. Smells the alcohol on his breath. The boss lifts her over his shoulder and carries her to the men's quarters. She's pleading, crying, but no one stirs. This is a regular occurrence they are powerless to prevent.

The boss's sons sit anxiously, together with the men from the Lands Department. They jeer and gasp as he removes her nightdress. The bird soars above the men's heads. One son takes to it with a broomstick, but the bird is too fast. It sits on the beam, mocking them.

The young woman tries to focus on the cracked windowpane. She would prefer to see anything other than the faces of the men who will brutalise her. Her eyes are met by a box of rippling muscle. Thick and long neck, whose face remains in darkness. Glass shatters. She closes her eyes to the sounds of yelling, stumbling and the boss loading his gun.

Opens her eyes to silence.

The rope that was burning her wrists lies in pieces. Lifeless bodies are islands surrounded by red coral.

Mistress's room reeks of death. She knows who he is. She's heard the stories from the old women in the camp. But she didn't believe he really was a giant. His arms are like the branches of a tree, but his hands are gentle. Long fingers touch her pallid face.

His warm grin is a doorway to kindness. But the young woman knows rage simmers just beneath the surface, like a geyser. He blows through his hands into her stunned face. Whispers words of hope. Since coming to this hell, she has always feared hope. But as she scampers from the homestead, she clings to it like sap to bark.

Bloodied feet greet her first morning of freedom. By the fourth day she's faint. Only dogged will moves her legs. On the fifth day she finally arrives at the camp. She's gripped by fear. The old woman is tiny and grey. Then she sees it: eyes flickering with recognition. Mother and daughter embrace.

The clever man's heart sings. He wants to stay, to drink in their happiness. Their strength. But the water spirits beckon. The invaders have infected the mighty river with poison, driving the fish to lunacy. Pink flesh on grinding metal has no respect for ancient secrets that live in the waters. Withered faces of mangroves cry for their spirit kin.

Do not fear.

Your time will come.

The business has begun.

'Bub, bub. You okay?'

Miranda's head is a snow dome that's just been shaken. Bile races to her tongue, but her body lacks the energy to run to the bathroom. She feels the rim of the bucket in her hands. Vomit stinks of wine.

'Auntie Ethel.'

'I'm here, bub.'

It hurts to open her eyes. Everything hurts. But the physical pain pales in comparison to the shame.

'What happened?'

Images flash like a neon sign. Two bottles of sauvignon blanc in each plastic bag. Sitting in the darkness, music turned low.

'You don't remember calling me? You were crying. That fuckin' Dan, I can't believe it.'

'I'm so sorry, Auntie.'

'He didn't deserve you, bub. But you can't keep doing this to yourself. You're better than that.'

'Auntie, I'm going to get help. I promise.'

Ethel takes the bucket and disappears into the bathroom. But the stench doesn't leave the room.

'Does Dad know?'

'No. I told him I was visiting Shirley.'

'And he believed you?'

'What do you think?'

Ethel looks over the room in disgust. Miranda can't remember the last time she ran the vacuum cleaner over the carpet.

Ethel stares at her, face awash with concern. 'Will you be able to go to work tomorrow?'

'I rang Andrew on Monday and we had a talk. He gave me the week off.' Miranda laughs nervously. 'I'm supposed to be checking out my options for treatment.'

'What about AA? Worked for your dad.'

'Hmm, sounds like another addiction to me.'

'Well it beats drinking yourself to death.'

Ethel's voice bristles with impatience.

'You're right, Auntie. I'll go.'

'Why don't you talk to Charlie?'

'No way. I need to do this myself.'

Miranda rests her head on the pillow. Ethel strokes her hair, the way she would when she first came to live with them.

'I had the strangest dream.'

'Really? Tell me about it,' Ethel says.

'It was back in the old days, this white family who lived on a station. And this huge blackfella killed them. The weird thing is, I've had dreams about him before.'

Ethel places a glass of water next to the window. Miranda nods groggily and returns to sleep.

Each yard is the size of a football field. Jason shakes his head at the sight of them. Some have artificial lakes, others have ponds with marble fountains in the centre. Long, winding drives are dotted with lampposts. The footpath is the width of the street. Hedges expertly pruned. Tradesmen's vehicles are parked in the street. Drop sheets and other equipment linger outside like crumbs next to cake. The price of living in this street, it seems, is constant maintenance. The mansions are ageing starlets.

Jason walks through the white arch-shaped gate of Lot number 144. Palm trees grow on either side of the lattice, resurrecting memories of *Fantasy Island*. He almost expects an eccentric host, dressed in white, to emerge from the pale blue stucco. Two imposing columns stand at the entrance to the house. In the centre is a dome-shaped window that reveals an internal staircase. There is no guard dog here. But security screens are on every window, even those on the second storey.

He looks back at the street; children sit on their bikes, watching the commotion. An old man with a terrier stands behind them, mouth wide open. Murder does not happen here. Eight Mile Plains is a suburb of mixed fortunes, but Dian Street is the high-class end of town. Not just any wealth, conspicuous wealth. Residents wear their money on their homes, like royalty wear jewelled crowns. Gates are like the door to a castle, but these castles have intercoms and signs warning of dangerous dogs. Private security firms only one phone call away.

The driveway is choked with police cars. Blue overalls from Scenes of Crime are working furiously, like bees constructing a hive. Doctor Thomas is standing outside his car. His face is grim.

Jason hears Higgins from beyond the gate and turns around. He's standing beside a television news van, letting off steam into sorry faces. The Commissioner won't be impressed, but both detectives know that's the least of their worries.

Diatribe finished, Higgins walks towards him, through the gate. He looks like someone who's spent days lost in the wilderness. Badly needs a shave. Shoulders are slouched; he looks exhausted. Body fuelled by cigarettes and coffee, no doubt.

'Don't take this personally, Matthews, but I'm sick of seeing you.'

'The feeling is mutual, my friend.'

The living room smells musty. A huge grandfather clock sits next to a portrait of a young boy. He looks like something out of a fairytale, with long blond ringlets and white stockings. Jason suspects his blue eyes might have a story to tell beyond the canvas. On the opposite wall hangs a velvet curtain.

Higgins looks around with mild disgust. 'Hard to believe only one person lived here.'

'You know, statistically, Australian homes have increased dramatically in size over the past thirty years. But the average number of occupants has decreased over the same time.'

'Matthews, I'm beginning to think that you don't have a life.'

'Check this out.' Jason points to a replica of an ancient goddess at the foot of the staircase. 'Themis, the Greek Goddess of natural law . . .'

Higgins has already lost interest. He takes the stairs, follows the sounds of cameras flashing.

The room conjures imagery of plantations from another time, another place. The four-poster bed is draped with white curtains, the pillows seem soft and generous, the satin sheets inviting. Jason figures the antique dresser is a family heirloom, as is the portrait of the woman above it. The geometry of the black and white rug has been overwhelmed by blood and feathers. He's lying face down, arms stretched as though making one final, desperate bid to escape.

'I always said I'd like to kill him,' Higgins says, side-stepping the body. 'But I never thought he'd end up like this.'

Harrison McPherson's courtroom antics were the stuff of legend. Someone told Jason he once kept a rape victim in the witness box for four days. By the end, she was adamant that she'd endured a second assault.

Higgins snorts. 'Always assumed he'd outlive us.'

Jason tries to remember the man. He never had so much as dark circles under his eyes. Always smug, James Bond of the legal profession. He looks around at the bars on the windows. 'Beats me how anyone would break into this place. It's Fort Knox.'

'It's our man,' Higgins says.

Their differences never cease to amuse Jason. While he tends to mull over his thoughts, seldom jumping to conclusions, Higgins charges like a bull. Jason looks sceptically at his partner.

'The press doesn't know about the feathers, Matthews – it can't be a copy cat. It has to be the same guy.'

A uniform enters the room. Early twenties. Keen to please. 'Higgins, it looks like we got a footprint, in the back garden.'

Jason picks up a packet of sugar-coated pastilles from a basket beside the bed.

'Thanks, officer. What you got, Matthews?'

Jason selects one with his gloved hand. The texture is wrong; lollies wear a dark coat. Sweet mingles with another scent: medicinal.

'I want to take another look at the living room.'

Beneath the velvet curtain they find a door.

Jason attacks the latch. 'I need help here – it's locked!'

The secret room is the size of a walk-in robe. It's bare apart from the tiny lounge suite and the entertainment unit. The plasma and DVD player are turned on at the wall. They recognise the baritone voice, but it's joined by crying. Child's crying.

FOURTEEN

'People, before we begin, I just want to say that I appreciate your efforts. I know some of you haven't spent time with your families for days.'

Higgins is trying to wear a brave face for his colleagues, but Jason can see it's about to crack. Higgins has just spent an hour being grilled by the Commissioner, who's under pressure from the minister, who just happens to be the Premier. To make matters worse, the media really are having a field day. One trashy current affairs program even paid for some ex-FBI agent come reality-TV star to fly out from Los Angeles. His offer of assistance was promptly declined, resulting in even more scorn from the tabloids. Everyone, from the lady at the newsagent to the barman at their favourite watering hole, has an opinion on the murders. Yet all Higgins can offer is a blank face. What he cannot disclose to anyone is that the police are up shit creek without a paddle.

Higgins looks unwell at the best of times. Today he looks like hell. His eyes are usually bloodshot, but now they're red almonds. Jason tries to pinpoint when his transformation into premature middle age began, but can't remember – it's like his skin has always been mottled. When Higgins removes his jacket, everyone notices the pools of sweat underneath his armpits. Last night's alcohol and this morning's greasy bacon are abandoning his body like it's a sinking ship, and who could blame them?

As Higgins scrawls on the whiteboard, Jason reflects on the shambles that is their investigation. In years past, a single strand of hair and even carpet fibres from the boot of a car led the police to their suspect. Where there's been a struggle it's common to find the killer's DNA beneath the victim's fingernails. Yet they've found no such evidence from any of the crime scenes. Absent were signs of forced entry. Did all three victims know their killer? So far, there's only one link between them. A nebulous link, taunting them to provide definition.

Witnesses are thin on the ground. It's not as though the police have not been contacted by members of the public. In fact, they have received several hundred calls since Brosnan's death just over two weeks ago. But many are 'psychics', the mentally disturbed or both. Higgins takes a seat and from his laptop projects three faces under the title 'Taskforce Themis'.

He looks up and is met with sallow faces, bodies that crave sleep. He focuses on Harrison McPherson.

'Okay. We've got a very rough estimate for the time of death – we're looking at between six and eleven pm.

'Henly, you've checked Sherene Payne's alibi?'

'Boss, she's been holed up at the family's property in Woodford for the last two days. Apparently, the press has been relentless. Her mother and father are staying with her, as well as her publicist.'

'Publicist?'

'Sign of the times,' Jason says, wryly.

Higgins points to the photograph of McPherson. 'The MO appears to be the same. What's new is the link to paedophilia. In all, there were three boys on the tapes. The tapes appear to have been made at the house. There was no means of identifying the children. I want to keep a lid on the tapes. At least for now. Lacey, I understand you've located Emma McPherson?'

'Yes, boss. She lives in the Northern Territory. They divorced fifteen years ago, haven't stayed in touch.'

'Watkins, what can you tell me about the footprint?'

'We're looking for a child, between eight and twelve years of age.'

Higgins pauses, rummaging through his thoughts. The further he delves into the briefing, the more agitated he's becoming. He wipes the sweat from his brow, expels a frustrated sigh.

'McPherson was found by his housekeeper, Vera Stanley, at nine o'clock in the morning. She was obviously very shaken yesterday. We'll be speaking with her again as soon as we can. She worked for McPherson for twelve years. She has to know more than she's letting on.'

Higgins stares down at his right hand, eyes wide. Jason sees it too, the shaking like an alarm clock. How much did Higgins drink last night? The DSS glares into their faces, faces shocked to see the fear in his.

'This is the most bizarre investigation I have ever worked on. The media are having a grand old time at our expense and the Police Commissioner is breathing down our throats. Welcome to the most fucked job on the planet.'

Higgins stops, sits down. Closes his weary eyes and rubs his forehead slowly. An uncomfortable silence seizes the room.

They've all faced unimaginable barbarity over the years: women beaten beyond recognition by men who had professed to love them. Blue faces of infants, sucked of life by adult hands, adults who had promised to keep them safe.

Mental fatigue is the unsophisticated lover who creeps into each one's bed at night, too shameful to ever reveal to family and friends. No one openly confesses to losing it, but Higgins is on the cusp. Jason grasps the reins of the briefing.

'As of now the only thing that links these three men is the Corrowa native title litigation. Lacey, tell us what you know about the note in Payne's mouth.'

'Sarge, it's possible that QUD61 is a reference to the Federal Court's number for the Corrowa's native title application. But it's missing the final two numbers – 83.'

'Okay. For the moment let's assume that the note is a reference to the Corrowa's native title claim. Why did the killer leave it under Payne's tongue? What's the killer telling us?'

Higgins drifts back to the conversation, his face wears a jaded grin. 'Revenge.'

Jason's pacing the carpet. 'All crime scenes had red feathers. Lacey tells us the feathers come from the Paradise Parrot. Let's put aside the fact that it's presumed extinct.' Jason turns to Lacey. 'Speak to Doctor Bernes again. We need to find out if there's any relationship between the Corrowa and the Paradise Parrot.'

Their faces are anxious for direction. He shrugs.

'Maybe it's their totem . . . whatever that is. Look, the killer might be a Corrowa or a student of Corrowa tradition. Given that there were no signs of forced entry, this person was presumably known by all three victims. So we're looking for someone who played a role in the litigation. Henly, I want you to go to the Native Title Tribunal. Find out everything you can about the Corrowa and the main players in the claim.'

He turns to Higgins. 'Boss, we've also got some news about the glass sample from Brosnan's kitchen. It's ochre. Its shiny appearance comes from Cinnabar or free mercury. Because of its compounds, it's possible it came from the Parachilna mine in the Flinders Ranges.'

'So we're looking for someone who has a link to South Australia?'

'Not necessarily. You can buy ochre over the internet these days.'

Higgins smiles at him across the table.

'What?' Jason smiles back. 'So I like to surf the net at home!'

She reminds Jason of the grandmothers on Palm Island. Her face glows with resilience. He knows the gentle façade hides a razor tongue.

'Miss Cobb?'

She examines him cautiously through the screen door. 'Who wants to know?'

'My name is Detective Sergeant Jason Matthews.'

'What do you want Detective Matthews?'

His name rolls off her tongue like a bird's-eye chilli.

'I'd like to ask you some questions.'

'What's this about?'

'Your native title case.'

'There were a number of people involved in that case. Why are you talking to me?'

'I've been told you're an elder.'

Her hands go to her hips, lips arch into a pout. 'Is that so?'

'Miss Cobb, three people have been murdered.'

'I tell you what. I'll call my lawyer and we'll take it from there.'

He watches her disappear down the hallway and return a few minutes later.

'My lawyer will be here in ten,' she says, and points to the wooden table and chairs. 'Take a seat. Can I get you a cup of tea?'

The woman is in her late thirties. Long blond hair tied up in a pigtail. Silver bands in her ears. Body hugged by black jeans. Eyes are glass marbles of peacock blue. They radiate the loathing he knows.

'Miranda Eversely, Miss Cobb's solicitor.'

On the phone she had the voice of a foghorn and kept stuttering.

Miranda reads the shock on his face and a blush spreads across her cheeks.

'Miranda . . . we've spoken on the phone. I'm Jason Matthews.'

'What's this about, detective?'

'Taskforce Themis.'

'Themis? Didn't she have something to do with the law?'

'That's right,' he says.

Her lips are red on the edges, as though she's wearing lipstick. They're curved into a half-smile.

'We're investigating the recent deaths of members of the legal profession.'

'Yes, Bruce Brosnan, Dick Payne.'

'And, as of yesterday, Harrison McPherson. All three were involved in the Corrowa litigation.'

'All three were involved in a number of native title matters.'

Jason responds with silence. He's not here to engage in an academic discussion.

'What do you want with my aunt?'

'I'd like to ask her what happened that day in Court and the community meeting afterwards. Perhaps she saw or heard something. In my experience such conversations can be very useful.'

'My aunt is exercising her right to decline your invitation.'

Jason places his card on the table between them. 'Here's my number if she changes her mind.'

As she watches him walk through the gate, Miranda has to admit that Detective Matthews is a handsome man.

'Did you know that fella, Miranda?'

'No, why do you ask?'

'He said you'd spoken on the phone.'

'I speak to police all the time. He was probably a Crown witness in one of my cases.' She lifts a white plastic bag to Ethel's face. 'Look what I brought.'

'Tim Tams! Oh, bub, you're a bad influence on me.'

Miranda winks. 'Everyone has the occasional slip.'

'I won't tell Charlie if you don't.'

'Deal,' Miranda says with a grin.

Ethel disappears into the kitchen to make tea, leaving Miranda in the living room. A black and white photograph of a football team hangs on the wall above the aged couch. The players are all young Aboriginal men and their long hair and headbands suggest the 1970s. She's seen this photograph so many times, but even now, there are things she hasn't noticed before. Miranda's struck by the ease behind Charlie's smile.

The door to the study is open. Miranda steps inside, peers at her old desk. It's the same size that it's always been. But now, the desk looks so tiny and battered.

'Have you been working on the computer, Aunt?'

'Yeah, I've been doing stuff to our website.'

'Whose website?'

'Oh, that Charlie likes to think it's his exclusive project, but where would he be without me?'

The home page promises a detailed history of the Corrowa, interviews with leaders from the Bjelke-Petersen era, archival footage. Miranda's intrigued by the feathers.

'Miri, are you right?'

'Of course, Auntie.'

'Well, hurry up. Where's those biscuits? I wanna have some before Charlie gets home.'

'I'm surprised he's not here.'

'Oh, he's at a board meeting for the Legal Service. Apparently the coppers have been giving our park mob a hard time. It's gotten worse since the murders.'

'He never told me.'

'That's probably because he's been busy organising the march.'

'But I could help. I'm a lawyer, after all.'

'Bub, I think you've got enough on your plate at the moment.'

As she polishes off her second biscuit, Miranda promises herself that she will have no more. And she mustn't leave the packet here, or Ethel will eat them all in the one night.

'So tell me, bub. What's troubling you?'

Miranda has said nothing, but Ethel's intuition is sharp.

'Auntie, are you afraid? You know, with everything that's been going on.'

Miranda doesn't want to speak the names of the dead. Somehow, it would be like inviting tragedy into their home.

'Now don't get me wrong. I have sympathy for the families

of those three, especially Dick Payne's family. It's sad that his kid will grow up without a dad. But bub, Payne had been doing terrible things to our mob for a very long time.'

'I didn't grieve for any of them.'

Ethel shakes her head and places her hands on Miranda's shoulders. 'Bub, what happened to those three was blackfella business. None of us has any control over that.'

They sit in quiet reflection, silence broken only by the rustling of the quickly depleting packet of Tim Tams.

'I've got some good news, Auntie.'

Ethel looks at her, eyes pleading.

'I've found an AA group in West End. Going to my first meeting tomorrow night.'

'Oh Miri, I'm so proud of you.'

Ethel grasps her fourth biscuit. Miranda guesses the rationale – she now has something to celebrate.

'It's nice having you here. It reminds me of when you were little.'

'I've never really thanked you for everything you did for us back then.'

Miranda feels a lump in her throat. It seems that tears are always just beneath the surface these days.

'Bub, I wouldn't have had it any other way. After my baby died, I promised myself there would never be any others.'

'I didn't know . . .'

'He was stillborn.'

'Oh, I'm so sorry, Auntie.'

Ethel smiles wistfully. 'He was perfect.'

Miranda wants to hug Ethel, but the old woman seems determined to finish what she has to say.

'Yes, it was very painful. Still is, every day.'

Ethel's voice is quivering. Miranda's face is hot, tears are not far.

'But then you came along, and I could smile again.'

Miranda wonders if this is the first time Ethel has spoken to anyone about her son. She can't imagine what it would be like to carry around such heartache for so long, without any support. Why hasn't Ethel told them before?

'He's with the old people now. He's grown to be a big fella. I got a new message from him, just the other day.'

Miranda marvels at Ethel. In spite of her pain, she still clings to her beliefs.

'And I'm learning more about our mob every day . . .You know I thought I had it tough. But no, Mum and Dad had it a lot tougher. Dad was taken to Palm.You know what for?'

Miranda smiles nervously.

'My dad told the protector that he wanted to see the money he'd been earning by working on a farm in Kingaroy.The bloody protector had been pocketing the money himself and he didn't want anyone to find out. So he shipped Dad off to Palm Island. Dad died a year later from typhoid.'

Ethel stares solemnly into space. 'Poor Mum. She left me with this couple she was working for. They promised to look after me, while she was trying to find out what had happened to Dad.' Ethel nurses her face with her palms. 'Can't even say what happened to Mum. It's too painful.'

Miranda holds her aunt while nursing her own confusion. All through the trial, Ethel had insisted she knew nothing of her life before the dormitory. Not even who her parents were.

'It's alright, love. Mum and Dad are looking after my boy. Everything's alright.'

'Aunt, who told you about your mum and dad?'

Ethel seems to freeze, and Miranda sees the glazed eyes. *Auntie, are you even here?*

'Bub, your father and I grew you up properly, not like that Dick Payne. That's why he won't come after you. Mind you, he follows you all the time. But he'd never hurt you. He promised me.'

'Auntie, who are you talking about?'

'You know . . . clever man.'

When she was a child, Ethel would allow Miranda to climb into her bed at night. Ethel would tell her stories about the clever men, sorcerers who exercised power over the weather, flew to ochre mines and guarded the narcotic, pituri. During the trial, Ethel had referred to them, but Harrison McPherson made her look like a fool who believed in fables. Afterwards, Miranda had been angry with herself for indulging Ethel. She'd always assumed that, like the boundary, the clever men lived only in past.

'My girl, we talk every day. That's how −'

'Where is he now?'

'If only you knew.'

'Auntie Ethel, if you know something about the murders, then we should tell the police.'

'I saw him last night.'

'Where?'

'Outside.'

The two of them walk out the back door and onto the verandah.

'Can you show me where he was? Auntie?'

Ethel points towards the roof. 'He was flying.'

FIFTEEN

The harsh sun of midday has yet to burst. Miranda sits on the grass beneath a tree, reflecting on the demonstrations of her childhood. The feeling of aunties sitting around her, Dad's voice booming from a microphone. It strikes her as odd that their march is starting here today, a park full of tributes to empire.

Metallic Queen Victoria stares down from her throne of sandstone. To her left is a trophy in the shape of a gun, an offering to the people of Queensland from King George V. The gun is aimed at George Street, warning colonials to stay away from hallowed ground. Across the street, dominoes etched in walls stand above pedestrians. Most saunter the footpath. They care little for monarchy, less for past.

The casino stands directly in front of the Queen's domain; with her stern face she silently admonishes those inside. The yellow and red sign 'Treasury Casino' sits above sandstone that bears the words 'Registrar General', two incarnations of the one body. Underneath Victoria's kingdom is the casino car park, its neon lights flashing like the gills of tropical fish.

At the base of Victoria's throne, a group of young men operate on the limbs of a PA system. Charlie stands above them, laughing. Miranda watches her father as he pauses to survey the crowd. There might be three hundred altogether. She guesses at least half of them are Corrowa, the rest belong to the Socialist Alliance, a few from the Greens. A small handful of the ALP rank and file sit on the grass, faith trampled by their Premier, but still breathing.

The Queen's palace is the old Land Administration Building, now a hotel. A man emerges from the glass door, like a soldier crab peering out from its shell. The long sleeves of his uniform are out of place in the heat. Television news vans are parked on the grass, indifferent to royal protocol. Journalists with perfect hair play elaborate games with microphones. Police stand at all four corners – foot soldiers sizing up prisoners of war.

Not all who enter the Queensland Police Service are racist. But racism invariably touches their souls. Like the residue of a discharged firearm. Miranda wonders who really gains from the war. Surely some cops thrive on power. But most spend their days just mopping up spilt humanity. Humanity that carries no political worth, holds no dollar signs.

The prisoners of war fill the void with whatever they can. Food, alcohol, amphetamines, every kind of addiction lingers in the crests of shell shock. Is it even possible to escape from the war? Dick Payne had tried to deny its existence, but it only corroded his psyche. He drowned in his own blood, but she suspected he'd been drowning in depression for years. She reflects on their final conversation, before inebriation emptied her brain of memory. Even as he was threatening her, Miranda felt some pity. Beneath the bravado and delusions was a black man filled with self-loathing. He may have gone to Harvard, but he spent his life delivering lines from others' scripts.

She hears a siren, but it's a fire engine, not a paramedic. Perhaps they will come later? She's read that glassing has become something of an epidemic. Or maybe it's just a media beat-up. She wonders what kind of beat-up the media will create over the Corrowa's march. Would they have even bothered turning up, if murder hadn't reared its head?

Death reveals so little.

What lies behind the masks of the living?

She may have never really known who Dick Payne was. But she knew even less about Bruce Brosnan and Harrison McPherson. Like most lawyers who have been around the

Federal Court, she'd heard of Brosnan's boasts of fighting in the trenches of the fledgling Aboriginal Legal Service. But it was obvious that the fire in Bruce Brosnan's belly had died long ago. McPherson, the Golden Tongue, seemed to thrive on professional jousts and destroying witnesses. But his personal life had been a mystery. Does it even matter?

Surely no one deserves to be murdered?

Rumour has scorched the Murri community like a bushfire. Yesterday morning, Boundary Street hummed with voices. Miranda imagined the aunties, sipping hot tea, speaking in hushed tones about a serial killer, who recently escaped from the 'psych ward' to discover his black roots. While watching the television news in his boardinghouse room, the killer became fixated with the story of the Corrowa. In his tormented mind, he determined that he would seek revenge. But by afternoon, the serial killer had transformed into a renegade cop, out to settle personal scores with a legal profession that cared little for those at the coalface. Today, he's probably a member of the Russian mafia.

Miranda sighs and looks up at the canopy of the tree. The shade reminds her of the old grey man in Meston Park, whose trunk now hides her shame. That morning, she found an empty can of mixed spirits that had been forced into its cavern. When Miranda had removed it, she noticed that the cavern was at least a foot deep. She threw the knife into it and scampered away, as quickly as her exhausted body allowed. She knows the police will be swarming all over Meston Park today. Will they find it?

'I've brought someone who wants to see you.' Ethel's voice is both chirpy and authoritative. She's wearing the Body Shop rose perfume that Miranda gave her.

The tiny silhouette behind Ethel's legs giggles.

'Linda!'

Miranda loves this little girl, whose parents both work as field officers for the Aboriginal Legal Service. Miranda usually dotes on her, but lately she's felt awkward. The sight of the beautiful child only makes her own disappointments more poignant.

'How come you've gone all coy, Miss Muffett?'

Ethel's gentle chastising has no real sting, but it's enough to bring Linda out of her shell. The little girl is wearing a white T-shirt and pink shorts, her curly brown hair divided into two braids.

'Can I leave this one with you? Her mum and dad are driving me to the hall. We've got to deliver some bread for the sandwiches. We'll only be fifteen minutes.'

'Actually, I was thinking of going across the road for a coffee.'

'Well you can't. The march is starting now. You'll have to take Linda. She wants to march, don't you?'

A grin from below reveals two missing top teeth.

'You've got your mobile, Miri, haven't you?'

Miranda smiles in defeat. When Ethel's in her element, it's impossible for anyone to refuse her.

As Ethel disappears into George Street, the crowd assembles into a makeshift line. Some children in the front carry a huge Aboriginal flag. Charlie is talking to them, no doubt telling them how proud they make him. A tear rolls down Miranda's cheek. She feels a gentle tug on her left hand and peers into the little face.

Miranda bends down and kisses her forehead. 'Come on, Miss Muffett, let's go.'

The demonstrators cross where Elizabeth Street meets William. To their left, the Performing Arts Centre celebrates twenty-five years. In the distance they can see the head of Kurilpa Bridge, pointing into the sky like the masts of the tall ships. They walk in silence, through cameras and bitumen. The sun hits them like a nail gun, but still they walk across the bridge. Journalists follow, shoving microphones into black faces.

The face of the river is chocolate, its ripples milk. Bridges like metal harnesses are choking Meanjin, Miranda thinks. The mangroves are cowering in shame, their branches bending into the water. Low tide cruelly reveals the newcomers' contempt: bottles, shopping trolleys and even household furniture wallow in the sediment.

They reach South Bank, the mutant child of World Expo '88. A multitude of identities pushed into the one brain that acknowledges only its shallow, recent past. A huge white ferris wheel stands alone, without the kin of an amusement park. The Nepalese pagoda remains among the artificial rainforest and synthetic beach. All on a riverbank where the homeless once slept.

Cranes hover above, guarding the steel skeletons of their new offspring. Every so often, the crowd pauses, allowing the stragglers to catch up. They jeer and laugh outside the South Bank Police Station. Its huge windows conceal the identities of those inside, together with their thoughts.

Wet cotton clings to Jason's chest like skin. The day is a furnace. The crowd is only a few hundred, a good number are elderly and young children. On a portable stage in the centre of the amphitheatre, a young man is throwing the lyrics of a rap song to the appreciative audience. White tents housing food stalls form a circle like a caravan of wagons.

As he walks down the hill into Meston Park, discomfort wells. There are scores of police on the fringes of the crowd. So many here hate the badge, but save their venom for the black men in blue.

Colleagues usually assume he'll go easy on blacks. At times however, Jason goes harder. When he was stationed at Palm Island, he lost it with a twelve-year-old. The kid had been throwing rocks the size of a baseball glove into the police compound. One night a projectile grazed Jason's face. He bound the boy's wrists with thick rope and held it through the window of his car. As he revved the engine, Jason grinned into a face smeared with tears and snot. After that night, Jason felt the weight of hate upon him.

He did nothing when Higgins beat Tipat to a pulp. He told himself it was because of the crime, but Jason had also wanted to prove his loyalty was not with a black child-killer. Jason's fidelity to the job is unquestionable. His skin only a vague tie to a family he's never known. Doesn't want to know.

Mum and Dad had tried to romanticise his black skin. When he was five, they took him to see *Stormboy*, ranted for ages about David Gulpilil's presence on the screen. In the lead-up to NAIDOC each year, they'd meet with the principal of Jason's school to discuss how the event would be celebrated. But they never really understood the terror and confusion that slowly cooked his emotions. Emotions that are now lifeless roots in the soil.

In his heart, Jason knew they were determined to give him the best they could. But life was never that precise. Their first inkling of the tumultuous path ahead occurred when he was six years old. While playing in the front yard the little boy noticed children descending upon the house next door that was adorned with balloons and streamers. Jason was the only child in their street who had not been invited to the birthday party. He felt a lump in his throat as he reflected on the memory of Dad's face. Complete powerlessness.

Jason's athletic prowess saw him play for the high school rugby league team. An aptitude for sport was ordinarily a ticket to teenage popularity, but Jason was acutely aware that he was different. One day, he overheard a group of girls behind him in Year Ten English. He immediately recognised Joanne Sutherland's voice. She was the most popular student in the school, with long legs and elegant blond curls. Like the other boys, Jason fancied her, but he felt protective of her. After all, they had been to kindergarten together and then primary school. Sitting behind her, he faintly heard Joanne whispering to her pack of understudies.

'Jason Matthews is so hot, but my dad would kill me if he ever caught me going out with a boong.'

Almost immediately, Joanne's fulsome lips shrivelled and her eyes grew cruel. Now he can only imagine her as an adult, standing at a clothesline with a cigarette between her lips. Yelling at a horde of children in a yard littered with broken toys, like discarded landmines.

From there on homework became a rarity. He began to truant, but soon tired of hiding in the bush behind their home. Miraculously, Jason finished school but with lacklustre grades. At seventeen years of age he didn't know what he wanted to do, in a world that had never really welcomed him. So he pursued one of the few careers open to him and, surprisingly, found his calling.

The aroma of the sausage sizzle is intoxicating. Sausages cooked on the barbecue always taste better, not that Jason eats a great deal of red meat these days. It's mostly fish and tofu for him. In the south-western corner of Meston Park he sees a bald black man sitting in a transparent box. He's wearing headphones and his fingers are working the sound equipment.

'Welcome to Black and Strong on 4MM. My name is Huey B and I'm your host. Today we're at beautiful Meston Park, in the heart of Corrowa country. The reason we are here – native title. As you all know, the Federal Court dismissed the Corrowa People's claim over Meston Park because, apparently, they weren't traditional enough. Hmm, it seems to me that the wrong question was being asked. When are they going to prove to us that we no longer have our sovereignty?'

A few in the crowd stop to listen, but most continue their business of greeting, laughing and earnest discussion. Plastic tables and chairs have been scattered in front of the stage. Ethel Cobb is at one of the few tables that has shade. Her face breaks into a grin when she sees him.

'Detective Matthews.'

Jason turns around.

Charlie Eversely is wearing the uniform that Jason has seen him in, many times on television – black land rights T-shirt, black shorts and thongs. He's shorter than Jason had imagined and older. Charlie's accompanied by a group of young men whose grey T-shirts identify them as security.

'Mr Eversely. How did you know my name?'

'I've seen you around.' Charlie's handshake is firm, genuine. 'It's good to see you here, son.'

'Thank you, Mr Eversely.'

'We'll see more of you, no doubt.'

Charlie continues on his way, leaving Jason to ponder the hidden meaning in their exchange.

'What are you doing here?'

'Oh, hi Miranda.'

She's casually dressed in a pair of black stretch jeans and a white T-shirt. A young child sits on her hip.

'You've got your hands full.'

'This is Linda. Linda, this is Uncle Jason.'

'She doesn't have to call me uncle.'

'Actually, she does. It's not right for Murri kids to be calling adults by their first names.'

Linda cries out to a nearby group of children and Miranda releases her to the ground. 'Actually, I'm glad you're here.'

'Really?'

'You know, it occurred to me yesterday that I didn't even ask where your people are from. That was rude of me, but in the circumstances . . .'

'Brisbane. We come from Brisbane.'

'Really, who are your parents?'

'Tom and Deborah Matthews.'

He laughs at the confusion on Miranda's face. 'They're my adoptive parents.' He pauses, uncertain of how much he should share. 'I don't know anything about my birth parents.'

'I'm sorry.'

Miranda seems awkward and he's relieved that she's finally showing some vulnerability. In the corner of his eye, he sees Ethel approaching, her tiny little arms in a runner's position. Jason feigns surprise.

'Boy, you disappoint me.'

He's been called 'boy' only a few times in his adult life. A couple of the old timers practically spat it at him. But Ethel's voice is coated with affection.

'Why's that, Miss Cobb?'

'I thought you'd see me before I crept up on you. You are a detective after all.'

'Who's saying I didn't?' Jason winks bashfully. 'This is a good turn-out,' he says, gesturing to the crowd.

Miranda looks around the park. 'Yeah, thanks to your friends the crowd has grown by at least a hundred.'

'We're glad to be of service.' He smiles into deep blue eyes that offer no reprieve.

Ethel pulls gently on his left shoulder. 'Boy, you and I need to talk.'

Anxiety washes over Miranda's face. 'Auntie, is this a good time? You've still got food to get ready.'

'It's done, girl. Now you leave me and the young fella alone. We got some talking to do.'

Miranda sighs in resignation and heads for the ramshackle playground.

Ethel gestures towards the table where she's been sitting. 'Sit down, boy. You look tired.'

From the way she speaks, Jason guesses Ethel is in her seventies. Her skin is surprisingly smooth for her age. The bob-cut parted in the middle of her crown is too severe, but he doubts there's a soul in the park, or anywhere for that matter, who would have the gall to tell her.

'So what do you think, Jason?'

'I think today's been a great success. You got lots of press and the people here seem to be having a good time.'

Jason casts the line, as he has done so many times. He will wait patiently until she's on the hook.

'Usually I'd ask where your people are from. But with you I don't have to ask,' Ethel says, grinning.

'Why's that, Auntie?'

'Because I already know.'

Jason shrugs, accepts her challenge.

'Aurukun.'

Jason is stunned. He's discussed his birth parents with no one. Not even Higgins. 'How did you know that?'

'Red Feathers told me.'

'Red what?'

'Red Feathers. He's your mob. At least, his father was your mob. But his mother was Corrowa.' Ethel laughs, slaps his shoulder. 'So I guess that means we're related!'

From behind his smile, Jason's brain is scrambling. Does Ethel know about the feathers at the crime scenes? Is that what she's telling him? They haven't told the press. They haven't told anyone. There is no way Ethel could know. Unless she was there.

'She doesn't know *anything*.'

He looks up to see Miranda standing over him. In the corner of his eye, he sees Ethel walking towards the stage. 'How can you be sure?'

Miranda sighs, as if the answer is self-evident. 'In all the time I've known her, Auntie Ethel has never so much as taken a fist to anyone. She's a Christian for crying out loud.'

The T-shirt is tight against her lace bra. Hour-glass figure wears those jeans like a glove. Jason notices that other men in the crowd are also looking in her direction. Miranda, however, appears oblivious.

He smiles. 'I think you and I started off on the wrong foot.'

'What makes you say that?'

'I have no desire to cause any harm. If anything, I want to work with your community.'

Miranda looks incredulous.

He checks his watch. 'It's three o'clock and I'm in desperate need of a good coffee.' He turns his head in the direction of Boundary Street. 'Join me.'

It was less a question than a command. He should have known Miranda wouldn't take kindly to orders.

'No, thanks. I have to get ready for an appointment.'

As Jason watches Miranda's svelte body disappear into the crowd, he resolves to shake every single cupboard in Ethel Cobb's life.

If that requires spending time with Miranda, he'll be the last to complain.

SIXTEEN

Miranda opens the door of the wardrobe, skims through her limited choices yet again. What she's wearing simply won't do. The tight white T-shirt makes her feel exposed. In the end, she settles on a loose blouse and black three-quarter length pants. As she walks out the door, Miranda laughs. Where she's going, no one will be concerned about fashion.

The front of Miranda's apartment is met by a new highrise complex. Sometimes, it feels like the highrise sits right on top of her front patio. She walks past Tegan's place, the converted flats. The landlord is an elderly Italian woman, who still lives on the top floor.

On a Sunday afternoon, the old lady usually potters in her vegetable garden. Tegan often works in the garden too. Miranda had once heard them marvelling over the sight of a bush turkey. Miranda realises she hasn't seen her neighbour since the exhibition. It was such an enjoyable night, until she ran into Dan and his fiancée.

Dan's not so spontaneous that he'd propose after a brief courtship. She knows that much. When they were together he'd take an eternity to mull over most decisions, from choosing the right brand of toothpaste to changing jobs. He was seeing them both, for sure. Weighing up the pros and cons each woman had to offer. All the while, Miranda was doing her utmost to make him happy.

But was *she* happy?

Dan would laugh freely at her wit and listen enthusiastically

165

to her chatter about her cases. Their lovemaking had been exciting, but as soon as it ended, he'd roll over without so much as a hug. He never had the courage to share his thoughts about their future, always placing some kind of barrier between them.

The white stucco house at the corner of her street looks as though it's lived through the generational change in West End. Probably bought for a pittance decades ago, it would now be worth a fortune. Branches laden with purple flowers lean beyond the yard and into the street. Miranda crouches to avoid their touch.

Boundary Street is a suburb contained in a street. Incense wafts from quirky gift shops that sell cheesecloth and crystals. Real estate agents have hung photographs of properties on their windows: she winces at five hundred thousand dollars for something 'cheap and a great start'. The luscious voice of a saxophone fills the air.

She continues up the hill, passing the Murri Hostel, quickening her pace as she creeps past Charlie and Ethel's home. The light in the kitchen is on and she can hear the faint trace of Huey B on the radio. She pauses at the top of the hill and turns to see the links in the chain from Boundary Street to the skyscrapers of Brisbane's CBD. As the pink and orange sky disappears into night's blanket, she walks on.

A dim light inside the church illuminates the image in the stained glass window. The saint's dress appears to be from the middle ages. He holds a sword above a Latin inscription. Miranda wonders if there is a patron saint for drinkers. A priest walks down the rickety steps and smiles.

Enclosed by chicken wire and overgrown shrubs, it's as though the hall is deliberately hiding. Miranda walks down the brief, worn path. A young man and a middle-aged woman stand outside the door. He appears to be in his mid twenties. He's handsome with chocolate eyes and a muscular physique. The woman is stout but not obese. Her hair is grey and cropped. The woman's clothes are casual but the fabric is expensive, designer label wear for slumming.

It's not too late for Miranda to turn around. But they have stopped talking. Both are now looking at her.

'Welcome,' the woman says, warmly. 'I'm Ann. We'll be starting in a couple of minutes.'

An urn bubbles furiously beside a pile of Styrofoam cups and a basket of teabags. Miranda makes a cup of milky tea and then walks to one of the orange chairs of hard plastic.

Most people stand in clusters, chatting animatedly, some are even laughing. But a few are like Miranda, alone and mirthless. The plain wheat biscuit tastes like cardboard, but at least it makes her look occupied.

She studies the large poster draped across the wall in front of a podium: The Twelve Steps. Does she even believe in God? Is alcoholism really just a hereditary disease? And what of the cure – a lifetime of meetings in places like this?

'Hey, stranger.'

Miranda turns to find Tegan sitting in the row behind. She radiates good health, her skin luminous. What on earth is she doing here?

'I know that look.'

'Sorry. I mean, if I look so surprised.'

'It's been eight years.'

'And you still come here?' Miranda says, incredulously.

'If I wasn't getting something out of it, I wouldn't be.'

'I don't really need this place . . . it's my boss.'

Tegan's laugh is earthy. 'This place achieved a miracle for me. It could do the same for you. But you have to want it.'

Tegan looks up to greet a young man; he'd been standing outside with Ann a little earlier. 'Ian, how are you, bro?'

They embrace tightly.

'Good to see you, sis.'

As Miranda settles into her first AA meeting, she feels a slight shift in her thinking. After all, Tegan seems happy. Is happiness a process that can be learnt? Perhaps it exists independently of good fortune?

But the more she listens, the more she feels confronted. Their stories bite into Miranda's conscience like termites on wood.

Jenny sobs as she recalls being arrested as she drove her twin boys to kindergarten. Her husband has since taken the children to Western Australia. Now Jenny sees her sons only twice a year, under the resentful eyes of her former mother-in-law. Her whole frame shudders as she speaks, like a dilapidated farmhouse abandoned by the family who had once breathed life inside it.

Ian's withdrawal was so painful he ended up in Emergency. Miranda has read that going cold turkey can be fatal, but till now she's never met anyone who's come close to dying from sobriety. She ponders the fingerprints that a daily cask of wine has left on his brain. Still too afraid to consider how alcohol has affected her own.

Ian's descent began with a childhood fractured by his mother's death and a heartbroken father who took to the bottle. By the time he was twelve, Ian's father was hardly ever home. Neighbours who had pitied them in the aftermath of the tragedy, began looking down on them. Before long, Ian was living on the streets. And a diet of plonk. When he could sell himself, he'd obliterate reality with vodka.

Ian hasn't imbibed for thirteen months. His face swells with pride as he describes his new life as a trainee administration officer in a government department. Only last week, he moved out of the hostel into his own flat. Miranda is charmed by the young man's sincerity. She wants to know when he hit rock bottom, so that swimming to the surface was his only option.

As if reading her mind, Ian describes his final drink. He can't remember how it began, only the epiphany when he woke in Meston Park. A dog licking his bloodied face. The few dollars in his wallet taken. No idea how he got there.

Her story.

She can't tell a soul. Never will.

Miranda coughs and splutters like a broken down car. Her lungs plead with her to stop.

I drink not because I have no control over my addiction. I drink because I have no control over my dreams.

Two teenagers shoot hoops on the beaten basketball court, underneath the streetlight.

She sits on top of the picnic table and cries.

Ethel wants to hold her, but it's pointless. It's a journey Miranda must travel, on her own. When they'd seen Miranda stumbling in Meston Park that night, Ethel had pleaded with Red Feathers to carry her girl home. But he wouldn't. Ethel understood his reasoning. Besides, he promised that no harm will ever come to Miranda. Red Feathers keeps his promises.

Ethel sits with Red Feathers behind the huge mud brick oven on the hill. It was an experiment built by a community group, several years ago. She once cooked a damper inside it, Ethel tells him, a flash one too with pumpkin seeds and parmesan cheese. On top of the oven the group built an eagle, each wing folding into seating for at least three people.

Ethel sits in one wing, Red Feathers the other. The mud brick is sheltered by a tin roof, which shields them from the streetlight.

'She's so sad, that one.'

Red Feathers shakes his head. Ethel knows Miranda's self-destruction has pained him too.

'Too much sorry business in this place.'

Smells of the community garden waft up the hill. Ethel breathes in thyme and basil.

'Hard to believe we been fighting the whole time you've

been gone.' She laughs in frustration. 'And it's the same bloody fight.'

Ethel knows the fight better than any of the living. Red Feathers had found her an empty vessel, but over time he had filled her with their stories.

It began in the palms of Biamee, he told her. It was Biamee's fingers that carved the people, his genius the source of the millions of beings who swam, flew and scurried across landscapes every colour of the sunsets he painted. Biamee loved them so dearly that he created the clever men. The clever men had promised to protect them from the newcomers. An impossible pledge.

At first relations between the two were civil. The Corrowa tried to impress upon the townspeople that some places were dangerous and best avoided, especially the ring. But the newcomers cared little for protocol. They extracted labour from the black men and women for which they paid them opium and alcohol. Gradually, the clever men left, in disgust. Only Red Feathers had stayed.

During the day, blacks could enter the town; indeed, they were expected to. Most white families employed black domestics, gardeners, cooks. But as night descended, West End's streets emptied of the Corrowa. Only the domestics stayed, quietly eating their dinner by the woodpile. The townspeople looked to the Corrowa's 'protector', Horace Downer, to strictly enforce the curfew.

Some were taken to faraway missions after the 'protection' Act passed in 1897. Those who remained held onto the old world. But the townspeople resented their presence. In time, contempt mutated into hysteria.

The Blacks are cunning. Like dingoes. You can see it in their eyes.
Don't trust the domestic with food. She'll lace it with arsenic.
Just as you poisoned her family?
Don't allow the boy near white women. He'll do to them . . .
What you did to his wife, his sister?
Remove the vermin.

Red Feathers was the first to fall.

After, from his dark prism, he watched the death marches. Survivors were cast around the State, like seeds in the wind. Red Feathers' family was spirited away to Yarrabah, but his wife never walked its pristine beach. She died during the journey and was laid to rest in an unmarked grave, far removed from Corrowa land. Their daughter would grow up in a dormitory, knowing nothing of her parents. Ethel's mother.

Red Feathers lived with the guilt for over a century. But he remained trapped in his prison of night. It was the force of Ethel's pain that brought him back, he told her, when the white man's law had denied her identity. Just as her grief over her dead son had brought him to her, all those years ago.

But time is of the essence.

Before, Red Feathers had been with her for only a month when his body began to disappear. At first, his left arm faded from her sight. Then his feet, followed by his legs, until finally even his head disappeared.

Tonight, Ethel can still see all of her grandfather. But she knows it's only a matter of time before his journey back to the darkness will begin.

She looks at him and frowns.

'Don't be wild with me.'

She shakes her head in frustration.

'Don't you see? I had to tell the young fella your name. Come on now, he's your mob.'

She waits for Red Feathers to reassure her, but he says nothing.

'You know I wouldn't have said anything otherwise.'

Ethel suppresses a sob. She gets so upset when she thinks she's disappointed him.

'I can so keep a secret.'

Ethel's voice has turned soft, childlike.

'Okay, okay, there was that one time. But Lesley and me, we were just kids.'

She wipes a tear from her cheek.

'We didn't have no one lookin' after us.'

They sit silently for a moment, welcoming the cool night air on their skin.

'You must have felt good today, seeing our mob at the march? You know, they're determined to stay at Meston Park in that tent embassy.'

Ethel rubs her forehead to relieve the pain. Soon the headaches will go, together with Red Feathers.

'What, you're not talking to me now?'

Red Feathers scratches his beard, the way he does whenever he's deep in thought.

'I know you don't want to. But you gotta do it.'

He frowns at Ethel.

'No one's gonna take any notice of us until you take him. Come on now. We talked about this.'

In the moonlight he can just make out the contours of her face. It's a solemn face that reminds him of his solemn duty.

'The Premier,' she murmurs softly.

Red Feathers nods reluctantly.

'He's next.'

PART THREE

SEVENTEEN

Mrs Stanley has been without Mr Stanley for some time, years perhaps, but she still nurses the pain. Jason doesn't have to ask her. He just knows. From the cream shirt that's too big, flowing black slacks that cover her bell shape. Every single grey hair has been swept from a face empty of make-up. Her peripheral vision sees only life's hard edges, too weary to capture lightness.

The house is neatly kept. No dirty dishes in the sink or yellowed newspapers lying about. But it's showing signs of disrepair. Walls carry the footprints of water damage and the screen door in the dining room is broken. Behind her steely façade, Mrs Stanley is falling off her hinges too. Throwing out her words at Higgins, like they're highly flammable. But Jason knows that if Higgins has to light a match, he will.

'How long had you worked for Mr McPherson?' Higgins says.

'Twelve years.'

'What kind of a boss was he?'

'Good.'

'Ever have any arguments?'

'Never.'

Higgins taps his fingers on the table. It's the only noise in this room. 'What was your routine?'

'I went to his house one morning a week. The days varied, according to Mr McPherson's instructions. I dusted, mopped the floors, vacuumed the carpets. That kind of thing.'

'How long would it usually take?'

She shrugs. 'It's a large house, so a few hours. Sometimes less.'

'Did you perform any other services for Mr McPherson?'

'I cleaned his chambers every Saturday.'

'Do you work for anyone else?'

'I do ad hoc jobs during the week.'

'So Mr McPherson was your only long-term client?'

'Yes.'

She hands Higgins a tray of biscuits. The rich base is filled with raspberry jam. Higgins declines. Jason assumes that he's too hung-over, too sick, to eat anything sugary. Jason doesn't care for sweets, but he accepts nonetheless. He notices her fingernails – chewed down to the pink.

'What will you do now?'

She pulls a face that's mostly confident. But anxiety lurks, like eels camouflaged by pond slime.

'What do you mean?'

Higgins offers a cynical grin.

'I've got savings.'

Higgins looks at the broken door and laughs. 'Really?'

She grimaces as though Higgins just crossed the invisible boundaries of decorum. 'Mr McPherson made it clear on a number of occasions that if anything happened to him, I would be looked after.'

'He was a very generous employer.'

'You could say that.'

Her voice has become stern, perhaps threatening. But Jason knows that it's wasted on Higgins, his hide is impervious.

'These days very few employers offer to look after an employee for life.'

'Mr McPherson was old school. Like me.'

Higgins waits. Jason's seen it before; he's giving her time to stew.

'Twelve years is a long time to work for the one person. The two of you must have become close.'

'Not really. Mr McPherson was seldom there.'

'Surely you must have spoken with him from time to time.'

'Mr McPherson usually wrote his instructions down on a note and left it on the kitchen table.'

'What kind of instructions?'

'Well, he'd specify what day he wanted me to come the following week. And if Mr McPherson didn't want me to go inside a room, he'd say so in a note.'

'Why would he do that?'

'Mr McPherson didn't pay me to ask questions.'

'I'm beginning to think he paid you precisely because you didn't ask questions.'

She purses her lips and her small eyes tell Jason they'll get nothing.

'Was there a particular room that concerned him?'

'A few times he told me not to go into his bedroom.' She pauses, appearing to mull over her thoughts. 'And he had specific instructions about the living room on the ground floor. I had to stay away from there.'

'Did you?'

'Of course.'

'Mrs Stanley, do you expect me to believe that in twelve years you never once allowed your curiosity to get the better of you?'

She looks sheepishly into her coffee. 'Once.'

'Once what?'

'I had a look beneath the curtain. I thought it odd to hang a curtain over a wall that didn't have a window.'

'What did you see?'

'A door. It was locked.'

Jason can feel it, the sixth sense that comes with the job. Broken bodies, remorseless killers and the sheer unfairness of life have all left a carbon print on his psyche that responds to lies like antennae to sound waves. He knows that Higgins has felt it too.

'I think you know more than you're telling me.'

She says nothing.

'Mrs Stanley, three men have been killed. Two of them had families.'

Her silence is a pencil, drawing disgust on their faces, in Higgins' voice.

'If I find out you covered for that paedophile, I'll do everything within my power to go after you!'

Higgins slams his hand so hard the glass tabletop almost shatters. It has the desired effect – her smugness is melting.

'There was one time, six months ago. I noticed the key had been left in the door.'

'And?'

'I needed that job. My husband took all of our money when he left. I would have lost this house.'

'Mrs Stanley, what did you see?'

'A video camera.'

'What else?'

Higgins is yelling now. He and Jason are exhausted. Neither can remember the last time that he had a decent night's sleep.

'Children's clothes.'

Her confidence has dissipated. Now she's afraid of eye contact.

'Did you speak to Mr McPherson about it?'

'No, of course not.'

'Did you ever see any children in the house?'

'No, no, I would have said something then. I swear.'

'You're not being frank with me, Mrs Stanley. You knew bad things were going on in that house!'

Mrs Stanley is cowering in her chair, like a newborn who's heard thunder for the first time. But she's on the hook now. Jason knows there is no way in hell Higgins will stop reeling her in.

'What of his associates?'

'You mean friends?'

'Yes! I mean friends!'

'I don't know anything. Please, I can't take this anymore.'

Higgins glowers into fresh tears. Lowers his voice to a whisper. 'Fuck with us and you won't see a cent from McPherson's estate.'

'You're lying.'

'Do you really want to take that chance?'

'Prick!'

Higgins rises from his chair. Jason watches with cool detachment as he kicks the screen door off its final hinge.

'How dare you!'

Higgins' smile is an icicle. 'If I were you I'd get that door fixed. In a few hours you're going to have news crews all over you. Every man and his dog will want to interview the woman who colluded with a paedophile.'

'Please, I beg you! Stop this.'

She looks at Jason, silently pleading with him to intervene. But Jason has no sympathy for a woman who turned a blind eye to horrific crimes against young boys. He walks outside and tramples on the screen door. Higgins laughs cruelly and stands over the sobbing woman.

'Tell me about his associates,' Higgins says.

'Dick Payne. I recognised him from TV,' she whimpers.

Two depressions scream from the centre of her forehead. Grey slithers in her eyebrows like old slugs. Miranda had been beautiful years ago. Men actually walked up to her in the street, to tell her so. Stale memories.

When the zipper fully reveals its teeth, Miranda is relieved that it's left her room to breathe. But when she looks back at the mirror, all she sees is an obese woman spilling out of a beautiful dress. The label read size eight. So why does she look so fat? At least the high heels make her feel a little better. Her squat legs always seem longer in these shoes.

Why has she always been so desperate to marry? The answer makes her cringe. Marriage meant she'd become 'somebody'.

In her mind, a wedding ring would have signified the point when she began to really live. Love would erase the need to drink, see her move into a home that felt like one. But sobriety, even punctured by the odd drunken slip, has become a microscope to Miranda's dark globe. It brings her confused axis into stark relief.

She always gets caught up in the giddiness of romance. But who are these men? It's only just beginning to dawn on Miranda that she never really knew any of her former partners. Never will. After that final call, each man had disappeared into the ether. The friendship that had supposedly underpinned the relationship disintegrated like burning paper.

For so many years, she has been building houses without ever bothering to lay a foundation. Whenever a house collapses into rocky terrain, Miranda just moves on to the next frame without concrete.

Why does she always travel the same route to the same toxic spill?

I'm already somebody.

I don't need to do this to myself.

Boundary Street bustles. On the footpath, an artist devours his canvas. He's a rare and endangered species in this harsh, new world. Beautiful people with beautiful wallets have immersed themselves in the atmosphere. They want to be a part of it so badly. You can see it in the animated hand gestures, the vowels that roll off their tongues.

When she was a child, West End had been a catchment area for those who were not welcome in Brisbane's middle-class suburbs: immigrants, artists, Murris. From the shared experience of exile a vibrant community had been born. But those days are passing, suffocating under a gold blanket.

His thick brown curls have been slicked back, and the white shirt highlights the contours of an athletic chest. He catches sight of her, smiles. She's surprised by how excited it makes her feel.

'Miranda, thanks for coming. I wasn't sure you'd make it.'

'Detective Matthews, you've made a great choice.'

'Please, call me Jason. I did a search on the internet and checked out a few menus. I liked this one the most.'

She smiles shyly, trying to hide how touched she is by his efforts. A bottle of sauvignon blanc sits in its cooler like a baby in a cot. Miranda declines. Jason pours himself a glass.

'Are you seriously telling me you don't drink? You must be the first lawyer I've ever seen refuse a glass of wine.'

'Actually, I'm on a health kick at the moment.'

I am capable of having dinner with a man without getting drunk. I can do this.

She looks around. 'I came here for dinner about two years ago. I've been meaning to come back. Guess I've been too busy.'

Is he nervous too?

'So, was the rally your first?'

'Was it that obvious?'

'No, of course not.'

I am so bad at small talk. Why am I only noticing this now?

'I can imagine it must get pretty tough in a community practice.'

'Sometimes, but surely no more stressful than Homicide.'

'I love my job. Can't imagine doing anything else. I've seen some horrific things. But I've also helped to give closure to grieving families.'

She breathes in his aftershave. Musk. Athletic.

'How about you? Did you always want to be a lawyer?'

'Sure. I grew up in the seventies, when the Aboriginal legal services were being set up. That really inspired me.'

'Could you imagine doing anything else?'

She shrugs. 'If I could have my life over again, I'd probably do something different. Health, maybe, or education.'

'Really?'

'The longer I stay in the law, the less I care for its blunt instruments.'

'Are you concerned about the law's instruments or the individuals who operate them?'

She realises why he's really here. Taskforce Themis. She looks down at her menu, conceals her disappointment.

A handsome man like Jason would never invite me to dinner, unless he had an ulterior purpose.

The waiter is not a day over twenty. Hair wears a net. Crooked smile wears attitude.

'Are you ready to order your mains?'

Their faces suddenly become question marks.

'I recommend the banquet,' he says, wryly.

'Okay.'

The waiter nods indifferently to the echo.

Silence wraps itself around their throats like invisible boas. Miranda eyes other tables, desserts encased in glass, even the till.

Anything but him.

'Your Auntie Ethel is a very special person.'

'She is indeed.'

Miranda stares longingly into her empty wine glass.

Snap out of it.

'Ethel moved into our house when I was eight, after my mother passed away. She practically raised me. Dad was pretty active in different community organisations back then. He didn't really have time to be a single father.'

'So she's been a big influence on you?'

'Of course.'

'From what I've seen, she's a very important person to your entire community.'

'Hmm, I think Auntie Ethel's got a soft spot for you. Usually she never speaks to police.'

'We don't always do the wrong thing, you know.'

His defensiveness is static electricity moving through her, exciting her. 'I agree that not all police should be painted with the same brush, but most have a bad habit of exercising their discretion to our disadvantage.'

'Some of us believe you can only change the system by working inside it.' He's surprised that he's swallowing her bait so easily. He's too shrewd for this.

'Some of us believe that the criminal justice system is inherently racist.'

'How can you practise law if you don't have faith?'

The arrival of a platter of dips and flat bread defuses the moment. Miranda is trying so hard to look poised but fails miserably when a large blob of eggplant falls on her chin. She's about to cry when he laughs. It's a warm laugh that puts her at ease.

'Sorry. I skipped lunch today. I'm starving.' She knows her face is undeniably the colour of embarrassment.

'Miranda, I know you do incredible work for your community. I want to help you. That's why I thought we should talk here, rather than at Headquarters.'

'Thanks. Greek cuisine is much nicer than those sterile interview rooms.'

'Yeah, we need to do something about that. Do you think more people would confess if we painted the walls lilac?'

'You don't strike me as someone who takes an interest in decor.'

'There's a lot about me you don't know. Just as I'm sure that there's a lot more to Miranda Eversely behind the lawyer's mask.'

'I guess you'll just have to find that out for yourself.'

'I intend to.'

He's intrigued by a neck that's long and graceful. Her honey skin is beautiful in that green dress that fits like a glove. But he's troubled by what's lurking below still waters. Jason has battled self-loathing for longer than he can remember. It's the enemy that never sleeps, never depletes its ammunition and never tries to broker peace. Now he's watching the war within Miranda. The sadness behind her eyes, the trepidation in her fingertips.

It surprises Jason, his concern. And for the first time in the job, he has no idea what his next move will be.

The banquet is sumptuous. He gorges himself with souvlaki and meatballs. It's such a change from his usual bland fuel for the gym. Miranda seems to examine every portion before placing it on her fork. After the final course, Jason looks at his watch. Cringes.

'What time is it?'

'Eleven. I'm usually in bed by now.'

'Me too.'

'Old age really does suck.'

She smiles, lowers her head.

'I guess we should get down to business.' She looks up but he can't read her expression. 'Miranda, this is going to be a private conversation between us. But we may need to do a formal interview in the fullness of time.'

She stares at him. For a moment her eyes seem empty behind the blue.

'Miranda, we need to talk about the real reason we're here.'

'Then we should get on with it. I have a busy day tomorrow.'

Jason feels the sting in her voice and briefly regrets his change in tack, before reminding himself that he's speaking to a person of interest.

'Okay. Dick Payne.'

'What about him?'

'You never explained why he called you that night. Several times, in fact.' Jason raises his hand, as though fanning her inevitable protest. 'I remember what you said – that the conversations were about the appeal. But I don't buy it.'

He pauses. Jason rummages over his words, grimaces as though he can't find what he's looking for.

'Were you having an affair with Dick Payne?' he says, finally.

'Are you serious?' Miranda scoffs, incredulous. 'Payne wanted to meet in his office that night. I declined. He wasn't used to people saying no to him. Hence the numerous calls.'

'Why did he want to see you?'

Miranda shrugs, looks towards the register.

'I'd prefer you told me in plain words. Body language is open to different interpretations.'

'I've already told you – our appeal.'

Jason offers a cynical frown.

'Look, I have no idea.'

'You should try harder.'

'I really don't know. Maybe he wanted to humiliate me.'

'Why would he want to do that?'

She raises her eyebrows. Is she mocking him?

'People in our community despised him, and for good reason. Dick's so-called reforms were all about blaming the victims of poverty, rather than building something positive. We've had that before, during the protection era, when this street was a boundary our mob couldn't cross at night.'

Jason knows he's losing the lead, lets her take it.

'I take it you hadn't heard of the boundary. My point is that Dick was all about treating our people like they're a problem to be controlled. And then, there was his lack of remorse over defeating native title claims. It's because of lawyers like him that the goalposts have been shifted beyond our reach.'

'Coffee?'

The waiter greets Jason's frown with a sarcastic grin.

'None for me. Miranda?'

'No. Thank you.'

Jason looks around. The other tables are being stripped of dirty dishes, and he's been watching the other patrons leave for hours. He knows he's lost her interest in Dick Payne.

But he's just getting started.

'I would have thought that someone who'd achieved as much as Payne did would be seen as a role model.'

'A role model for whom?'

'Kids, adults, everyone. After all, he succeeded in the corporate world and I imagine he could have spent his life making money on the backs of wealthy clients. Instead, he put his mind to solving problems in Aboriginal communities.'

She rubs her eyes, and he knows it's genuine fatigue.

'Regardless of what Dick set out to do, by the end he was the poster boy for the new assimilation agenda.'

'That still doesn't explain why Dick wanted you to meet with him in his office.'

She sighs deeply. 'Payne took differences of opinion personally.'

'I still don't understand why he would want to humiliate you. He'd just won the Corrowa case and the government was backing his reforms. What else did he have to prove?'

Her laughter ripples with bitterness. 'You didn't know Dick.'

'And you did?'

'I'd heard the stories. Dick expected people to worship him and when they refused, he held a grudge. His grudges were the stuff of legend.'

'Obviously, you didn't worship him.'

'No, I did not.'

'What about Ethel?'

She wears the expression of someone who's just swallowed a lemon whole.

'Auntie Ethel hated the guy! But she was never rude to him. At the beginning, he tried to persuade all of us to withdraw the native title claim in exchange for a pathetic compensation package. Apparently, our young people would get token jobs, building a shopping centre on their own land. Ethel told him very politely that we would stand our ground.'

Jason draws his chin into his palm, processing every word, every gesture. He knows she's not being straight with him.

He breathes in deeply. 'Where were you on the night that Dick was killed?'

'I was at home.'

'Was anyone else with you?'

She shakes her head.

'Where were you last Wednesday night?'

'I was at an exhibition.'

'What time did you leave?'

'I don't know. Nine o'clock, I guess.'

Miranda unhooks her handbag from the back of the chair.

'What did you do after that?'

She unzips her purse, throws a fifty on the table and looks at Jason squarely.

'I went home.'

As Miranda welcomes the cool night air on busy Boundary Street, she feels a sudden tightness around her wrist and looks up.

'Miranda.'

'What are you doing here, Dad?'

'I saw you come out of . . . What's wrong?'

'Ah nothing, I . . .'

'Miranda, why are you lying to me? Tell me what's wrong.'

Her anger at her father has always been suppressed. But now it's coalescing with fear that's given it legs.

'Why would I talk to you about anything? You've always been there for everyone else, but never me!'

'Miranda, that's a horrible thing to say.'

'No, Dad. The horrible thing is that you wished it was me who died, instead of Mum.'

As he watches her disappear into the night, Charlie allows the tears to flow. A group of Murris are nearby. Ordinarily, they would stop and say hello. But tonight they know better. The brother is in a world of pain.

Miranda stares at the bottle in her hands, as though she's waiting to hear its voice.

Her mind is a cacophony of imagery: schoolmates huddled in front of a bonfire, excitedly watching airborne corks. University parties where cocktails were served from plastic bins. A decade ago, her old drinking buddies changed, their lives bore fruit. Their careers brought wealth. Partners gave them children who filled their homes with laughter. But Miranda remains locked in her grim inertia. No longer cute in her drunkenness, she drinks alone.

She hears a knock on the door and wonders who the hell it could be. She quickly places the bottle in the cabinet beneath the kitchen sink. She knows it's ridiculous to still be hiding alcohol at her age, in her own home. A home she shares with no one.

She opens her apartment door and steps back.

'What do you want, detective?'

Jason's tongue is gentle, lightly caresses. It happens so quickly that later she marvels at how easily he removed her dress. Knows she'll never remember how they made it to her bed. Will always remember how good it felt to be desired.

How good it felt to be reminded that things could still happen for her.

EIGHTEEN

The light fittings are ice cubes at the bottom of a glass, melting from the bonfire. They're dressed in suits, but it's pomp in a puppy pen. Hansard records more clichés than a trashy romance novel. Absorbs more punches than a world title fight. It's like a schoolyard brawl; everyone wants to breathe the excitement, but no one wants to bleed.

Elegant façades are everywhere around Parliament. Desks carved from precious wood. Gold jugs that quench hateful tongues. Blue and green carpets are like leaves on a forest floor, but without their cleansing scent. This place smells of pluck served cold. And road kill. Their words are claws, tearing away at each other's humanity.

The Speaker sits below the coat of arms, resting his chin in his hand. Every few minutes, he implores them to come to order. In a monotone voice, he orders them to refrain from using 'unparliamentary' language.

Iron lattice houses the public gallery. Journalists fold their arms and occasionally chuckle. Schoolchildren watch with interest; their presence does nothing to douse the flames below. Public servants drift in and out. Among them is Lesley Tagem. She's alternately muttering and glancing behind her, as though expecting someone or something to crash through the heavy blinds.

The monitor on the wall informs the Premier that he has two minutes left on his feet. His face is a beetroot simmering in its own juices. Beads of sweat sit at the roots of his hair. They stare in amusement, willing steam from his ears.

'As I stated at my press conference, I am committed to ensuring that the Dick Payne Memorial Program will be a success. In fact, immediately after my press conference I made arrangements for my Senior Indigenous Adviser, Lesley Tagem, to work directly with staff in the office of the Minister for Indigenous Affairs. They've formed a working group. Coconut Holdings is on standby. They want to employ sixty Indigenous people to work on the Meston Park site, by the end of the month. I am determined that will happen.'

Lesley watches the tirade, like a punter at the races. She's invested so much in this horse.

What else will I lose before this race is over?

The Premier retires to his seat. Ignores the smiles of his sycophants that have become as familiar as the gold trim on the walls.

'Premier, that sounds very impressive. But how can Coconut Holdings possibly commence construction when their property rights are not being respected?'

The Leader of the Opposition is a mere apprentice of thirty-two years. Tall and scrawny. His short black hair holds a cup of gel like a baby seal who's just been rescued from an oil slick. Minute pieces of tissue are constellations illuminating the shaving cuts on his face.

'For the past week, members of the Corrowa tribe have been living in tents in Meston Park. Their leader, the notorious radical Charlie Eversely, insists that Meston Park belongs to them. Surely, we cannot allow this anarchy to continue. The Federal Court determined that the Corrowa People's native title was extinguished. I ask the Premier, when will the Corrowa People be forced to respect the umpire's decision?'

His confidence is flying and he wears the grin of the victim of schoolyard bullies who has finally turned the tables.

The Premier grimaces at the young fool. 'Like all other reasonable Queenslanders, I have been surprised and saddened by the refusal of this particular group to accept the Federal Court's decision. My department is currently in negotiations with

Coconut Holdings and representatives of the protesters, with a view to resolving this situation amicably. I have been informed that the negotiations are progressing satisfactorily. Indeed, I am confident that the dispute will be resolved by the end of the week.'

Lesley suppresses the urge to laugh. She's the one whom the Premier has entrusted to 'negotiate'. But that mob in Meston Park won't listen. Not to her. Not to anybody. Except that fuckin' old coot.

Ethel's swinging her finger to and fro, like the chimes in a grand-father clock.

Used to do that when we were girls.

Bossing everyone around, even then.

'Lesley, you can't mess with the business.'

Lesley loosens the knot under her chin that's holding the shawl over her head. She's been losing clumps of hair for the past two days. Her doctor offered no solutions, only a referral to a specialist. Who can't see her for two months!

The Premier's opponent clears his throat and resumes his attack. 'Mr Speaker, I understand the police have been called to that camp several times in the past week. They've had to remove drunks and drug addicts in the interests of public safety. This has been to the dismay of many in the Queensland Police Service, which is already suffering from being short-changed by this government. Mr Speaker, sources within the Queensland Police Service claim that Taskforce Themis is being compromised by inadequate resources. Can the Premier please explain why his government has seen fit not to value their work?'

The young man's meteoric rise through the ranks of the Opposition owed more to a lack of talented competition than political acumen, but during rare moments of clarity, he can fight. All morning, he's been like a Jack Russell with an invisible death grip on the Premier's ankles. The Premier scoffs.

'My government is the only one in living memory to pro-vide the Queensland Police Service with sufficient resources to fulfil its responsibilities to the people of Queensland. Furthermore, such criticism from the Leader of the Opposition is a bit rich, given the legacies of former Coalition Governments. I should not have to spell out those legacies to the Leader of the Opposition. After all, the Fitzgerald Report is still publicly available. I can ask my secretary to download it from the internet for him, as I assume he didn't have enough pocket money to purchase a copy from the first print run.'

The chamber is awash with laughter. But the Jack Russell won't be deterred. He'll just pursue a different target, one that's smaller and dim-witted.

'Mr Speaker, murder is no laughing matter and neither is the granting of privileges to spoilt minorities. I ask the Minister for Indigenous Affairs, what is the Indigenous community doing to assist Taskforce Themis?'

The Minister for Indigenous Affairs, Belinda Field, is a rabbit staring down the barrel of a gun. In spite of spending thousands on botox, her forehead is creased in fear. She's sitting in a deflating lifeboat, which is being circled by great white sharks, in the face of an imminent tsunami. This is the first time Field has been asked a question in Parliament.

At least the woman's dressed for the occasion. In fact, she's the only politician who can wear Prada. Some of the older women try, but the Prada just ends up wearing them. Belinda knows how to work it. Her long legs scream out from beneath her tight black dress. And those Jimmy Choo shoes just set the whole outfit off.

How the press love her. Of course, she's invested hundreds of hours into developing the right poses. Her favourite involves cupping her chin in her right hand and, through elegant Armani frames, locking her eyes in steely determination. But answering questions in Parliament? Well, that just isn't her thing.

Looking great is a different story. Why, that's kept her well fed for most of her adult life. Not that she ever eats more than a few morsels. Starvation is just part and parcel of being a model.

And it was modelling that brought Field here. That heavenly body gave her a public profile. Using it in a devilish way got her married to the horniest millionaire in Brisbane. It also brought her to the exotic world of Indigenous affairs.

In her first press conference following the announcement of her bid for pre-selection, Belinda was asked why she chose politics after retiring from the catwalk. She said she'd had a spiritual awakening while filming a commercial at Uluru. She'd engaged in telepathic communication with members of the Mutitjulu community, apparently, and was convinced she'd found her calling. Some dowdy journalist spread a rumour that the epiphany was actually the result of the empty wine bottles her former assistant had seen in her hotel room. But Field didn't allow such pettiness to get her down. After all, she was on a mission.

The Labor Party hadn't needed much seducing. Field was already a minor celebrity and Labor was in short supply of glamour. But the movers and shakers weren't prepared to make a huge investment in Field. After all, she wasn't terribly bright. So they gave her a seat in the heart of conservative territory. But what Field lacked in intelligence, she made up for with enthusiasm. She knocked on doors until her knuckles were raw. She batted her eyelashes at every male in her path, kissed babies who smelt of diarrhoea.

Her opponent, on the other hand, had held his seat for so long that he took his electorate for granted. He didn't knock on a single door, being content to leave that business to the volunteers from the Young Liberals. How he spent his time outside Parliament, no one knew. His wife often made cynical comments as he walked out the door each morning.

'Going to work on another crossword love? Enjoy your nap in the office, Mike.'

They both knew that she was more resentful over his lacklustre career than he was.

'Mike is such a disappointment, he could have been Premier

you know', she'd confide to her colleagues on a Friday afternoon, over a gin and tonic.

When the Premier rang to offer his congratulations for seizing victory in enemy heartlands, Field gushed about her spiritual awakening in the desert. So the die was cast. She was the only politician in Labor history who had requested the portfolio of Indigenous Affairs, a job the Feds had once likened to being a toilet cleaner on the *Titanic*. She was so thrilled by her appointment that she visited the Premier, to thank him personally.

Since becoming a minister, Belinda has endured a few tumbles. Like when she asked an old pensioner at Manoah whether she preferred Prada or Chanel. It was meant to be a joke, but unfortunately some bitchy journalist overheard their conversation. The Premier dragged her over the coals for the gaffe. Now, he's giving her the look he gives when she moans too loudly during their lovemaking. It only lasts for a few seconds, before he turns to his opponent.

'How low is the Leader of the Opposition prepared to sink? I cannot believe he's attempting to use Taskforce Themis for his own selfish purposes. As if that wasn't bad enough, he's stereotyping all Indigenous Queenslanders.'

The Premier waves his finger in the air. 'Dick Payne would have been disgusted.'

The Opposition is a school of greedy toadfish. Mesmerised by the sight of fresh meat. The Leader of the Opposition snarls. 'Why is the Premier answering a question that was directed to the Minister for Indigenous Affairs?'

Suddenly Field stands, her whole body shaking.

'Oh my God, she's having a fit.' Whispers echo through the chamber.

'What should we do?'

'Call an ambulance.'

The puppies cease trading blows, all paws to the ground, to see the minister's crumpled body, her svelte legs crossed demurely.

★ ★ ★

The Premier closes his eyes as his body sinks into the car's plush leather. Savours the carbonated water gliding on his tongue. His head is pounding. His throat has been dry all week, his voice hoarse. It happens whenever Parliament sits. When he gets home, Madeline will attempt to nag him into seeing their family doctor, but to no avail.

He chuckles as he reflects on Belinda's performance. That woman will do anything for him – even fake a seizure. Christ, it was effective. Tomorrow, the state's taxpayers will wake to photographs of paramedics fussing over Belinda. The press will forget all about the fiscal dilemmas of the police force, at least, for now.

The Premier is on the nose with the electorate. Labor is as welcome in Queensland as a plague-carrying rat in a restaurant. People are ready to embrace change for the sheer sake of it. Only one thing stands between him and defeat – fear that the Opposition will turn out to be as incompetent as it looks.

Fear is the Premier's signature dish. Over coming months, he will bombard the electorate with a snowstorm of accusation and innuendo. Unable to see the road ahead, they will have little choice but to spend the bitter winter of the election in limbo, waiting for him to rescue them.

He knows his cronies think he's an enigma: a chameleon that seamlessly alternates between statesman and assassin. To his enemies, the Premier is out of control. Destroying careers, belittling journalists, feeding his advisers a diet of arrogance and sleep deprivation.

The Premier believes he's the same man he was before. But the demands of the job have required him to shed unnecessary skin. The Premier still has the same moral compass from his heyday of student politics, but its face has faded, so that it's no longer legible. Morality is now an apparition whose presence is felt, but whose hands can never touch him. Over the years, he's watched colleagues breathe in the air of ground zero, until it gradually enfeebles them. Bodies become heavy and slow, eyes lose lustre, speech a shell without its soul of conviction. But not him. The

Premier never makes the mistake of peering into the aftermath of one of his explosions.

But the punishing hours are finally exacting their payment. He feels like he's navigating a hulk through a cyclone. His patience is just as haggard as the torn sails and his body weak from constantly bailing water. At Madeline's urging he will make an effort to take an interest in the children's milestones over dinner. Kylie recently triumphed in her school debating championships. Darren, on the other hand, was caught smoking pot in the bathroom, again.

'Thank crikey this week's over, eh?'

Even though he studied with the finest minds at Oxford, the Premier is careful to avoid any hint of intellectual prowess. Tall poppy syndrome can be fatal.

The driver does not respond, preferring to raise the volume of the radio. The reggae music is like a mating call to the jackhammer in the Premier's head.

'Change stations. I want to listen to Alexander Johns on Green and Gold FM.'

The driver tilts his head, he's speaking, but not to the Premier. His voice occasionally breaks into laughter, but it's otherwise inaudible.

'I said, change stations.'

His demand is met once again with cool indifference.

Who the fuck does he think he is? I'm the Premier! This guy can't take a piss without asking me first! Harry knows that.

Ordinarily, Harry drives him everywhere. Old gold, reliable Harry, who barely murmurs a word, other than to remind the Premier that his dear old mum was a Labor voter. But Harry rang in sick this morning.

The driver's neck is thick and long. The Premier imagines the rest of him must be enormous. Woolly brown curls have been cut to the edges of his scalp. He's never had a black driver before. The latest stunt at employing Aborigines in the public service? Isn't the Dick Payne Memorial Program enough for those people?

An old woman breaks into a run. She makes it to the safety of the traffic island, but she's clearly in pain, rubbing her back with one hand, making a fist with the other.

'My God, man! You could have killed her!'

The Premier expects a profuse apology, at the very least an explanation. But he's ignored. Again.

'Are you deaf? I said you could have killed that woman. You listen to me, boy. From now on you will do exactly as I say!'

The driver sways his head to the rhythms of Bob Marley. His movement is weightless. He's oblivious to the Premier's anger, or more likely, contemptuous.

'That's it! I've had enough. Pull over *now*! If you don't stop this vehicle, I will personally see to it that you never work in this state again!'

The Premier feels for the mobile phone in the pocket of his suit coat, but finds nothing. He rifles through his briefcase as the car increases its speed and he hurtles back into the seat. His heart sinks as they pass his street.

'You fucking coon! Stop this car!'

The car finally slows at some traffic lights. Adrenalin rushes, the Premier inhales deeply.

This is his chance.

His head spins when he discovers that both doors are jammed tight. The Premier bangs on the window like a dog that's been caged in a pet shop for too long. Only a young boy notices him. The child's mother is preoccupied, blustering into a mobile phone. That's when the Premier sees a million stars.

NINETEEN

Adelaide Street yawns. The city's manic pace grinds everything to exhaustion. Council buses are old draught horses. Voices deep as they haul their restless cargo. Lesley cringes into the empty plate. There are only crumbs left of her fifteen-dollar 'breakfast' – one stingy piece of sourdough with avocado and feta. Four little mushrooms on the side. Four! And they serve rocket with every bloody thing these days. The café is called 'Insect'. Lesley figures she'll be a stick insect if she continues to eat here.

Concrete floors speak understated wealth. They mutter and groan whenever cutlery drops, chair legs shift. Bulbs encased in gigantic black eggcups hang parallel to rows of smaller lights that remind her of a film studio. It's casual dining that only the rich can afford. And Lesley. She's down to her final ten dollars. Payday isn't until tomorrow afternoon. But she'll have a big win on the pokies tonight. Can feel it in her bones.

She thinks back to her conversation with Parkes yesterday and cringes at the little twerp.

'Lesley, the boss thinks you should take some time off. It looks bad for you to be here, when your people need to go through, what is it?' Parkes tilted his chin, rubbing his whiskers in concentration. 'That's right, sorry business.'

He wore the grin of the child prodigy who'd just bamboozled the maths teacher.

'But isn't the working group meeting next week?' she said. 'I should be at that meeting. After all, the CEO of Coconut Holdings knows me. We're mates.'

'Lesley, you should know better than to argue with the boss.'

Now, Lesley looks around. Suits always appear busy, their conversations permanently important. And they have an alphabet of gadgets, from geospatial technology to heartrate monitors. They shoot the occasional glance at the old black woman sitting on the barstool. With her tiny frame, Lesley knows they think she looks like an infant in a high chair.

She brings the blackfellas to the table and then the men take over. No one ever gives her credit. Not even Harrison McPherson gave her credit when they won. He wanted to disown her that day in his office. Would've kicked her out, had she not seen it.

Death bird's feather in his mouth.

A man with a crown of silver sparks makes his way towards the exit, pauses at Lesley's table. 'Hello, my name is Roger Corbett.'

She cautiously shakes his hand. 'Hello, Roger.'

'I just wanted to say that I'm very sorry for your loss. Dick Payne was one of the most articulate men I have ever heard. Your entire community must be grieving. He was such an amazing advocate for your people.' His handsome face turns crimson. 'I'm sorry. I promised myself I wouldn't rant, but, evidently, I have. I just wanted to say what a wonderful leader he was. This country will be poorer for his absence.'

Ordinarily, Lesley would be touched. Roger seems like a good man, she thinks. But today her arteries are circulating dread instead of blood. She's so damned tired. Last night she only slept in short bursts. 'Thanks, luvie. That's very kind of you.'

As Lesley watches Roger disappear through the glass doors, she wonders what he, or anyone, really knew about Dick. As much as she loved him, Lesley had to admit that Dick didn't offer new ideas. He dished out saccharine that made audiences giddy.

Aboriginal people must develop a work ethic.

Governments have to turn off the tap of sit-down money.

Aboriginal parents have to learn to be responsible.

But what did any of it mean? Empty words. His public life had been carefully scripted, from the Dorothy Dixer questions on Green and Gold FM, to the clothes he wore each day. Like all good actors, Dick kept his real self hidden in a fortress. But its walls were cracking. She'd heard of his exploits with Harrison, how they'd drunk to oblivion, snorted coke. How Dick had slept around. If he were alive, she knew the young fella would be unrepentant. His work was all about resurrecting pride in black communities. The problem was, the way Dick conducted his affairs left no room for pride.

It's all gone to shit. Maybe it always was. She's got no one now. Not even Alisha.

Names are cries of seagulls, heard between waves of applause. Eyes glisten beneath flashing bulbs. Must be a thousand people inside this hall. Alisha's shoulders are too tiny for the black gown, can barely see the dress that cost the earth.

'Baby, I'm so proud of you.'

Everything I've done has been for you.

Lesley feels the heat on her scalp as she steps into George Street. The blue scarf is wrapped tightly around her head. It's become land that's yielded too many crops. Barren with the exception of a few scattered thickets.

Most people on the street avoid eye contact with strangers. So Lesley is surprised by the young woman's smile. She's pretty with honey-coloured hair and knee-high boots beneath a black skirt. Not a day over twenty. The same age as Lesley, when she first arrived from Manoah. One of the many black kitchen hands in the bustling public hospital. In those days, black women were allowed to prepare the patients' food, but couldn't give birth in the same ward. She never really thought about it at the time. After all, the white people at Manoah lived in separate houses, ate in their own dining hall. The work was dreary, but the other girls made her feel welcome. And she had Ethel, but Ethel was getting all political. Lesley didn't care for politics back then. She lived for Saturday night dances. The old dilapidated hall in Turbot Street came alive that one night of the week for the sharpest black folk in Brisbane. But that too has disappeared, replaced by a car park.

Back then Lesley would never have spent fifteen dollars on one stingy piece of toast. Probably could have lived on fifteen dollars for an entire week. She barely knows this city anymore. Brisbane is following in the footsteps of its sophisticated siblings, Sydney and Melbourne, she thinks. They've got too much choice – that's their bloody problem. Coffee is a kaleidoscope: latte, flat white, cappuccino, caramel mocha, extra hot! What happened to plain old black or white?

Smiles and laughter ripple through the chic markets. But the wares inside the stalls are a foreign language that has no meaning for Lesley. Certified organic orange juice. Organic rye sourdough. Organic chocolate spelt muffins. Lesley breathes in the scent of butter melting on corn. Grimaces at the price.

It's all gone to shit since he died. But he hasn't really left her. Came again this morning.

'How are you, darl?'

The security guard is in his early sixties. Leather face offers a smile. Eyes are genuinely warm, in spite of what they must have seen.

'Oh battling on, bub. Battling on.'

The stench of disinfectant invades her nostrils as she reaches the top stair. But it quickly evaporates into the familiar excitement on her tongue. Every room, every corner is dim. Neon lights in the ceiling are snakes of orange and green. Lesley can see snakes everywhere, even in the faded blue carpet.

Naked and surrounded by red dust.

Crying and waving his hands in the air like he's trying to warn me, but I can't hear him.

There's more scrub on the perimeters.

No swings or wooden seats stuck to the ground.

The old mansions above the hill wear fresh paint.

No sports cars parked in the kerb; no cars at all in the dusty street.

Black women in white dresses are outside the wooden fences, baskets dangling on their hips.

They cower in fear when they see the men on horseback. They draw their horses to a standstill at the top of the hill.

Ethel's wearing that sour face she's had since we were girls.

'I told you, Lesley. Didn't I tell you?'

I want to tear her hair out, but they've broken into a gallop.

They're coming for us.

The bar is a wasteland. Last New Year's Eve Lesley was one of hundreds in this place, dousing failed expectations with alcohol and synthetic laughter. There were so many people on the dance floor that her arms were pinned to her sides, as she swayed to the music. But now it's just Lesley and the jaded waitress.

The waitress has the virus. Lesley can see it in the boredom that's taken hold of her face like cement. The virus doesn't just live in people. Even the plastic palm fronds in the main gaming room are being slowly deprived of oxygen.

She enters one of the catacombs for the living dead. Motorbikes are suspended from the walls, offering the ultimate freedom. Freedom they lost long ago in their glass tombs. In the mornings, this room is like a school bus that's almost come to the end of its run. There's only a few passengers remaining and each has claimed a buffer zone of several seats.

Lesley recognises the woman in the far right corner. They've never spoken, but they exchange the occasional smile. Sometimes, she comes with a friend, but most of the time she's alone. Lesley doesn't know her story, only her name. Mavis.

Mavis lives in blue jeans and a red parka that she wears irrespective of the weather outside. When Mavis is with a friend, she'll rub her hands together, and say, 'Right, let's win some money.'

Mavis' eyes are glued to the machine. Three coffee cups and a discarded bag of potato chips sit on the table beside her. Lesley figures that Mavis has been here all morning. Once, both she and Mavis stayed in this room for ten straight hours, with only toilet breaks in between.

The cowboy's face is rugged handsome, and he wears a white hat with an exaggerated brim. The Indian is mostly naked apart from his headdress and leather pants.

This is it. I can feel it in my bones.

The phone in her slacks vibrates, and she reads the caller ID. Alisha.

Oh thank God. My baby has finally called.

The twang of coins flooding the receptacle could have come from an angel, creating precious melodies with its harp. Lesley feels faint when she reads the numbers on the screen.

Two hundred thousand.

She hears sobbing and yelling and then realises it's her. Moments ago, only an earthquake would have shifted Mavis from her seat. But now, she's next to Lesley, alternately hugging her and throwing fists into the air. They're performing an impromptu dance that requires no music, no choreography. The dance of the faithful.

I'll take the money.

Make a fresh start.

Not like the last time.

She pauses for a final lingering glance of the catacomb. But this place is no longer coated in misery's dust. It's vibrant and kind. Oh so kind. Where else would an old woman down on her luck, down to her final ten dollars, make so much money?

I'm not like those other blacks.

I have a go.

I never give up.

I'm a doer.

The image is vivid; she can taste it. Sees it every morning as she walks to her bus stop. Massive two-storey house of grey and white opposite Orleigh Park. Half the top storey is on stilts. Its wall-length windows look onto the huge old grandfather trees and the river. Lesley has spent hours sitting in Orleigh Park, imagining waking in that house. How it would feel to sip her tea on the ample balcony, drinking in the sights and sounds of wealth. I've worked my entire life. Ethel and the others are clinging to broken dreams. But not me.

I always have a go.

That's why I took the money from Coconut Holdings in the first place. If you don't take advantage of an opportunity, you're a loser. They should listen to me, but they never do. No one does.

I'll show them all.

Adrenalin is soaking Lesley's body like a sponge. She expects to see sparks when she places that coin in the slot.

'Oh my God! Another fifty thousand.'

Mavis' eyes are ping pong balls. 'You've had your turn, Lesley. Let someone else try that machine.'

Lesley glares at Mavis, her voice resonates poison. 'Now, you listen to me. I've spent more time sitting right here than you've had hot dinners. I've earned this. You just fuck off!'

Mavis shrinks. Lesley doesn't even notice her leave.

'Oh my Lord! Another twenty thousand.'

'Sweet Jesus! One hundred thousand.'

The cardigan she wore here is now overflowing with coins. The knapsack that held her lunch box is full, as is the lunch box. The scarf that was hiding her balding head has also become a makeshift bag. One cup of Lesley's bra is packed with loot, the other waiting.

That house is mine. I deserve this.

The chill is eating through her. Lesley wants to empty her bra of the cold money, but there's no way she'll let go. She's determined to cling to every single dollar.

Lesley looks around and wonders why she's the only one here. Ordinarily, other punters are drawn to winners, in the hope that luck is contagious. At the very least, someone from management should have come over by now, to either congratulate or interrogate her.

She knows the laughter behind the doorway.

'Why can't you let me have this?'

Hears the spill of coins, but Lesley can't move.

So it's true.

The cold air on the Premier's skin tells him it's night-time. His teeth chatter in unison with trees that are shivering violently. He knows a storm is brewing. Noises abound but he has no idea what or who is making them. Animals. Wind.

When he opens his eyes, he knows he's far from the city. Night's fabric is lined with stars and there are no skyscrapers to dull its gemstones. He rubs his hands up and down opposite arms, knees against each other. But nothing will breathe warmth into his body. Fear lives behind the chill and it's so much worse.

It hurts to swallow, his mouth is so dry. He blinks slowly. It's like he's regaining consciousness after an operation. The anaesthetic has taken him to a protective fortress and he's still in the throes of the journey to present.

I'm going to die.

He's naked, in the foetal position. When Katie was a baby she would cry for hours, and sometimes all through the night. They took her to different experts in order to find out what was wrong with her, but no one knew.

Katie's hairdryer roars from behind the bathroom door.

Mobile phone screeches.

'Parkes, what now?'

'It's Coconut Holdings. They're losing patience with the protesters.'

'So am I. Get on to the Commissioner. Now.'

Why didn't I say goodbye before I left?

As he rolls onto his back, the Premier hears the chatter of pebbles. His body is an orchestra of pain, especially the drums in his back. But it's not as bad as the cold.

Why didn't they leave my clothes?

He knows that smell. Pungent whiff of the dam on his farm, when it hasn't rained for months. His haven. He's spent weekends fencing, travelling along its boundaries on his rider mower. Years ago, he and Madeline had a picnic beside the dam and made love on their old rug, while the children were at riding school. If he was on his land, he'd know it. He'd feel the touch of its memories. Taste its welcome.

He surveys his body. No gashes.

His head vibrates like a beehive when he stands. Shoulders are an abacus whose frame has warped. With each step another bead shrieks in pain.

What kind of drugs did they give me?

The Premier's mind is a light bulb going dead. It flickers back to what happened just before he got into the car.

Parkes' voice has become a thick growl.

'Boss, I spoke to the Commissioner. They're ready to move on those blacks.'

'Good work, Parkes. Tell the Commissioner to do whatever it takes. But he needs to keep it in mind that I've got a fucking election to worry about.'

'Don't worry, boss. They'll do it tonight. There'll be no journos lurking around.'

He hears the crunch of stones, but the Premier is no longer moving.

'Who is that?'

Nobody responds.

'I know you're there. Show yourself!'

The blow to his head is so powerful he becomes airborne. Darkness drains his mind before it has an opportunity to tally the damage.

He knows the box is wooden. He feels the splinters in his toes. Smells some kind of varnish. Then searing pain all over. There must be bull ants in here.

Jesus Christ!

Something stings at the nape of his neck. The pain is so intense he imagines the poison seeping into the bone. Darkness.

Woken by the heat on his feet. He's taken back to the

camping trips of his childhood. In spite of his mother's scolding, he loved to feel the breath of the campfire on his feet. The heat grows in intensity. Tongues of fire are shooting up from below.

If there is a God, I beg you, kill me quickly.

The inferno is suddenly gone. As though it never was.

What have they done to me? Who are they? What do they want? How much of this is real?

He's bathed in luminescent red. It coats his skin, even beneath his fingernails. Cool to touch. It's a kind of rain. It falls on his tongue – tastes of a creek bed. He could be back where this misery began. He can see the trees shaking, gemstones in the sky. But the ring is new. Its edges are like a saucer, smooth as ceramic.

She's standing with her back to him. Naked with only mud covering her.

'I'm deadly. I'm deadly. I'm deadly.'

The voice is soft, almost soothing. A voice he knows.

'Is that you?'

'I'm deadly. I'm deadly. I'm deadly.'

'Lesley, it's really you.'

TWENTY

The waiter smiles at her for just a little too long. Higgins feels slighted, but he too is a little mesmerised. Sherene's eyes are amber charms, nose delicate. She is too refined to be anywhere or with anyone common.

'Thanks for making time to see me.'

'I'm glad to help, detective.'

Then why did it take you three days to return my calls?

'How are you?'

The Sherene who found her husband's body had a face squeezed of life. Long grey and brown hair was knotted, wet. Body hidden in a tracksuit and sneakers.

'I'm alright. Thank you for asking.'

Sherene's hair is now shorter and tousled. The grey has vanished into a rich dark brown. Her clothes are elegant. White silk blouse tucked into a black skirt with knee-high boots. Perfume is smooth and sensual. Expensive.

'To be honest, I've never been busier. I've had so many invitations to become involved in different causes.'

'Oh really?'

'Yes, the Minister for Indigenous Affairs asked me to chair the working group for the implementation of Dick's program. Belinda's an old school friend.'

She pauses, expecting him to be impressed by her connection to the former model, but Higgins is nonplussed.

'Wasn't she in the paper the other day?'

'Yes, she had a health scare. But she's fine now.'

The couple at the table next to them stand to leave. Now they're alone in the courtyard.

'The Wexley Institute also invited me to join their board. Ironically, I was always resentful that Dick spent so much time doing work for them.'

Sherene doesn't wince when she mentions his name. It's as though her husband has been dead for years, faded into distant past.

'What exactly does the Wexley Institute do?'

'You haven't seen one of our columns in the *Queensland Daily*?'

'I tend to go straight to the sports section.'

Laughter reveals teeth as flawless as her pale skin.

'We pose new solutions for problems in Aboriginal communities.'

The waiter returns with their coffees, cappuccino for Higgins and a skinny latte for Sherene.

'Right, so you work with Indigenous researchers?'

'Ah, not exactly, but we do visit Indigenous communities from time to time. We're a non-profit association, so our travel budget is quite small.'

'Who exactly is the Wexley Institute?'

'Actually, it was just Dick, my father and a few others. The institute has some office space at Dick's law firm.'

'What's going to happen now?'

'The firm is still very committed. We'll just go on.'

'What's next on the cards for the institute?'

'Well, we're going to lobby the Commonwealth to make some changes to social security legislation. Under our plan, all welfare recipients will be forced to accept any job they're offered, anywhere in the country. Those who remain on welfare will be subject to government supervision.'

'What kind of supervision?'

'Their spending will be tightly controlled, for essential items only. Public housing tenants will also be subject to good behaviour covenants.'

'That sounds harsh.'

'So you're happy for people who don't even work to waste your taxes on addictions?'

He offers a grin. 'Enough of my income is spent on satisfying my own addictions.'

Her laugh is demure, sexy.

'So this was all Dick's grand plan?'

'Yes. That's right.'

'Did Dick live like a monk too?'

'I don't see how that's relevant.'

He's gazed into her face for too long: the light pink eye shadow and blush.

'It's for a photo shoot.'

Dark red lips are curved into a half-moon.

'For which magazine?'

'*Chic.*'

He's seen the magazine sitting on the coffee table at home, even flicked through one. Dense with celebrity gossip.

'They're going to publish a story on our marriage, give a reconciliation theme to it. In lieu of paying me a fee, the magazine will establish a scholarship fund. We're going to send Aboriginal children to boarding schools.'

'That sounds exciting.'

Sherene ignores his cynicism.

She must be sick of death, sick of mourning. A butterfly that refuses to look back at its cocoon.

'We're in the process of getting corporate backers. Some big names have expressed interest. There's even talk of a rock concert next year, in the mould of Live Aid.'

'Sounds like you'll need a punchy slogan.'

'What a coincidence. I was discussing that very issue with my agent, only yesterday.' She creases her forehead, mocking frustration. 'The Firsts?' Sherene laughs at his confused face. 'Our slogan – it's about creating the first generation of Aboriginal Australians to enjoy equality of access to education.'

'And you're sure boarding school is what Aboriginal people actually want?'

'Well, Dick went to boarding school and he was probably the greatest leader they've ever had.'

She frowns at her diamond-encrusted watch. 'Oh dear, I have to go to the photographer's studio.'

'But I need to ask you some questions.'

'I don't want to be late.'

Higgins sits back in his chair, folds his hands behind his head.

'I know you're busy. So busy, in fact, that you haven't contacted me once since your husband's death. Most people in your situation ring us daily, anxious for any information.'

She stares wistfully at the concrete Buddha in the garden, turns back to Higgins, eyes moist.

'Why haven't you asked me about the investigation, Sherene? Don't you want us to find your husband's killer?'

'I refuse to dignify that question with a response.'

She's biting her lip; her strong façade crumbling beneath his glare.

'I've already made a statement. I really don't know what else you could possibly want from me.'

Higgins purses his lips and wriggles his nose, as though he's buried in concentration. But it's all part of the theatrics.

'It's my experience that most people never recover when a loved one is murdered. They try to move on, but life is never the same. You, however, are an enigma. In the space of only a few weeks, you lost a lover *and* a husband. Yet, here you are, posing for magazines and joining boards.'

His smile is ice. 'You take my breath away, Sherene.'

'I'm just trying to create something positive from the tragedies.' She reaches for a tissue from her skirt pocket. 'How on earth can you condemn me when I'm only making an effort to turn my husband's dream into a reality?'

'From where I'm standing, Dick's dream is looking an awful lot like Sherene's ambition.'

'How dare you!' She springs from the chair, drives its legs into the tiles.

Higgins' laughter oozes confidence. 'I'm really looking forward to reading the article.'

'Why on earth would you be interested in reading a women's magazine?'

'I want to know what you're going to disclose about your marriage.' His tired eyes are sparkling. Higgins can feel her on the hook. 'Are you going to talk about the times Dick beat you? Or perhaps you'll tell them about Dick's friendship with Harrison McPherson?'

She throws her voluminous handbag on the table, takes out her iPhone. 'Don, hi – it's Sherene. Unfortunately, I've been delayed. Can we reschedule?' She waves for the waiter. 'Thanks, Don. See you then.'

For the waiter, Sherene has the rigid smile of a corpse. 'May I have another skinny latte?'

The chair legs screech as she plants herself back down, but Sherene won't look into his eyes. She plays with keys of her phone like a sullen teenager.

Higgins smiles at the waiter. 'I'll have another cappuccino, thanks.'

The waiter is barely out of school. His nose is freckled and fine brown hair too long. He smirks at Higgins, suspecting a lover's tiff. Higgins reflects the warmth of a grizzly bear.

'Are you sure you don't want a Scotch?' she says, tartly.

'At this time of the morning, no,' he replies casually, unwilling to take her bait.

The construction in Albert Street is a huge metal cage, an ant colony of workers with hardhats. The drilling and banging have melded with the sounds of the traffic. A man walks past their table, heaving a trolley containing replacement bottles for water coolers. He imagines Sherene standing by a water cooler, breathing in the fumes of office politics.

'You've had quite a transformation, Sherene.'

'It's called a make-over, detective.' Her smile is cool, confident. 'You could do with one yourself.'

He laughs assuredly, but Higgins is tiring of this game. The Commissioner has become his shadow and his marriage is in its dying days. Matthews wants to screw him over.

'The real life story, that's what I want. None of this airbrushing rubbish.'

She expels a sigh and he can tell it's more resignation than a plea for relief. She meets his eyes across the table and he knows he's broken through.

'We were happy, at first,' Sherene says. 'We met at uni, got married after graduation. Then Dick went away to Harvard and came back with a public profile. Once he began his love affair with the press, our marriage began to deteriorate. By the end, I barely knew him ... And once Dick started having affairs, the train leapt off the tracks.'

He tries to suppress thoughts of Lisa, but it's pointless. This is too close to home. You make so many promises when you're young, assume that she'll always forgive.

'Did he ever discuss the Corrowa case?'

'No, but I know he had a great deal of animosity towards the Corrowa, especially Charlie Eversely.'

Higgins feels the adrenalin, but his face remains expressionless. 'Why's that?'

She shrugs. 'I'm the wrong person to ask. I don't know anything about black politics.'

It's an odd remark coming from a director of the Wexley Institute, Higgins thinks, but these days people rarely let a lack of knowledge deter them from anything. Jury members think they're Perry Mason. The neighbour tells him he should watch *CSI*.

'What kind of things did Dick say about Eversely?'

'Oh, the usual. Eversely had his head stuck in the sand. They could never go back to the '70s. I think Dick was hurt, as well. In the early days, some of the older activists looked down on him . . . and responding well to criticism was never Dick's forte.'

'Harrison McPherson?'

'What about him?'

'How well did you know him?'

'Barely. He didn't practise family law and I do. So I never had reason to brief him.'

'But Dick worked closely with him?'

She waits, murmurs thank you to the waiter for her second coffee. 'Dick and I went to some Christmas parties at his chambers, but I always left before things got out of hand.'

He lifts his eyebrows – a silent question mark that hangs in the air.

'Two years ago I received a telephone call from one of Harrison's former secretaries. It was the morning after the Christmas party. She'd been matching Harrison drink for drink. The next thing she knew, she was naked, on top of his desk. The men were taking turns.'

'What did you tell her?'

'To go to the police.'

'Did she?'

'No.'

'Did you discuss it with Dick?'

'By then I knew better,' she says, wryly. 'I didn't want to end up with another broken arm.'

'Why didn't you leave him?'

She stares to the ground, shakes her head. Once again, Higgins' mind drifts to his own marriage. It's the lock of hair that won't be tamed.

'How much time did Dick spend with McPherson?'

'Harrison often called Dick at home. I overheard Dick making plans for drinks, dinner.' She pauses, reflecting. 'I was never invited, of course.' Bitterness resounds in her voice. 'And Harrison always attended Dick's public lectures; those were really the only times I saw him. Even then I tried to avoid him.'

'After what happened at the Christmas party, I can understand why you wouldn't want to be in the same room as that animal.'

'Actually, I'd always felt that way about him.'

She stares at the waterfall in the corner, drinks in the reflection of luminescent orange. 'Have you ever met someone you just know is dangerous?'

'I'm a cop. Instinct plays a huge part in my job.'

'I think there are some people in this world who are pure evil. McPherson was one of them.'

She sips her coffee.

'I've only ever met one other person like that,' he says, leaning into the table. He lowers his voice. 'And one thing I've learnt over the years is that holding onto a secret can be an incredible burden.'

His eyes dangle over the hint of white lace beneath her blouse, follow the contours of her breasts. Higgins can't understand how someone so beautiful and sophisticated could allow herself to remain in a marriage that was crushing her. Embraces the familiar pull in his chest, it niggles like a toothache.

I should send the baby to Mum for the night.

Take Lisa out for dinner.

Life's too short.

'Sherene, I know there's something you want to tell me.'

'You'll think I'm deranged.'

'The truth is you're one of the most intelligent women I've ever met.'

She laughs softly. Higgins would have said anything to get her to this point. But his words are true.

'When Dick and I were first married, we went to his home town, Mount Isa.'

'I know the Isa well.'

He smiles, encouraging her.

'Dick didn't want to go but I insisted. In those days, my opinions still meant something. On our first night, we went to a barbecue at his aunt's house. His family was polite, but I could tell something wasn't right.'

'What do you mean?'

'The way they acted around us. It was as though they were frightened of something. No one looked me in the eyes and each one of them was reluctant to hug me.'

Her phone shrieks. Sherene ignores it.

'The next day, Dick took me to this creek. It was quite a way out of town. I was struck by how cold it was. Here we are in Mount Isa, in the middle of January, and I was shivering. That's when I saw him.'

'Who?'

'I don't know who or what he was. The water was so deep, but he was standing. He was glaring at Dick, like they knew each other. I've never been more terrified.'

'What happened?'

'Dick took my hand and we practically ran to the car. We didn't speak a word about it on the way back to town.'

'Did you ever find out who the man was?'

'That's the thing . . .'

'Go on.'

'You're going to think I'm crazy.'

'Sherene!'

She shakes her head, already dismissing words still unspoken.

'Ever since Dick passed away, I've dreamt about that . . . man. I don't think he's in Mount Isa anymore.'

Tiny hands mask Lesley's face with soggy paper. The ink on the paper has run but the Premier can still see the departmental logo. They're briefing notes. Her name is printed in bold at the top of each page. He's only read one of her briefs – she'd weathered criticisms about his government at some community meeting. He was furious with her. The last thing he needed that day was a barely legible note about bickering blacks.

The grey tea-cosy is matted and streaked with red. Her body is how he'd imagined it, slack and dimpled. Neither one of them is embarrassed by their nakedness. He's still uncertain if Lesley is even aware of his presence.

'Lesley!'

'Shhh.'

'Lesley.'

He begins to whisper then curses himself. 'Lesley, it's me, the Premier!'

One of the papers falls from her hands. The note is dated two days ago. Its heading reads, 'Negotiations with Protesters at Meston Park'. The note confirms what he already knows – there will be no negotiated solution to the impasse.

'Lesley, is this why we're here?'

'You can't mess with the business.' Her voice is earnest, calm.

'Lesley, do you know who you are?'

'What a silly question. I'm a coconut!'

'Lesley, how did we get here?'

'I'm a cooocooonuttt!'

The Premier snatches the papers from her hands, only to be confronted by emptied sockets where eyes had once lived.

Why isn't she in pain?

We must be dead.

Hundred-dollar notes appear to be glued to her lips. Lesley suddenly shrieks, but it's euphoria rather than pain.

'I'm getting that house!'

'Fuck those other blacks!'

'I'm a doer!'

Stale cigarette smoke wafts, together with cheap wine that's too sweet, too young. Snakes are everywhere, in the carpet, the ceiling. Neon snakes. He imagines himself watching the earth spinning on its axis. It comes to a sudden halt when his body hits the ground.

Once again, he feels the chill. His heart sinks to the soles of his feet. And it's heavy with guilt.

'Why are you staring at me?'

Madeline's eyes are playful.

I take her hand. 'What do you think of marriage?'

'Are you asking me to marry you?' She smiles coyly.

'Yes. Yes, I want to marry you.'

'Darling, I have something to tell you.'

'Madeline, I have to go to a branch meeting. I'm already late. Can't it wait?'

She looks down at her svelte waist. 'This is important too.'

Car keys shriek when I throw them on the kitchen bench. 'Go on then. Spill!'

She runs to our bedroom. I can hear her crying behind the door.

Politics is an elegant cesspit. The constant mud-slinging, the rumours, the lies – I grit my teeth and swallow.

My family has no choice.

It always seemed inevitable that Darren would be the first to crumble. Even when he was a baby, Darren's foundations were brittle, his gumption only dust. He'd cry whenever Madeline left him, even if only for a few minutes. Irrespective of expensive schools, stern reprimands and heartfelt advice, he knows Darren will probably always struggle. Kylie, on the other hand, is the prodigal daughter, with consistently high grades and admirable community spirit. Already one of the rising stars of Young Labor. But he knows there are occasions when she too feels the strain.

Madeline is a lioness, too protective, wants to wrap them in cotton wool.

'Kylie just came home.'

I check my watch, just after midday. 'Has she come down with flu?'

'She came home because she was upset.'

'Oh really?'

'Some of the girls at school were teasing her.'

'What about?'

'The article in the Queensland Daily *about you. And Belinda Field.'*

That's when I see the ice in her eyes, the hate.

'I don't care who you fuck, but you keep it away from our children.'

'I don't like the sound . . .'

'Shut up! Just shut up! I have raised our children, mostly as a single parent! I have supported your career! But I will not allow you to destroy our children!'

Payne's laughter is thick, melodic. 'Mate, I've always admired you.'

Lesley stands with her back to us, pouring coffee, but I know she's listening. She'd hear an ant crawling through the carpet.

'Do you know why?' he says.

'I could suggest several reasons. Perhaps you should save time by telling me yourself.'

Lesley chuckles softly.

Payne smirks. 'I admire you because you walked away from a multi-million-dollar practice to serve the people of Queensland.'

'I'm not exactly struggling, Dick.'

'But you can't afford to holiday in Monaco.'

'I can't say I've ever felt a desire to go to Monaco.'

Payne grins and lifts a suitcase onto the desk. It's similar to Madeline's old Louis Vuitton, but this one is brand new. 'Mate, I think you should treat yourself. Take Madeline.' He winks. 'Or Belinda.'

I open the suitcase.

Must be a million dollars in here.

The man's footsteps are slow and laboured. 'The black man has been ruined,' he mutters. He stops at the Premier's feet, shakes his head. 'Ruined by welfare dependency.'

The Premier gasps in disbelief. Payne's waist is a forest of stretch marks that hangs above shrunken genitals. Spittle runs down the corners of his mouth.

'The black man is a child, carried for so long on the back of its indulgent mother that he has forgotten how to walk.'

'Dick, who are you talking to?'

'The question of rights is preposterous. Deadbeat parents should lose all rights to their children.'

'Dick, listen to me!'

Payne claps his hands, mesmerised by a rhythm only he can hear. 'Anathema a-n-a-t-h-e-m-a.'

'Dick, please! I need to know. Am I dead?'

Dick's about to speak when Lesley runs into him, head crouched down, arms in front of her. She bounces off his buttocks and crashes to the ground.

'He's a comin', ooooooh, bub – he's comin'!'

Built as he is tall. Arms are out of proportion with his body, hands lie on the ground like two ends of a scarf. A belt of leather clothes his loins.

Dick glumly kneels beside Lesley. Both stare into the ground, as though waiting for something. They each hold a metal plate attached to a chain. The stranger stands in front of Lesley and grimaces at the hysterical woman. He takes the chain from her hands and places it over Lesley's head. When the plate touches her chest, she screeches as though the metal is burning her.

It's Dick's turn. He too is sobbing now. The stranger speaks to him in a foreign tongue. When the plate touches his breasts, Dick screams out gibberish and violently shakes his head, as though he's unrepentant.

Fathomless eyes turn to the Premier.

He's not real, none of this is real.

It's all in his mind. A mind that's dying.

Am I already dead?

In public he always claimed to be a devout Catholic. But privately, the Premier was certain that death was the end. Accounts of bright lights and reunions with long-departed loved ones were simply the brain winding down. Heaven was an invention, designed to smother fear of death. As if reading his thoughts, the stranger shakes his head in chastisement. He points his hands at the Premier's knees.

The pain is excruciating.

White goalposts stand at a distorted angle, rippling slightly in the air. Abuse hurtles from the crowd, drowned out by the referee's whistle. Dad's crouching over him, face all panic. In a few hours, a doctor will tell him that he'll never play football again.

He's losing his mind. Is this what the brain does when you're dying?

He just wants one opportunity to say sorry to Madeline and the kids.

After that, I'll go.

The smell isn't unpleasant but sanitary, like the disinfectants used in his mother's nursing home. The Premier can feel his family around him, but their bodies are distorted like amoeba.

'Dad, I got a B- for English.'

'Darren, sweetheart, it's time to go.'

Madeline's beautiful voice. He smells her strong perfume.

'Okay, I love you, Dad.'

'Kylie, darling, it's time to say goodbye.'

'Bye, Dad. I love you.'

His words bash the doors of his mouth, desperate to escape.

'Darling, what's that?' Madeline leans in close.

'Oh my God. Nurse, nurse! There's something wrong!'

Rubber soles screech on the floor. 'Step away, please.'

'What's wrong, doctor?'

The darkness begins to fill the Premier's mind. Suddenly he's drowning in darkness.

TWENTY-ONE

The light is dim, the smell musty. Walls are mostly bare, with the exception of faded posters advertising long-forgotten political rallies. The hard plastic chairs argue with concrete whenever anyone moves. The urn in the corner occasionally hisses, as the passion boils over.

Ordinarily, Charlie would be conscious that he's the only black person in the room. He'd expect distance, protective body language from the others. But not here. Most have been coming to these meetings since ANTaR was born in the grubby furnace of the Wik debate. Charlie has no time for the name 'Australians for Native Title and Reconciliation'. Native title has been little more than a poisonous diversion, and reconciliation, well, who the hell really knows what that means?

But he admires them nonetheless. For so many years, they've been meeting in this church basement. Writing letters to politicians demanding that they implement the recommendations of all but forgotten enquiries, raising money for health campaigns, turning up to demonstrations and community meetings. Most of the time, they receive little thanks for their efforts.

He's old enough to know that for these few hours, those in this room will only ever reveal one side of the prisms that are their hearts. Charlie will never know what kind of partners, parents and siblings these people are. He will never know if they are kind to their colleagues or welcoming of their neighbours. But he cherishes the sincerity in the room, drinks it until his body can hold no more.

'If one of my relatives had their wages taken away from them by the government, I'd be furious. I wouldn't be satisfied until they were fully compensated.'

Janet is five years younger than Charlie, but her heart knows the same fire. She's been wearing the same mini-skirts for the last thirty years. Hair has stayed the same angry shock of red. She was one of the early volunteers at the Aboriginal Medical Service. And a friend of his late wife, Carys.

'And as for opposing your native title claim, well that just beggars belief. Why should you have to prove who you are anyway? What happened to land rights? I just can't get over this Labor Government. Is there any difference between them and the conservatives?'

Jim's been a member of Labor since he was a teenager. Now he's leaning on his walking stick, fury dancing in those hazel eyes.

'Charlie, what I want to know is, how do you keep fighting? I mean, it must be so frustrating to survive decades of conservative governments, only to be fucked over by Labor.'

'Language, mate, language!'

'Sorry, Janet.'

The students in the front row giggle. Charlie suppresses a grin. He wants to tell them that anger is a virtue. But the true test of courage is an enduring belief in the goodness of others, even when the past gives you no reason to believe.

'Charlie, where have you been?' Ethel stands at the back of the room. 'Charlie, I've been trying to call you!'

His phone is turned off, as it always is during meetings.

The pan of leek and garlic releases the shrill laughter of a coven. The aroma of the vegetable lasagna in the oven is intoxicating, its warmth melding with the night breeze that enters through the old windows above the sink. Classical music drifts from the dining room like exquisite perfume. This is the life Miranda had imagined would belong to her by now.

Jonathon is standing behind the granite bench, slicing a loaf of olive bread. The black T-shirt caresses toned muscles in his chest. Jonathon's skin is luminous as are his blue eyes. Miranda refuses to envy her dear friend, but she craves his obvious happiness. His vitality.

Why do I hold onto pain much more than other people do?

It's not as though Jonathon has never known pain. You don't live into your late thirties without making its acquaintance. But whereas people like Jonathon allowed pain to wash over them, Miranda clings to it, allows it to overwhelm her until she douses it with alcohol.

'Is this the first time you've been here?'

'I think it is, yeah.'

They've been friends for twenty years, but rarely have they been in each other's homes. Miranda is loath to invite anyone inside her apartment, apart from Ethel and Charlie, and that's only because Ethel insists. She's embarrassed, but not by the broken furniture or dusty carpet. She's ashamed of the smell of defeat.

'It's beautiful here.'

Jonathon's house is a little smaller than Charlie's, but it hails from the same era. The walls have been recently painted eggshell white. The smell of paint still wafts through the airy rooms.

'How are Charlie and Ethel?'

'Okay, thanks.'

'I imagine the press must be hounding Charlie?'

'Yeah, but Dad's been doing this for thirty years.'

'You know, you're pretty lucky.'

'How's that?'

'My father has no interest whatsoever in social justice. He thinks my practice is a joke.'

She's tempted to talk about her strained relationship with Charlie, but decides against it. Tonight is for good conversation, laughter.

Instead, she says, 'I think all families are complicated.'

Jonathan smiles. 'You're not wrong.'

He pours some balsamic vinegar and olive oil into white triangular dishes. 'Here, dip the bread into this. It's delicious.'

'Where did you get the bread?' she says.

'That organic bakery down the road.'

'The new one that opened a couple of weeks ago?'

'Mmm, it's fantastic.'

Jonathon takes a bottle of red wine from the cupboard. Miranda isn't familiar with the brand. The organic logo suggests it's expensive. He pours himself a glass and offers one to Miranda.

'No, thank you. I'm taking a break from drinking.'

'Good for you. By the way, you look great at the moment.'

'Thank you.'

This morning she got up at six, feeling refreshed, was even excited to go to work. Jason had left at five-thirty; she'd felt the gentle press of his lips on her cheek.

'Would you like a glass of mineral water?'

'Yes, please.'

Miranda welcomes the bubbles on the roof of her tongue. Jonathon raises his glass of wine.

'A toast – to the law.'

'And what's so great about the law?'

Jonathon smiles, his mind ticks over. 'Alright. To the noble people who try to inject compassion into the law.'

'Do you really think that's possible?'

'You can never afford to lose hope, Miranda.'

'Speaking of hope, it's a good thing we got the notice of appeal filed in time,' she says.

He sips his wine, shakes his head. 'What a terrible time, hey? I was shocked when Brosnan was murdered, but then, to see Payne and McPherson as well. What the hell is going on?'

He takes another sip. 'Have the police been in touch with you?'

'Yes.'

'Me too.'

'Oh really? Who interviewed you?'

'I can't remember his name. That's terrible, I'm usually pretty good at remembering names.'

Jonathon removes the lasagna from the oven; they inhale the luscious sauce and eggplant.

'It was some Aboriginal detective.'

'Oh right.'

Miranda has never been good at disguising her feelings, but right now she's doing everything she can to remain a closed book.

Jonathon frowns, his eyes projecting concern.

Oh no, he knows.

He's going to think I'm such an idiot.

'Did that detective mention anything to you about taking precautions?'

Of course we've been taking precautions.

'What precautions?'

'Miranda, the murders are obviously related to the Corrowa claim.'

Exasperation rings in his voice.

'So?'

'So we need to be careful. Perhaps you should stay with Charlie and Ethel until the police catch this guy.'

'Why do you assume that it's a man?'

'Miranda, don't change the subject. I don't know if it's safe for you to be on your own right now.'

'Actually, I am being careful. I'll be fine.'

Jonathon pours himself another glass of wine. He's nervous tonight, too anxious to fill any potholes in their conversation, too willing to admonish her.

They take the dishes into the dining room. It's tastefully furnished and understated, with a cabinet holding wine glasses and china dishes. The huge mahogany table consumes most of the room.

'This is beautiful.'

Miranda is emphatic. She's so proud of him, for having a successful career, an elegant home.

'We like it here.'

'We?'

Jonathon's smile seems anxious.

'What is it?'

'I have a new partner.'

'That's wonderful news.'

Miranda tries to sound excited, will do anything to hide her disappointment, her jealousy. Over the years, Jonathon has dated several women, each beautiful and brilliant. When every relationship ended, he seemed to move on easily. Jonathon was rarely one to hold on to past. He surely tasted bitterness, but he never swallowed it whole.

'And does this partner have a name?'

He offers her the bowl of rocket and parmesan salad.

'Why so secretive?'

'You're on a mission. Aren't you?'

'Well I'm not about to let you off the hook.'

'Okay. *His* name is Rod.'

'Oh right,' Miranda says too quickly, betraying her awkwardness.

'That's all you can say – "Oh right."'

'Okay, I'm a little shocked. Just give me some time.'

They smile into each other's eyes for a few moments before she's able to break the ice.

'To be honest, I'm shocked you didn't tell me sooner.'

'Why?'

'Because I'm your friend. I could have supported you.'

'Miranda, you know I love you dearly. But to be brutally honest, you're not exactly capable of offering emotional support to anyone.'

'That's a little harsh.'

'Harsh but true. You, my dear, don't even like yourself.'

'Ow! I'm wounded.'

He plays with his lasagna, while musing over thoughts.

'I've seen self-loathing in my own community, Miranda. I've carried it too, but I can't anymore. It's destructive.'

'You? I don't believe that. You're the most together person I know.'

'Life is never easy, for anyone. But you . . . Miranda you live as though you're waiting for some magic cure that's going to take the pain out of life. Trust me – it doesn't exist.'

'Just hold on a minute. I've known you for almost twenty years, and only two minutes ago you tell me for the first time that you're gay. Now *you're* subjecting *me* to psychoanalysis. Jonathon, you need to slow down.'

Miranda is simmering inside. She knows he's speaking the truth. But how do you change something that's been with you forever? Where do you begin?

'I told my family a few weeks ago. Now it's your turn. I want you to meet him.'

'I already know he's amazing. Only someone incredible could possibly deserve you.'

Jonathon smiles at her lovingly. 'He's one of the good guys.'

'So how come Mr Good Guy isn't here?'

'Rod's a doctor, works gruelling night shifts at the PA Hospital.'

'A doctor, huh? I'm impressed.'

He places his hand over hers, runs his fingers over her knuckles.

She feels a sudden emptiness. 'I'm sorry for not being there for you.'

The grating beep of her mobile phone goes off.

'I should have turned that off.'

'Answer it. It might be Ethel and heaven knows I don't want to get in her bad books.'

She studies the caller ID.

'You're right.'

* * *

The skylight is ugly, a relic of the loud and gaudy 1980s. It stands behind Meston Park like a rocket waiting, pleading, for take-off. The torches in the camp are fireflies on the wall of the city. Small enough to ignore, but never completely. The adults and young children have planted their roots in front of the fire. Teenagers are draping their bodies across the still warm cricket pitch.

The Corrowa's camp is a circle of five canopies with stretched, white skin. Smaller tents surround them. Two days ago they were almost overwhelmed by a storm, but all that is left of that fury is a scattering of puddles. Birds are silent, so that now there is only the hum of traffic, but that too has died down to a lull.

They've just eaten dinner and the air is still heavy with sausage and fried onion. A billy simmers on the barbecue plate, holding enough water to fill the enormous teapot. A gust of wind shakes the trees, mingling with the softly spoken rumours that envelop the flames. No one mentions the names of the dead. But their suspicions are the same.

Clever man's back.

Jason is nervous. The green young men want this too badly. The dim lights of the mansions across the street are mists that surround another world. A world he doesn't know, but is surely less complicated than this one. Higgins is a phantom. Jason can barely see the grooves in his face, the lips curved in a half-smile. But the violence is glowing like a flare.

'We don't have to do this, you know.'

'Matthews, if you have a problem . . .'

'Listen to me. The killer knew the victims – they welcomed the killer into their homes. There were no robberies either. Higgins, this was personal!'

Higgins spits to the ground, points at the camp. 'That mob takes this native title bullshit personally.'

'Where is your judgment? Most of the people in that camp

are poor. There is no way any of them move in the same circles as McPherson, Payne and Brosnan. And they'd have stood out in their prissy neighbourhoods – someone would have seen them. The killer is someone who passes through that world, unnoticed. Higgins, can't you see that?'

Higgins throws his cigarette to the ground. Orange splinters vanish into his shoe.

'Orders from above. You don't like it – leave.'

Grass rustles beneath pounding feet. The mangy dog hears them first, its pained bark a distress signal. But it's pointless. Negotiation has no place in the darkness. There is no discussion about the illegal fire. Not even the pretence of the time-honoured trifecta. Canopies are snapped, makeshift tables thrown from their legs.

Higgins' hands are wrapped around a scrawny neck like a boa constrictor that's pounced on a chicken. The boy is barely into his teens. His feet are just above the ground and he's struggling in vain to be set free. He spits into Higgins' face; it's a match thrown into gasoline. Higgins slaps his face, sending him flying through the air. Others try to help, but they're pummelled with batons. Bodies are piled into nearby police vans, like conveyor belts in a soulless factory. And Jason stands watching, wondering if he too is soulless.

Miranda smells the hurt before she sees the broken canopies. The remains of the barbecue are scattered throughout the camp. A mother tries to soothe the baby in her arms. She stands beside another woman, whose arm is in a sling.

Dad's face is calm, too calm. He's listening, but she knows he's struggling to keep a lid on the anger. Ethel is standing behind him, her face full of anxiety. Miranda can't hear what Jason is saying to them. But his solemn eyes tell her that the fragile peace has been broken.

TWENTY-TWO

'Heart attack, eh?'

'Hmm.'

'What page did you say it was on?'

'Nine.'

Ethel scans the *Queensland Daily* for a few seconds before she finds the article. It's only ten lines, in the bottom right-hand corner above an advertisement for bank loans.

'I'm surprised we didn't hear about it earlier,' she says. 'Murri grapevine must be getting rusty.'

'Well, she'd been out of the community for a long time.' Charlie walks into the pantry and returns with a jar of honey. 'Didn't she have a daughter?'

'Oh, I haven't seen Alisha for years. Last I heard, she was working in Sydney.'

The crumpet hisses as Charlie smothers it with honey. 'Who's her father?'

'Mitchell, his name was Mitchell. But I don't remember anything else about him. He took off before Alisha was born.'

The morning light filters through the generous window-panes. Ethel loves this time of the day, sipping milky tea, eating toast saturated with butter and vegemite. But this morning her mind is a construction site; so much is going on, she can't hear herself over the din of voices. Thousands of spirits looking to her, to Red Feathers. Spirits that don't understand how power-less they were to intervene last night. She heard them in the river this morning, whispering, mocking.

No, they don't understand.

It's all happening according to plan, but she's surprised by how drained she feels. Crying for no reason, constant exhaustion, excruciating headaches.

'Doesn't say when the funeral will be,' she says.

'We'll have to keep an eye on the funeral notices.'

She gulps her tea. Hopes that its warmth will soothe her pain. 'It'll probably be at Manoah.'

'Expect many people to turn up?'

'Probably. That mob at Manoah aren't too political.'

'You going?'

'Not sure.' She feels the tears running down her cheeks; Charlie hands her a box of tissues. 'I just don't want to be a hypocrite.'

'What do you mean?'

'All that mob will be singing Lesley's praises. No one will be talking about the bribe she took from Coconut Holdings.'

'Well, we don't know for sure that she took a bribe.'

'I don't know, Charlie, why do they do it?' she says, throwing her hands in the air. 'Why do they turn their backs on us?'

'We can't judge, Ethel. I learnt that a long time ago.'

'Why not? You spent your life fighting, Charlie, and then someone like Lesley comes along. She didn't believe in anything.'

'People like Lesley never have any credibility in the community. I felt sorry for her. Imagine what it would be like to be a pariah among your own mob?'

'But that was her choice.'

'And she ended up wasting precious years because of that choice.'

He finishes the last of his crumpet, seems to savour the honey. 'You and I are the lucky ones. We can walk into any community meeting and we'll be welcome.'

Charlie stands at the doorway to the study. 'I'm giving my interview now. I'll be free in about an hour.'

'What, you're not going to the studio?' she says, surprised.

'Too busy. I need to stay in today. Besides, I want to see how many hits are on the website.' He offers her a wink.

'Oh, I didn't know you could do that.'

Charlie looks at his watch.

'Gotta go.'

'Alright, bub.'

'*Good morning to our wonderful audience. My name is Huey B and you're listening to Black and Strong. This morning our guest is Charlie Eversely, Chair of the Brisbane Aboriginal Legal Service and a longstanding advocate for the Murri community. Good morning, Charlie.*'

'*Morning, Huey.*'

'*Charlie, I understand you were at Meston Park last night.*'

'*Yes, Huey, that's right.*'

'*We've heard that police conducted a raid on the Corrowa camp just after nine. What can you tell us about the raid?*'

'*I didn't arrive until the police had left, so I can't give you an eye-witness account of what happened during the raid. But I can tell you I was shocked by what I saw. It looked like a cyclone had gone through that camp.*'

'*Were there any arrests?*'

'*Huey, I do know that fifteen people were arrested and charged with trivial offences, like trespass and committing a public nuisance.*'

'*Police are still arresting people for trivial offences?*'

'*More often than not it's our people they're arresting.*'

'*Charlie, do you know the reason for the police raid?*'

'*This raid was clearly an attempt to intimidate our people, so that Coconut Holdings and the State Government can get on with their grubby deal, and desecrate our land by building a multi-million-dollar eye-sore.*'

'*Charlie, can you tell us what's in store for those who were arrested last night.*'

'Huey, the Legal Service is attending on them as we speak. They expect to be making bail applications in the Magistrate's Court this morning.'

'Were you surprised by the raid, Charlie?'

'No, I wasn't surprised. But I was disappointed. Last night was a clear example of police abusing their powers in order to intimidate our people. We fought against these kinds of practices thirty years ago. It sickens me to think that so little has changed.'

'Charlie's still got it,' Ethel says, her eyes glowing. 'I know, bub.'

Even though she can see only Red Feathers' reflection in the window, Ethel feels his sadness.

'Everything will be alright.'

She wearily shakes her head.

'Yes, it's easy for me to say, but there's no point in worrying about things we can't change.'

Ethel takes the dirty dishes to the sink, watches the suds bloom in hot water.

'What's that, bub?'

'I'm sorry too.'

She smiles lovingly into the window.

'I wonder what our girl is doing.'

The psychologist said to call her Gina, but Miranda's not sure that she wants to know her on a first-name basis. She appreciates the irony. Over the coming months, Miranda will open her soul to this woman. In this room, her secrets will gain a life of their own, far from what they are now, which is dust on her brain. But she's still clinging to the security of formalities.

'I don't believe in therapy for the sake of it. I don't want to be coming here indefinitely.'

Gina speaks slowly, in a voice that's both friendly and judicious. 'Then you'll be pleased to hear that I have very few long-term clients. Judging by what you've told me so far, I'd say we can cure you in eight sessions.'

Miranda doesn't like the word 'cure'; it sounds too perfect. Life is never perfect.

'I think the best treatment for you would be Eye Movement Desensitisation and Reprocessing Therapy, or EMDR.'

She hands Miranda a brochure.

'This mentions post-traumatic stress disorder. Do I have that?'

'I don't think so. I'm recommending EMDR because it's effective and it works quickly.'

The chairs are old and the upholstery is torn, a desk in the corner is piled high with manila folders. Miranda knows the windows stare into the street, but the blinds are down. In the movies, the neurotic client is reposed on a couch, but Gina doesn't tell her to lie down.

The hour passes quickly.

When she walks out into Boundary Street, Miranda feels the tears welling, tears of joy. She's proud of herself for making it through her first counselling session. But her happiness fades when she realises there are no messages on her phone.

As she climbs the faded carpet of the stairwell that leads to her office, Miranda's mind is a carousel.

He hasn't called since yesterday.

He saw me there last night. Why did he ignore me?

Angela seems happier than usual. She follows Miranda into her office, her hands folded behind her back.

'I have some news,' she says. Angela's cheeks are rosy, face brimming with excitement. 'I'm pregnant.'

Miranda quickly offers a heartfelt embrace. 'Congratulations. That's wonderful news. Paul must be thrilled.'

'We've only been trying for a few months. I thought it'd take longer. After all, we're not exactly young.'

She wants to remind Angela that twenty-five is not old. But Miranda resists. This is, after all, Angela's moment.

'Miranda, I'm so lucky. You know, I've got friends in their late thirties who are going through hell trying to get pregnant.'

Angela checks her watch. 'Ouch, I've got to be in court in half an hour.'

'Will I see you when you get back?'

'Probably not. I have a doctor's appointment this afternoon.'

'Okay, well, once again, congratulations.'

As she takes her seat, Miranda reflects on Jonathon's relationship, Angela's pregnancy. They're good people who deserve to taste life's fruit. But the pain niggles inside her.

When is it going to be my turn?

O'Neill bursts through the door like a gust of wind. 'Mate, how did it go?'

'Good, thanks.'

He perches himself on the chair facing her, reminding Miranda of a parrot. 'I know a few people who've been to see Gina. She helped them through some really tough times. And given that her office is only a block away from here, it makes sense for you to see her.'

His face is suddenly sheepish. 'I don't expect you to tell me the details . . . unless, you want to.'

'I'll be fine, thanks.' Miranda can feel her cheeks burning. So much is happening, she craves time alone.

'I just wanted you to know that I'm proud of you,' he says.

O'Neill has never been one to wear his heart on his sleeve; it makes the gesture all the more touching.

'Thank you.'

Her voice seems to be disappearing, drowned out by human traffic. She's an island, watching other people's lives speed ahead.

Jonathon's in love.

Angela's having a baby.

'To be honest, I'm exhausted. I didn't get much sleep last night and then there was this morning's business.'

She can't yet use the word 'psychologist' in relation to herself.

'Is it okay if I work from home this afternoon?'

'Do you have any appointments with clients?'

'No. I have to draft some affidavits. If I work from home, I'll have fewer distractions and get them finished.'

'Okay, mate. You do what you think is best.' He's about to leave, when he pauses. 'Mate, you heard Angela's news?'

She smiles into uncertain eyes.

'Yes, it's wonderful.'

Boundary Street is a universe of smells – curries, noodles, espresso, kebabs. Miranda is suddenly ravenous; she hasn't eaten since early morning. There's some cold pizza in the fridge; she'll zap it in the microwave. She walks past the old flats next door. Tegan's husky voice mingles with the sounds of the guitar. Her door is always open, something Miranda would never do. She empties the mailbox, only bills and brochures.

Her knapsack is heavy with files. All for family law clients. She's thinking she might get out of family law. Miranda gains little satisfaction from the work anymore. In fact, some of her more difficult clients have made her fearful for her safety. But she's not sure where to go to from here. She'll need to discuss it with O'Neill.

Miranda suddenly feels exhilarated. This is the first time she's considered the possibility of making a change in her life. A light bulb has been switched on – she doesn't have to stay mired in the quicksand. It's a choice.

Miranda places the knapsack on the couch. She's opening her telephone bill when she sees the feathers. They're arranged in a circle beneath the kitchen table. She hears the scream. Her own.

'Miranda!'

It takes her a moment to realise that Jason is pulling her arm.

'Miranda, listen to me! You need to follow me. Now!'

The bottles are different shapes and colours, from turquoise to incandescent red. The orange light behind them is a sun, wielding the power to give warmth and take it away. Miranda studies

Jason's reflection in the huge mirror above the bar, his chocolate skin, slender nose. The rebellious curls on his forehead that have escaped the grasp of hair gel. Her own face appears a little thinner than usual, and her skin seems to have gained a healthy glow.

Jason is rummaging over the mess that his seemingly structured life is rapidly becoming. Yes, he should have made the call. Yes, Miranda's apartment should be searched. She should be questioned. Before last night, he wouldn't have hesitated. What he saw bombarded his usual instincts with glue.

Jason knows that he is far more than a casual observer of Higgins' violence; at times, he's been complicit. But last night was different. Those people were not paedophiles. They were not killers. They were simply in the wrong place, at the wrong time.

'How's your father?' he says, cutting his own thoughts dead.

'I don't know. I haven't spoken to him today.'

'Did you speak to him at the camp last night?'

'For a little while. After you left.'

Neither one of them wants to raise the fact that he ignored her last night. Jason just wasn't up to dealing with her at the time. Is never quite ready for dealing with any woman.

'Can I buy you a drink?'

'I'm taking a break from drinking.'

'Oh yeah, sorry. I forgot.'

Jason nods at the bartender, orders a rum and coke.

The chandelier above them is a colony of light, imprisoned in crystal and silver. It sits uncomfortably with the flock of slender television screens that stare down at them like gargoyles. Each news program is flashing the same photograph – the Premier smiles into his daughter's eyes. His arms are wrapped around his wife's waist. Their son's long hair is unkempt, but stylish in the way that youngsters wear it now. The photograph vanishes, replaced by a pummelled car.

'Why do they always have to show photographs from crash scenes on TV?' Miranda shakes her head. 'It's so disrespectful.'

'It's what people want to see,' Jason says, casually.

'That doesn't make it right.'

'I didn't realise you were such a big fan of our late Premier.'

'I wasn't. But there's a principle at stake.'

'Which is?'

'We should be respectful of the family. This kind of footage must be distressing for them.'

'They can choose to turn the TV off.'

Miranda doesn't know if he's being serious or not. Wonders if he's always this flippant.

'They practically ignored the fact that the Premier's driver was killed too. His name was Harry Wilson. He'd been the Premier's driver for ten years.'

Jason ignores her. She can tell he's tiring of this conversation. Or perhaps he's tiring of her.

She gazes around the bar, pretending to be preoccupied. On the walls are geometric plants in various shades of purple, black tiles underneath their feet. Miranda doesn't recognise the music, but it's soft. Predictable. A young man croons about his broken heart. Patrons speak of property, property, property.

Years ago, the air choked on smoke and spilt beer. This place was a graveyard for those who stopped living before they stopped breathing. But like the old geography of West End, the barflies are gone. Now the Melbourne Hotel caters for a more refined crowd that enjoys tapas with their boutique beers. She looks back at Jason.

'I didn't know you were a rum drinker.'

'You're hardly in any position to judge.'

'What do you mean by that?'

His smirk is cold. They sit quietly, but the tension between them is like hail. She wonders what she did to make him angry. He's stressed from work, that's it. Bullshit. She's back in the place she always ends up.

Why do I go out of my way to please men like Jason? Men like Dan? Why do I need to be with them?

Why am I always so reckless?

When she was three years old, Miranda ran into a department store lift while she was shopping with her mother. Carys scampered from floor to floor, frantically searching for her daughter. Miranda bided her time clutching the hand of a Good Samaritan, oblivious to her mother's ordeal. When she was in her twenties, Miranda lived for the moment. She once drank herself into a stupor at the Regatta Hotel, and when she'd spent all her money, she casually announced that she was swimming home. Bystanders gasped in disbelief as Miranda plunged into the Brisbane River.

As she grew older, Miranda became more inhibited and she remained hidden in her apartment. But the carelessness remained. During her first week as a solicitor, one client broke down and threw a chair at her. Another threatened to attack her with a syringe apparently filled with contaminated blood. Miranda calmly responded to each incident by going home to another bottle of wine.

People ordinarily assume that she's just brave. Auntie Ethel calls it 'backbone'. But Miranda knows it's recklessness born of self-loathing. If she truly liked herself, she wouldn't take so many risks.

I wouldn't be sleeping with a man I barely know.

Jason's eyes see straight through her, like he's stealing her thoughts. 'Can I ask you something?' he says.

'Sure.'

'Why were you afraid of the feathers in your apartment?'

She shrugs.

'Had you seen them before?'

'Maybe.'

Jason gulps down the last of his rum and coke, gestures to the barman for another.

'Would you mind not looking at me that way, Miranda?'

'Sorry.'

'How long since your last drink?'

'Six days.' She's surprised by the pride in her voice. She hadn't wanted to make it so obvious.

'Well congratulations.'

'You're not the most sensitive person, are you?'

'Sorry.'

His sarcasm is a bitter aftertaste.

'So tell me, why did those feathers scare you?'

'Am I speaking to Detective Sergeant Matthews or Jason?'

'Baby, why don't you pick?'

The barman is an artist whose genre is hypnosis. She's fascinated by the way he pours the champagne, so that only a thin layer of white floats at the top of the elegant glass.

'Should I buy you a drink?' Jason says. 'I hear sauvignon blanc is a personal favourite.'

Miranda feels like she's shrinking, she's so embarrassed. She tries to turn away, but her eyes won't leave the bar.

The barmaid is beautiful and vivacious, her storm of blond hair scooped up in a bun. She offers a flirtatious smile to Jason. Miranda feels the sting of humiliation when he reciprocates. She desperately wants to run, delete his phone number, never speak to him again. But she's drawn to the crisp white wine in front of her.

The bar staff refuse to serve her. Even in her drunkenness, Miranda is horrified by the stares of the other patrons. Her legs are spaghetti. She grasps the metal railing as she slowly descends the stairs.

The cool night air bites her skin and she hopes it will propel her into sobriety. What did she tell Jason about the feathers on her father's website? Did she tell him anything? She can't remember. She *needs* to remember.

She hears the coins as they hit the ground, sees her make-up and brush strewn across the footpath.

Looks up into her dad's face.

He's sobbing.

TWENTY-THREE

Waves chatter as they break over the wreckage. Miranda's arms are draped across the wood like a foam kickboard. The red dress is taffeta and clings to her like a layer of film. Perhaps she was a passenger on one of those massive cruise ships that holds a citadel in its palm. But if that were the case, where are the other passengers? It's more likely she fell from a cliff and the head injury has wiped her memory clean, like it happens in the movies. The fin is a speck at first, which makes her conscious of her legs, exposed. The shark has the finesse of a semi-trailer. She's blinded by the sheen of its teeth, smells its hunger.

Waves disappear into the arms of the ceiling fan. It's on the maximum setting, too cold for Miranda. She feels around the bed for a blanket, but there's only the thin sheet. Her head is a thunderstorm, her mouth a drought. Charlie's kept the room much the same since she moved out fifteen years ago. Textbooks from high school and university are still on the shelf. The radio she played while doing her homework still sits in the corner. The footprints of old Blu-Tack remain on the walls. The smell of freshly cut grass wafts through the window, ameliorating the mothball smell.

She's wearing one of Auntie Ethel's T-shirts. It demands land rights in '88 and Miranda wonders why she held onto it. Wonders why Auntie Ethel is such a hoarder and what does that say of her personality? Miranda comes from the disposable generation; she loathes clutter. Few things carry so much sentiment that they cannot be discarded.

The bathroom smells of lavender detergent that makes her even more nauseous. As she purges the sugary wine, Miranda feels relief. But she's so dehydrated she imagines her body desiccated, so that she is only a bag of bones. Her knees ache. Both are grazed and speckled with dried blood.

Where's Dad? He's waiting, biding his time.

He'll explode, she knows it.

Miranda waits to hear a voice, the sounds of the radio. Nothing. She returns to bed, to visions of taffeta and sharks.

Jason sips his third coffee this morning and grimaces. Cheap instant that's so bitter he had to add three teaspoons of sugar. Two hours of sleep last night; his head is a lead balloon. He knows that his eyes are bloodshot, feels them reeling from the glare of the computer screen.

'When was this website launched?'

'Three days ago, Miranda said.'

Jason smells the spirits on Higgins' breath. Higgins is a ticking bomb. The explosion is imminent. Jason knows he'll take casualties with him.

'What does Eversely have to say about himself?'

Jason clicks the mouse over one of the icons and leans in.

'The usual – community activist, old-timer from the Bjelke-Petersen years.'

Higgins scoffs. 'Someone give the man a fucking medal.'

The Corrowa Portal implores visitors to learn about their history and culture. News updates have links to various articles on the Corrowa's native title claim, their impending appeal and the protest camp. The Resources Page contains a history of the boundary and a list of references for articles in historical journals. But it's the logo on the homepage that's got them intrigued – red feathers.

'This is nothing,' Henly says, shaking his head.

Higgins stares at him icily. 'Bullshit! We've kept a lid on the

243

feathers. There's only one way Eversely could know about the feathers.'

'I don't think he acted alone,' Jason says quietly, standing to face Higgins. 'Miranda must have something to do with it.'

'What are you talking about?'

'She knew all three victims.'

'So did her father.'

'I can't imagine either the judge or McPherson opening their doors to Charlie Eversely. Can you? Miranda's in a different category. They'd see her as a professional acquaintance, albeit a junior one.'

Jason can see the dead end Higgins is hurtling down, can smell the rubber from his burning tyres. He'll keep trying to prevent the collision, however hopeless that might be.

'Look, Higgins, we don't have enough to make a circumstantial case against Charlie Eversely. Not yet, anyway.' Jason looks across the table and feels relieved to see that sandbags are under Lacey's eyes too. 'Were you able to find anything that linked the Paradise Parrot to Corrowa tradition?'

'I've spoken to Doctor Bernes a few times.'

'And?'

'Nothing. Even before the Paradise Parrot became extinct, it wasn't common to south-east Queensland. It was more prevalent up north.'

Jason paces the faded carpet. Searches the crevices in his mind for something, anything. 'I think we should question them all, including Ethel Cobb.'

Higgins scratches his stubble, but Jason knows he's only pretending to muse over his thoughts.

'I agree,' Higgins says. 'Finally, you've made a useful contribution.'

Jason ignores the rebuke, knows the old game play. He looks at Higgins squarely. 'But we can't have a repeat of what happened at Meston Park.'

'Don't play games with me, Matthews. You're not so innocent.'

'What do you mean by that?'

'You've spent more time with the charming Miss Eversely than anyone else.'

Higgins' menacing eyes say it: they all know he's been sleeping with Miranda. He's only got himself to blame.

'Once a terrorist always a terrorist,' Higgins says.

'What the –'

Higgins slams his hand on the desk, sending Jason's cup of instant flying. The others watch in disbelief as streams of coffee run down the whiteboard.

'Eversely was with that fuckin' embassy in the '70s. He's nothing but a public nuisance, someone who should have been put away a long time ago.'

Jason heads for the door. He won't have any more blood on his hands, hands that carry too much now.

'Matthews, sit the fuck down! You want to stay in this job then you better sit the fuck down!' Higgins' eyes are a lighthouse beacon. The ships in this dim room follow his light without question. Only Jason will risk crashing into the rocks. Because Jason finally knows what Higgins' eyes are saying. Jason is just another fuckin' coon who'll get promoted beyond his capabilities soon enough. Their friendship is over, if it ever existed.

'We don't know what kind of weapons are in Eversely's house,' Higgins says, 'but we all know he's a dangerous man.'

Jason watches helplessly. He smells the napalm but he'd give anything to pretend that it's not hanging in the air, poisoning all of them. He knows that Higgins' treachery is most potent just before the violence is unleashed. This is the time when he'll lie, blackmail, bend the rules until they fracture.

Miranda wakes to the sounds of his footsteps in the hallway. The gentle light behind the curtain informs her that it's late morning. The thunderstorm in her head has settled to a lull, but she still feels exhausted. Miranda prepares herself. She'll offer nothing in defence; she has no excuse.

He's swimming in his old land rights T-shirt and black board shorts. When did Dad lose all of that weight? And he's exhausted. There's no scorn in his eyes, only sadness. Charlie sits on the bed, combs strands of hair away from her forehead with his fingers. She can't remember the last time he touched her. 'When you were born you were the most beautiful little girl in the maternity ward. Mum and I used to take you to all our community meetings. The aunties would make such a fuss over you. But true God, you had a temper. Still do. And I wouldn't have it any other way.'

They both laugh gently, but uncertainty lingers.

'Darlin', I know I haven't always been a good father to you.'

'That's not true.'

Charlie smiles sadly, shakes his head. 'I had no business bringing grog into our home. No business at all.'

'Dad, I know you had a lot of problems back then.'

'I just need you to know that I love you very much and I have always been proud of –'

'Dad . . .'

'For once in your life, Miranda, don't interrupt. You need to start looking after yourself, not for me, not for Mum or Auntie Ethel, but for *you*.'

'I'm sorry, Dad.'

'You got nothing to be sorry for. When your mum passed away, I turned to grog. That's how I taught you to work through your problems . . . and I never, ever wished that you'd died instead of her.'

Tears roll down her cheeks, she feels the lump in her throat. 'I know.'

She cherishes his words, desperately wants to savour them. But the bashing on the front door drowns out everything.

'Police!'

Charlie waits, uncertain.

'Police! Open the door!'

'I'll get it, love.'

He tries to sound calm, but he knows that something is wrong. Miranda stands behind her father when he opens the door to a smug Higgins. Jason is standing beside him. Miranda tries to make eye contact with Jason, he resists.

'We have a warrant to search the premises,' Higgins says.

Miranda snatches the piece of paper from his hands. 'What's this about?'

'Just let us do our job, Miranda.' She hears the unease in Jason's voice, but she knows he'll do nothing to help them.

Police ascend the stairs, a silent procession enters the hallway. All ignore the two dumbfounded faces. Miranda wonders why the hell they've brought their guns, tasers.

'What's going on?'

Ethel is dressed in her power-walking suit of black lycra. Sweat drenches the hair on her forehead.

'Miss Cobb, we need to speak to you too.'

Ethel ignores Higgins and turns to Jason. 'Boy, you should be ashamed. How can you do this to your own mob?'

Jason refuses to look into her eyes, grits his teeth. 'You people are not my mob!'

They hear a series of thuds from the study. Drawers are being ripped from the desk, thrown to the floor. Miranda turns but Jason stands in her way.

'Don't you touch my daughter!'

Higgins' laugh is cold, taunting. 'Old man, it's way too late for that.'

'You bastard!' Miranda slaps Jason's face.

He stares at her coldly and grasps her shoulders. 'Listen to me. You just do what we say and everything will be alright!'

'Let go of me, you bastard!'

She kicks his feet, and the other officers chuckle.

In his youth Charlie took so many strikes from police officers but he had always found some way to resist. Once, he even forced his fingers down his throat, so that he would spoil the wax on the car his face was being bashed against.

We fought so hard.

Can't go on like this forever.

When is this going to stop?

'What do you think you're doing coming into my house?'

Higgins seems to relish the opportunity to confront Charlie. He draws so close, Charlie can smell the rum on his breath.

'Just do it. Go on, boy!'

'Back off, Higgins!'

Higgins grins at Jason's nervous face. Higgins wants Charlie's blood. He must have a hundred tactics up his sleeve and Jason knows he'll use every single one of them if he has to.

'Why don't you handle Miranda, Matthews? You seem to be good at it.'

'You prick!'

Higgins turns to Miranda. 'That's one count of obscene language. You're coming with me.'

'You're not taking my daughter anywhere.'

'Old man, I'm afraid you don't have any say.'

Charlie knows the copper's gone too far. He won't see Miranda in a watch house. Won't allow anyone to lay a finger on his baby girl. Charlie's left hook connects with Higgins' jaw. He sees a spurt of blood, feels the electric current of the taser enter his body.

Time speeds mercilessly as the chaos unfolds.

Higgins calls Jason to help drag Charlie's slumped body, but Jason cannot hear his words. He can only hear Miranda sobbing. She's struggling with some uniforms, pleading to be allowed to go with her father. Ethel is standing alone in a corner, looks almost catatonic. As he follows Higgins through the door, Jason fights every instinct he has to run.

TWENTY-FOUR

'He's had enough.'

The constable is used to wielding power over the powerless. He's kicked a drone, taken money from a dead man's wallet. But that façade can't breathe in this cell. Stinking hot during the day, but its light never penetrates the concrete. Nothing lives in this desert apart from the stale air that's smothering him with grim reality.

'Higgins, I mean it. He's had enough.'

The constable is too young to carry a gun. But not too young to have smelt the corpses of teenage junkies, or given comfort to the brutalised, who will never know any. None of it compares to this.

Blood and sputum have formed a grotesque portrait on the hefty telephone book. It shudders and buckles beneath the force of white knuckles. The prisoner grimaces before collapsing.

'I'm not prepared to lose my job, Higgins.'

Milestones flash through the constable's brain: graduation, proposing to Tina, buying their first home. And it's all about to fade under the flashing lights of the press.

'Did you hear me? I won't lose my job for you.'

Higgins pauses and laughs, reeks of old bitterness. 'You don't know jack shit.'

The constable's beady eyes are reptilian, ever watchful of predators. He knows now that Higgins is the worst kind of predator. Loved by his colleagues, but secretly feared. They'll cheer as he throws a torch, and when the scorched earth is cold they will lie for him.

Exposing the demon that lit the inferno is unthinkable.

'What about the videotape?'

'We'll doctor it, constable.'

Higgins ploughs his right foot into the prisoner's side, drawing cries of pain. 'Ruined my family, you fuck!'

He spits onto the prisoner's forehead. 'We've got unfinished business. Haven't we, boy!'

'Higgins, for Christ . . .'

'What about the man your father killed? He had a family too.'

Higgins pauses, plants his hands on his hips. 'What did you say, boong?'

Charlie knows his body will never recover. He'll be a cripple, if he survives.

Take as much blood as you want. But I won't give you a drop of my dignity.

Higgins kicks Charlie's head in like a football. Fragments of his teeth become airborne.

'You know what, old man? It wasn't just Matthews who had fun with your daughter. I left a big pile of red feathers inside her apartment yesterday. Should have seen her and Matthews take the bolt.'

The concrete stinks of urine and vomit. But Charlie notices there's something else. It's more pungent than death. This place is a vacuum that sucks all humanity, all hope.

I promised Carys I'd look after our baby.

Charlie tries to lift his ballooned head from the stench. But he doesn't have to any longer. They're telling him.

It's time. Mother is so beautiful; tears burn her face as she holds out her hands to him. He'd only ever seen photographs of his father, but he knows him.

Carys is no longer the shadow he said goodbye to in that

hospital ward. She's still got those wild auburn tresses and that heart-shaped smile.

Our baby's grown.

Did the best I could.

So hard without you.

Higgins puffs on a cigarette, takes a swig of the Jim Beam. He's enjoying the warming sensation, the lightness creeping through his bones.

'What's he saying?'

Higgins laughs as the constable holds his breath to look into the old man's bloody face.

He swings around when he hears the cell door, but it's too late. Matthews' gun is already pressed firmly against his neck.

'Matthews, mate. This is another Tipat.'

'Tipat was a paedophile, Higgins.'

'This piece of shit destroyed my old man.'

'That doesn't give you the right to kill.'

Jason turns to the constable, who's gone sickly white. 'Check him.'

He feels for Charlie's pulse. Shakes his head.

She's been coming to this watch house for the past ten years. Could come for another ten and still it would remain unknowable. She loathes the artificial light, the industrial smell.

The innocents only become hardened, the shipwrecks push their hate closer to the surface.

'My name is Miranda Eversely. I've come for my father, Charlie Eversely.'

'You need ID.'

Miranda produces her driver's licence for the camera.

'What was the prisoner's name again?' The female voice on the intercom is indifferent.

'Eversely. Charlie Eversely.'

The pause makes her nervous.

'You have to wait.'

The Aboriginal flag outside Parliament House is tattered and faded, a child who has known only neglect. It's been left outside to suffer the elements, acknowledged rarely and even then, grudgingly. But Miranda expects nothing more from those who co-opt the most enduring symbol of Aboriginal sovereignty, while simultaneously denying that Aboriginal sovereignty lives, breathes.

George Street ends in a mouth of traffic. On one side is the Parliament, three storeys of sandstone, surrounded by green spikes. Iron lattice is rusted like an old relic. Scraggly palm trees grow inside the fence. They too are withered and tired. The most destructive gamblers don't lurk in the casino. They're here.

Parliament faces the Botanical Gardens. A calm oasis. Between heaven and hell, cars come in and out of the mouth, those inside ignore the demonstrators. They live in a parallel dimension, a place where Charlie's murder only exists as thirty-second sound bites.

Ethel stands across the street, outside the Queensland Club. Built for wealthy, white men in the nineteenth century, it scorns its youthful neighbours. Huge columns look like something from America's Deep South.

Miri, everything's going to be okay.

I'll take care of everything.

I promise.

The National Australia Bank logo adorns the blood bank caravan that's parked outside the Parliament; donors swim around it like tadpoles. Inside a fruit stall two Chinese men sit slouched in deck chairs, expressionless faces watching students dawdle to the nearby campus. The students hasten their pace as they approach the demonstrators. All decline invitations to sign the petition.

The Socialist Alliance flag is draped across a makeshift table.

Those behind it are the final vestige of activism in this place, a university for the 'real world'. A small media contingent has turned up, but today they have a different tack. They stand watching the speakers, silently, even respectfully.

Miranda's brain is newspaper on microfiche, reeling over death without meaning. Without cause. Daniel Yock, the beautiful young dancer who didn't live to see twenty. Mulrunji Doomadgee. Arrested for singing.

Perhaps both would have lived had the recommendations of the Royal Commission been implemented. Those voluminous reports now just gather dust, along with the principle that arrest should be an option of final resort. Years ago, another version of those inside the sandstone promised to breathe reality into the vision of the Royal Commission. But the bureaucrats took the Commonwealth money and built new watch houses, jails.

Miranda looks back towards the demonstrators. *Why did it have to happen to Dad? Dad believed in people. He'd learnt how to get rid of his anger, made his peace.*

He was a teacher.

Even as a child, Miranda knew that police were to be feared. That word appeared like a boil in the atmosphere, on the occasions that Charlie had a swollen mouth and painful limp. She'd seen them waiting outside the front door. Enormous men who seemed to give life to Jack and the Beanstalk. As she grew older, Miranda learnt of the true horrors of that time.

Bjelke-Petersen was determined to run the black settlements as prison camps. Cops regularly tortured the radical blacks who said 'no more'. When Miranda grew up, Charlie told her of the black men who had taken 'accidental falls' through the windows of police stations. Black women who had been raped by cops. His own beatings. She knew then, it was a war.

Had Charlie been wounded while fighting in a military uniform, he would have received treatment for his psychological injuries and, perhaps, he might have been paid compensation. But there was nothing for the black men and women who suffered all kinds of scars at the hands of their own government. Their own police force that was supposed to keep them safe.

She thinks about the new Premier sitting in her office with the Police Commissioner, their phalanx of advisers in tow. Their faces will still be dressed in synthetic composure, even though the press conference ended an hour ago.

'Mr Eversely's death is being investigated by experienced homicide detectives and members of the Internal Investigations Branch,' the Premier said. But Detective Senior Sergeant Andrew Higgins would not be stood down during the investigation. The Police Commissioner had deemed it inappropriate. The Premier concluded: 'I have complete confidence in the men and women of the Queensland Police Service.'

Miranda hasn't been surprised by Labor's surge in the polls since the Premier's death. The *Queensland Daily* regularly prints photographs of the statuesque blonde on its front page. She wonders if it bothers Belinda Field that so much attention is placed on her looks, and so little on her competence.

The loudspeaker has an ugly pitch, the voice an unwelcome intruder.

'I first met Charlie at the Embassy in '72. The two of us were just kids. But we learnt from the best of them. Uncle Chicka, Gary Foley, Dennis Walker.'

Wiry and grey. In other circumstances, he'd be enjoying watching grandchildren grow. As he looks into Miranda's face, she feels his thoughts.

We paid such an enormous price.

'When I was growing up, the mission manager used to come to our home unannounced, to give my parents the run around. We all felt the humiliation, but did nothing. Everyone was just so disempowered. But when I got to the Embassy it was like a religious awakening. They refused to bow to anyone. That was where Charlie cut his teeth.'

The crowd cheers in earnest. They relish the memories of leaders who danced on air, fought without fear.

'When we finally got a Labor Government in Queensland, we thought things would get better. At last, we'd be treated as citizens of this State.'

A long and bony finger points at the Parliament.

'But nothing changes under Labor – they're just as bad as the mob they replaced. It's been one week since our brother was murdered and not one of those responsible has been brought in to line. In fact, they're still going to work every day.'

His voice is thick with anger.

'If one of those coppers had died, do you think our brother would have been allowed to walk away? No way! Brothers and sisters, I'm sick and tired. Sick of our people dying needlessly in police custody. Tired of racists walking away with impunity.'

The speaker's voice is a barometer of the crowd. The brother radiates the frustration that's become palpable. Police stand at the end of George Street. Locked jaws silently plead for the demonstrators to light the spark.

Ethel watches Red Feathers flying above the topmost branch of the old grey tree. She pleads with him to come to her. As her eyes bore into his sadness, she knows. A coke bottle soars through the air, and she knows.

Powder keg's been lit.

The child's screams pierce the speaker's words. A woman holds her hand on his scalp to stem the bleeding. They're surrounded so quickly they're barely visible through the jungle of arms and legs. The air is dense with anxious whispers that suck all reason, all control.

The police are an endless stream of toy soldiers. Each row followed by another. A young black man writhes on the ground like the body of a snake whose head has been severed. A man in overalls nurses a broken nose, while his friend holds back his forehead.

The police dogs' snarls should have made them cower in fear. But the crowd doesn't blink. A young woman runs through the gate of the Botanical Gardens. The rock she's carrying is the size of her head, but the weight has no impact on her agility. She throws it into the vortex.

Miranda's feet are fused to the bitumen.

Stop, please stop. Dad wouldn't want this.

The little boy is now sobbing as blood streams down his face. The woman has disappeared. Miranda's hands are on his shoulders before she's even conscious of her own movement.

'Don't worry, you'll be okay.'

She sees the fear in the child's eyes.

'We have to find your mum. Where did she go?'

Miranda hears the collapse of the baton. Feels a lightning bolt of pain scorch the back of her head. She's trying to reassure him, but her head is swimming.

His cries disappear into the darkness of her mind.

Red Feathers clutches Ethel's wriggling body.

'We gotta do something,' she says.

Her heart aches when she sees the tears rolling down his cheeks. 'You're losing it, aren't you? I knew it. When I saw you this morning, I couldn't see your feet.'

Ethel stares bitterly into the crowd. A woman in a Socialist Alliance T-shirt is nursing Miranda's head in her lap. Another is standing above her, speaking into a mobile phone.

'You know what this is, don't you?'

He nods sombrely.

'That's right. That fuckin' boundary is still here.'

He looks slowly around the crowd and back at Ethel.

'Don't worry, bub. I'll be more prepared next time you come. All of us will be.'

TWENTY-FIVE

Her fingers are gentle, caressing Miranda's forehead like water gliding across a stone.

'I don't want to.' Mum's voice is just how she remembers. Soft and pleasant on the ear. 'Charlie, can't we stay just a little longer?'

Dad looks up at the giant sitting on the other side of her hospital bed. His arms are resting on the floor, head pushed against the ceiling like a bag of tomatoes.

'We have to go.'

Mum kisses her softly on the forehead. Smells of sandalwood.

Dad runs his hand across her cheek. 'Baby girl, I want you to remember that if you open your eyes, you can find a reason for hope.'

He bends down and kisses her cheek. 'Don't ever stop believing in people.'

Miranda imagines a shooting star, a million explosions inside her skull. The mattress is hard, the sheets too thin. Her nose catches the hospital smell. Chemicals to clean, to heal, and, when all else fails, to soothe the dying. Her memories of Carys' time in hospital are silhouettes of reality. But in her heart, Miranda has always known that Mum's final days should have been spent sitting in her cherished garden, surrounded by family. Not in a cold and sanitised place, filled with strangers and machines.

She doesn't know of any Murris who are comfortable in hospitals. One of the old uncles from Meston Park had even absconded soon after receiving surgery for throat cancer. He bolted with a drip still in his arm. Miranda can understand his reasoning. This place is for the sick, the dying.

Staring through a veil of sleep.

But still, I can see her sadness.

She's holding something deep within, sits on the bottom of her soul, dragging her down.

She hears the snapping of surgical tape and feels a sting in her hand.

'Can I get you anything?' The nurse has a shrill voice.

'No. I'll be fine, thank you.'

Ethel's hand is on her forehead. It's clammy and Miranda can feel her anxiety, as though its essence has been shifted into that one hand.

'Everything is going to be okay, bub. I've taken care of everything.' Her voice dwindles to a whisper. 'Me and Red Feathers had a good talk. You don't know him, yet. But he's a clever man. Bub, he said it's okay for me to tell you.'

Miranda might be groggy, but that doesn't stop the fear pulsing through her veins. Memories are flooding her mind, but they have no order. It's as though she's surrounded by reels of film that have been spliced, jumbled. She knows only the scenes, but has no real grasp of the story. Remembers the fighting, the fear, but no recollection of how she arrived here.

Ethel's eyes are glazed. She's wearing the same expression from the day she told Miranda about her son. The newborn who died and has since grown into an adult.

'Everything is going to be okay, Auntie,' Miranda says without believing it to be true.

'I'm the one who used to say that to you, when you were a little girl.' Ethel's sob is air escaping from a bottle. 'You were very sad for those first few months.'

Miranda's mouth is parched. Ethel gives her a glass of water.

'Pretty scary time.'

'They were, Miri, but we had some good times too. When

I came to Brisbane, a lot of the mob thought I was a Johnny Come Lately. The only one who didn't judge me was Charlie. I bet you didn't know that about your dad?'

'No.' Miranda is not sure if she's ready to talk about her dad just yet, but Ethel goes on, as though she's speaking to herself.

'That's why I moved in. A lot of us were worried that Charlie would drink himself to death after Carys passed away. But he pulled through.' Ethel is nodding now, her eyes staring vacantly into space. 'Yeah, Charlie did alright.'

'We couldn't have pulled through without you, Auntie.'

Glazed eyes turn to Miranda.

'Bub, you mean the world to me. That's why I have to tell you the truth. It won't be easy for you to hear this, but you must. I did it, bub. I killed all of them.'

It's her calmness that terrifies Miranda. Has she gone mad? She really is crazy.

'I don't believe you!'

'And why not?' Ethel shakes her head in disgust. 'People assume that just because I'm an old woman, an auntie, I don't have the same feelings, the same desires as everyone else.'

Miranda's head is swimming, body wracked with pain. She's desperate to wake up and leave this nightmare.

'Why?'

'I've had to fight my entire life, proving to people who I am. I wasn't going to let them take my identity away from me.'

Ethel forms a rock with her right hand and holds it to her chest. 'My identity is all that I have.'

'We've filed an appeal . . . we're fighting this, Auntie.'

'But we'll never win, bub. That's not what this native title business is about.'

Miranda feels like she's standing beside a dyke rifled with holes. She's sticking a finger in each hole. But it's pointless. Any minute now, the wall will come crashing down. Life as they know it will be under water. Disappeared.

'What will God think of this?' Miranda says.

Ethel makes a raspberry with her mouth. 'He forgot about us blackfellas a long time ago.'

'But you . . .'

'I still go to church, 'cause I've got a lot of friends there. Besides, we do good charitable work in the community. But I stopped believing in the big fella a long time ago.'

The nurse glances at them as she walks past, but Miranda ignores her. Regardless of what happens in the future, her life will always be divided between before this moment, and after.

'So when did you decide to tell me?'

'Yesterday, after what they did to you.'

Miranda feels a new jackhammer in the back of her head, as if her body is reminding her that it too has suffered.

'Got even worse this morning, bub. The coppers carried out dawn raids on people's homes. They put guns in kids' faces, tasered people who weren't even putting up a fight. They'll keep hounding our mob, till they get what they want.'

Ethel reaches for her black handbag on the floor. She rests it on the foot of Miranda's bed and opens the zipper. Lifts out the knife.

'Where did you get that?' Miranda says, aghast.

'Where you left it, bub.'

The blood has dried, but it's still on the blade. Miranda is shaking now. 'How did you know?'

'Red Feathers,' Ethel whispers.

'You didn't tell me about the knife!' It's Jason. He storms through the doorway, his body ablaze with anger.

Ethel smiles at him. 'I was going to, in my own time.'

'Put the knife down, Ethel.'

She looks hurt. 'Do you think I'm going to harm my little girl?'

'Just put the knife down.'

As she hears the click of the handcuffs, Miranda notices the resignation on Ethel's face. Insanity has been replaced by reason.

She knew this was coming.

O'Neill feels uncomfortable in a suit that smells of old sweat. It should have gone to the drycleaner this morning, but after he got the call, he put on the first suit he could find, straight from the pungent laundry basket. The Aboriginal Legal Service was run off its feet and in need of more troops. So he spent several hours in the watch house, taking instructions from the scores of Murris and other activists who'd been arrested.

He's been doing this for thirty years. Sitting next to clients who share their secrets. He doesn't see any point in it. It's the role of the police, the DPP, to produce evidence that will establish guilt beyond reasonable doubt. Why help them by confessing? He's never met a compassionate prosecutor. Doubts he ever will.

Ethel offers him a friendly smile. 'How's that lovely wife of yours?'

'She's fine, thanks.'

'Good to hear.'

He's always known that she's resilient. Could see her strength during the litigation, marvelled at how she kept everyone under control. Even when the Golden Tongue was ruthlessly interrogating her genealogy, Ethel remained calm. But this is the first time that her coolness has made him feel ill at ease.

Ethel has never been in an interview room before. But she knows its harshness, felt it when she was arrested during the Commonwealth Games. The Magistrate's Court was full of people that day. Unfriendly people. At least there were other Murris in the dock, their laughter bringing light to the darkness.

Jason is finding it hard to breathe. He's like a patient who has an ache that no doctor can explain. Each expert dismisses him as a hypochondriac, but intuition keeps telling him that it's terminal. Not that he has much confidence in his judgment now. He's been on stress leave since Charlie died. He was sitting at home, in front of the television, when he got Ethel's call.

'Jason, I'm at the PA Hospital.'

'What are you doing there?'

'It's Miranda.'

He offered only silence. He felt ashamed. He knew that he should have called Miranda, to express his sympathy, but Jason didn't have the strength for it.

'She got king-hit by a copper yesterday,' Ethel continued. 'She blacked out.'

'That's terrible.'

'Bub, I need you to meet me at the hospital.'

'Why?'

'Because all of this has to come to an end.'

Now, across the table, Jason looks squarely at Ethel. 'My name is Detective Sergeant Jason Matthews.' He gestures towards her.

'My name is Ethel Irene Cobb.'

'My name is Andrew James O'Neill.'

'Ethel, do you agree that you have come here of your own free will?' Jason says.

'Yes.'

'And you understand that anything you say could be used against you in a court of law?'

'Yes, I understand.'

The interview was the easiest he'd ever done. Ethel made full confessions. Now, they have only to take her to the crime scenes, where she will deconstruct each murder.

O'Neill looks exhausted. Jason should feel victorious. At the very least, he should be relieved that a dangerous killer has been apprehended. Grieving relatives might now begin to move forward, even though the ache will never be pacified. But something niggles.

'Cat got your tongue?'

There's a new spark in Ethel's eyes. Jason is incredulous. After everything that's happened, she still wants to challenge him.

'What do you mean?'

'Don't play games with me. You want to ask me something.'

'*Ethel*,' O'Neill says anxiously. He too has seen the demon in her eyes.

'Shut up.' She laughs to herself; it's a boastful laugh. 'Go on, boy – fire away.'

Jason has never been one to decline a challenge, but he too is fearful. 'Alright. I don't believe any of the victims allowed you into their homes, especially Bruce Brosnan. I think he would have been very alarmed to find you on his doorstep. I think he would have called the police.'

'You're right.'

'Ethel, hold on.'

She glares at O'Neill; it's a blowtorch on his confidence. O'Neill shrinks into his seat.

She turns to Jason. 'What else?'

'I also think you had an accomplice.'

'Yes.'

'What?' Jason gasps.

'Gee, you're deadly.'

O'Neill almost chokes when she offers Jason a wink.

'I had a co-worker. He got me through each door. He also told me about their dirty little secrets. How Bruce Brosnan was fucking Sherene Payne, while her husband was filling his nose with drugs. He saw McPherson taking those boys to his house. Oh, I knew about all of it.'

Ethel is a starlet of the stage, breathing life into a part that has been written just for her. Jason wonders if she's plain forgotten about O'Neill, whose face is an explosion of nerves and sweat.

'Who was your accomplice, Ethel?'

'Red Feathers.'

'Who is Red Feathers?'

'You know, I told you already.'

She gives him a quizzical look.

'That day at Meston Park, you know. I told you then that he's your mob.'

'Who is Red Feathers, Ethel?' Jason says, anxiously.

'My grandfather.'

Jason frowns, confused. 'But he must be well over a hundred years old.'

Jason and O'Neill exchange uncertain glances, but Ethel is unshaken.

'Where is Red Feathers now?' Jason says.

'He's standing right next to you.'

TWENTY-SIX

Six months later

The real estate agent is a crocodile with an angel's voice. Miranda is taken back to childhood, listening to Ethel read *Little Red Riding Hood*. The agent's long, pointy jaw reminded her of a wolf's.

'Yes, I'll be buying,' Miranda says. 'I'm just not sure when.'

As Miranda ends the phone call, the reality that the house now belongs to someone else finally hits. But in her heart, Miranda knows that Charlie would not be angry with her. That place holds too many painful memories for Miranda to ever live there again. The same goes for her old apartment. For the last few weeks she's been renting a studio apartment in the city. Everything but her clothing is in storage.

She stares at the old battered sign across the street. She imagines O'Neill and his crew inside, frantically rowing against the current. Doing everything they possibly can to keep the dream alive. But that dream is no longer Miranda's. Perhaps it never was.

O'Neill's face had been sincere when she told him her decision, but he too knew it was time.

'Mate,' he said, 'are you sure you want to go?'

She smiled. 'Yes, I'm sure.'

'And the appeal?'

'There's no point in seeking a new trial – Ethel was our most important witness.'

'How is she?'

She shrugged. 'I visited her yesterday. I don't think she even knew I was there.'

She gave a final lingering glance at her old desk.

'What happens now?' he asked.

'We go on and do what we've always done. West End, Meston Park, they'll always be in here.' She pointed to her chest. 'That's where our real strength is.'

Miranda shakes her head and walks away. She can never go back to that office. That life is already her past.

An hour ago, her bank account swelled with more money than she earned in ten years of practising law. She isn't ready to retire, but she's not sure what to do next. One minute, she's enrolling in a bridging course to get into medicine. The next it's overseas travel, perhaps to Europe. About once a month, she considers applying to become a foster parent.

She's dating again and, for the first time, Miranda is embracing the experience. Once a week, she enjoys a delicious meal and good conversation. Meeting men in their forties is exciting. Her dates have travelled, achieved, have a story to tell. And they want to know Miranda's story. But she's still writing that manuscript, uncertain of what pages she should reveal.

When she reaches the café, she finds he's beaten her there.

Jason watches her approach the table. Miranda's physique has become athletic. But there's something else. She seems more at ease with herself.

When he stands, she gives him a half-smile. Not quite friendly, not quite antagonistic. He catches a waft of her floral perfume, it's familiar.

'Thanks for coming, Miranda.'

Her face is luminous. The dark circles under her eyes have vanished.

'Have you had breakfast?' he says. 'They have amazing pancakes here.'

'Great. I had my long run this morning – I'm ravenous.'

'Long run?'

'I'm training for the Noosa Marathon. It's going to be my first.'

'Wow, I'm impressed.'

'I'm not doing it to impress you.'

He's deflated but then shakes himself out of it. After all, he didn't expect Miranda to run into his arms.

'Coffee?'

'Thanks, Jason. I can order myself.'

Miranda gestures to the waitress.

'How's Ethel?' His face is earnest.

'She's deteriorated very quickly.' He nods sadly, but Miranda shakes her head. 'I can't wallow in self-pity. Other people have suffered too. The Brosnans, Sherene Payne and her daughter.'

'I never believed Ethel was solely responsible, and I certainly didn't buy that story . . .' His words shock him. This meeting isn't supposed to be about the investigation. But it lives on his brain like invisible ink.

'Sorry, I didn't mean . . .'

'There's no point raking over it.'

Jason's surprised by her resolve, but says nothing.

'So are you still Detective Sergeant Matthews?'

'I am, but I've taken leave.'

'How long for?'

'Twelve months initially.' He pauses, uncertain of how much he should tell her. How much is too painful for her to hear. 'They'll do whatever they can to intimidate me into changing my story. I won't be able to go back after Charlie's inquest.'

Miranda grimaces into her coffee. She doesn't want any part of this conversation. 'It'll just be another whitewash.'

'You'll get the truth, Miranda. I promise you that.'

'And what of Higgins?'

'Desk duties.'

She laughs bitterly. 'The Royal Commission studied

ninety-nine black deaths in custody. Not one copper was held responsible. Not *one!*'

Dad died alone, without anyone to tell him that he was loved.

Why, why did it have to happen to him?

She's about to yell, but the epiphany hits. Bitterness may not have made her an alcoholic, but it kept her there, for too many years. She looks into Jason's crimson face; he's struggling.

'I asked you to come here so that I could apologise,' he says. 'I'm truly sorry for what happened to Charlie.'

'I forgive you.'

He's stunned.

'I know you tried to save him.'

A lightness comes into his eyes. 'Miranda, please believe me when I say this – I won't be intimidated by anyone. Besides, I have no reason to lie at the inquest. My career's over.'

'Mine too.'

Miranda laughs into his confused face. 'Best thing that could have happened. I think I was the most miserable lawyer in Brisbane.'

Jason laughs softly and shakes his head. 'Look at us. Burnt out and we're not even middle aged yet. We'd make a good couple.'

Miranda wriggles in her chair. She's still attracted to him, but too much has happened.

'Can I write to you?' he says.

'Sure. But I can't promise a reply.'

'Good enough.'

Jason watches her disappear into Boundary Street. He's never been in love, probably wouldn't know if he was. But right now he wants her more than he's wanted any other woman.

Then it hits him. Miranda's perfume – he smelt it in Brosnan's kitchen that night.

Jason starts driving but doesn't realise where he's heading until he turns down the familiar street. He sits in the car outside the house for a long while. He knows the place could not have possibly shrunk. But it has. The soil in the flower beds seems dry and rocky. Even the macadamia trees have lost their magic. As a boy he'd spent hours hitting a tennis ball across the wooden planks of the garage, but it too seems somehow smaller.

He reflects on the last time he was here, but the memories are jumbled. Dad hovering above the Weber, a bird protecting its eggs. Mum's gentle laughter over the dinner table. Words spoken that he never meant, but can't take back.

A huge fist seizes his chest and he knows that knocking on that door will take everything he has.

But Mum has pre-empted him. She's standing inside the doorway. Her hair now a silver sheen and much shorter than he remembers.

Jason hears himself whimper. Hugs her tightly.

TWENTY-SEVEN

A cool breeze says goodbye to summer. Meston Park seems to Miranda like an island in the midst of a bustling port. They're surrounded by traffic at all hours, but it's always 'out there', on the periphery. The grass has been freshly mown, rubbish picked up. Lone bottles are like buoys in the ocean.

Construction has begun in the north-western corner. The Coconut Holdings earthmover reveals a smile of silver teeth each time it makes a deposit into the white truck. It stands on top of a sink that holds all of the Corrowa's tragedies and achievements in its plug. But something has changed in Miranda. Before, her eyes felt the bitter taste of defeat. Now, she knows they are stronger. Every day they wake is a victory.

For so long as they believe they are Corrowa, they will never swallow defeat.

Their lodgings are simple: white tents gathered in a circle. In the centre are some plastic chairs and tables. The abandoned playground has come alive with children, their precious laughter carried by the wind. The Corrowa will stay here until their bodies are dragged away. In a week. Perhaps a month. But it will happen. When it does, they will dust themselves off, salve their wounds, return.

Cars bearing the insignia of various community organisations travel up the dusty path. Miranda sees the logo of the Aboriginal Legal Service and embraces the familiar clench. Charlie would be proud. Is proud. She can feel him here. He's the one pushing her feet forward. Dreadlocks sit beneath their shoulders like dead weights. Each holds a tin mug in his hand. They recognise her, nod in acknowledgment. She wants to cry, run away.

A black Corolla hurtles along the path and pulls up next to the Aboriginal Legal Service car. Ian's white business shirt looks like it's wearing half a bottle of starch. Tegan is sitting in the back seat, squashed between the door and the enormous cooler. She hasn't seen either of them since their last AA meeting.

'We thought you guys might need some supplies,' he calls out. 'We've got a curry, lasagna and about five hundred sandwiches.'

Tegan laughs and gestures to Ian. 'He took the morning off work, just so he could find out the verdict on the lasagna.' She offers a mocking grin. 'Apparently, he's an expert.'

Tegan gives Miranda an enormous hug, the kind that makes you grateful for living, while struggling to breathe. Words are trapped beneath the lump in Miranda's throat.

As she walks alongside her friends, Miranda says a silent prayer.

Dad, you were right. I really can find a reason for hope. Always could. Just had to open my eyes.

She looks up and sees a bird stretch out his wings, admires his cloak of emerald and red as he soars into the heavens.

ACKNOWLEDGMENTS

Mum, Dad, Chamsta, Scott and Russell. Thank you for your love and support. And thank you to Bruce Sims and Rebecca Roberts for great editorial advice.